PENGUIN CLASSICS

THE PASTURES OF HEAVEN

Born in Salinas, California, in 1902, John Steinbeck grew up in a fertile agricultural valley about twenty-five miles from the Pacific Coast—and both valley and coast would serve as settings for some of his best fiction. In 1919 he went to Stanford University, where he intermittently enrolled in literature and writing courses until he left in 1925 without taking a degree. During the next five years he supported himself as a laborer and journalist in New York City, all the time working on his first novel, *Cup of Gold* (1929). After marriage and a move to Pacific Grove, he published two California books, *The Pastures of Heaven* (1932) and *To a God Unknown* (1933), and worked on short stories later collected in *The Long Valley* (1938). Popular success and financial security came only with *Tortilla Flat* (1935), stories about Monterey's paisanos. A ceaseless experimenter throughout his career, Steinbeck changed courses regularly. Three powerful novels of the late 1930s focused on the California laboring class: *In Dubious Battle* (1936), *Of Mice and Men* (1937), and the book considered by many his finest, *The Grapes of Wrath* (1939). Early in the 1940s, Steinbeck became a filmmaker with *The Forgotten Village* (1941) and a serious student of marine biology with *Sea of Cortez* (1941). He devoted his services to the war, writing *Bombs Away* (1942) and the controversial play-novelette *The Moon Is Down* (1942). *Cannery Row* (1945), *The Wayward Bus* (1948), another experimental drama, *Burning Bright* (1950), and *The Log from The Sea of Cortez* (1951) preceded publication of the monumental *East of Eden* (1952), an ambitious saga of the Salinas Valley and his own family's history. The last decades of his life were spent in New York City and Sag Harbor with his third wife, with whom he traveled widely. Later books include *Sweet Thursday* (1954), *The Short Reign of Pippin IV: A Fabrication* (1957), *Once There Was a War* (1958), *The Winter of Our Discontent* (1961), *Travels with Charley in Search of America* (1962), *America and Americans* (1966), and the posthumously published *Journal of a Novel: The* East of Eden *Letters* (1969), *Viva Zapata!* (1975), *The Acts of King Arthur and His Noble Knights* (1976), and *Working Days: The Journals of* The Grapes of Wrath (1989). He died in 1968, having won a Nobel Prize in 1962.

James Nagel is the first J. O. Eidson Distinguished Professor of American Literature at the University of Georgia. He founded the scholarly journal

Studies in American Fiction and edited it for twenty years; he is the general editor of the *Critical Essays on American Literature* series, published by Macmillan in New York; and he serves as the executive coordinator of the American Literature Association. Among his dozen books are *Stephen Crane and Literary Impressionism, Ernest Hemingway: The Writer in Context*, and *Hemingway in Love and War*, which was selected by the *New York Times* as one of the notable books of the year in 1989. He has published over fifty articles in scholarly journals, and he has lectured on American literature in twelve countries. His current projects include a study of the contemporary short-story cycle and a book about Ernest Hemingway's *The Sun Also Rises*.

CONTENTS

INTRODUCTION

I

When *The Pastures of Heaven* was first published in the autumn of 1932, almost no one knew his name. John Steinbeck was not then the established writer he was to become later in the decade with the appearance of *The Grapes of Wrath*, and he was a long way from the celebrity status he was to enjoy with the award of the Nobel Prize for Literature in 1962. In the early 1930s he was a struggling writer committed to a literary life but still searching for a subject and a style. He found the first in the area he knew best, the farm country near his home in Salinas, California, and the simple people who settled there. This was the subject that was to inform the best of his work and to underlie his reputation as a writer of intellectual substance and social significance. In the writing of a series of stories about this area, he refined his fictional prose and a new method of organization, and he was well on the way to developing the consummate craft of his greatest work.

John Ernst Steinbeck was born on February 27, 1902, in Salinas, California. His father's family, the Grossteinbecks, had come from Germany in the nineteenth century, settling briefly in Jerusalem before moving to Florida and then California, simplifying their name on the journey. The father, whose name was the same as his son's, worked at several occupations, milling flour and serving as treasurer of Monterey County. Steinbeck's mother, Olive Hamilton, came from an Irish family that had settled on a ranch near Monterey before the Civil War, and she had been a schoolteacher prior to her marriage. John and Olive established a home in the Salinas Valley, between the Gabilan Mountains to the east and the Santa Lucia range to the west. This was the area of John Steinbeck's youth and the terrain he was to capture in the best of his early work, especially in *Of Mice and Men*, "The Red Pony," and his masterpiece, *The Grapes of Wrath*.

But there was little in his early life to suggest the status he was later to attain. He was not an outstanding student in Salinas High School, from which he graduated in 1919, but he did have strong personal interests in science and classical literature. His experiences in an Episcopal Sunday school gave him a good background in Scripture, one he was to use in his fiction the rest of his life. At Stanford University his record was less than exemplary; he attended sporadically from 1920 to 1925, taking courses in zoology and the classics and devoting himself to his training in creative writing, the only area in which he excelled. As Jackson Benson has pointed out, Steinbeck is unique in his generation for having studied the craft of writing fiction at a university. But some semesters he dropped out of school and worked as a common laboror, learning the ways of ranch hands and migrant workers, and later returned to Stanford for a semester or two; he left the university without graduating.

He made an unsuccessful attempt to establish himself as a writer in New York City, but he ended up pushing wheelbarrows filled with concrete for the foundation of Madison Square Garden. He returned to California broke but determined to pursue a literary career. His first book, *Cup of Gold*, was an adventure tale about a pirate, inspired in part by the success of Rafael Sabatini's *Captain Blood*, published in 1922 and made into a popular movie in 1925. Steinbeck had attempted to combine the tradition of the buccaneering romance with the Grail legend, but this first novel attracted scant attention. He worked at his next major project for five years, a novel later titled *To a God Unknown*, but this endeavor to meld Arthurian legend into a tale about a California farmer's struggle against the elements was temporarily abandoned.

It was set aside early in 1931 so that he could begin work on a volume of short stories prompted by Elizabeth Ingels's comment that she was going to write a volume of interconnected tales similar to what Sherwood Anderson had done in *Winesburg, Ohio* in 1919. She had grown up in a valley to the west of Salinas called Corral de Tierra, "the fence of earth," and had the idea of doing a series of stories about the development of a young girl interacting with the strange families of this confined environment. Steinbeck was inspired, for here was a subject closer to home than anything he had thus far attempted, and he quickly adapted Beth Ingels's idea into the project that was to become *The Pastures of Heaven.*

His idea for the new book was to remain largely constant throughout its development, although he changed several details and ultimately deleted a few of the original stories. In the spring of 1931 he wrote to his friend Ted Miller to say that he was at work on *The Pastures of Heaven*: "Now this is a series of related stories each one dealing with a family in the Pasturas." As the manuscripts indicate, his initial idea was to begin with the description of the valley, then move on to stories depicting roughly ten families, then to introduce the Munroes, the key family that would influence the lives of the others in the concluding group of stories. As his work progressed on the first draft, however, he seems to have felt that the separate stories lacked unity, and he decided to introduce the Munroe family at the beginning, immediately after his description of the valley, thus unifying all of the following stories by the interventions of the Munroes. By May 8 he was far enough along to write to his new literary agent, Mavis McIntosh, explaining the basic plan for the volume:

> The present work interests me and perhaps falls in the "aspects" theme you mention. There is, about twelve miles from Monterey, a valley in the hills called Corral de Tierra. Because I am using its people I have named it Las Pasturas del Cielo. The valley was for years known as the happy valley because of the unique harmony which existed among its twenty families. About ten years ago a new family moved in on one of the ranches. They were ordinary people, ill-educated but honest and as kindly as any. In fact, in their whole history I cannot find that they have committed a really malicious act nor an act which was not dictated by honorable expediency or out-and-out altruism. But about the Morans there was a flavor of evil. Everyone they came in contact with was injured. Every place they went dissension sprang up. There have been two murders, a suicide, many quarrels and a great deal of unhappiness in the Pastures of Heaven, and all of these things can be traced directly to the influence of the Morans. So much is true.

As he developed the group of stories, he took the central idea beyond what Beth Ingels had originally suggested, making the material his own. In creating the schoolteacher named Molly Morgan, he drew on the experiences of his mother in the early years of her career. For the senior Whiteside, he utilized his father's interests in classical literature. He took a story about a pair of sisters who become reluctant prostitutes from another book he was planning and merged it into the structure of his new volume.

By the autumn of 1931 he had finished the composition of the stories, and his wife, Carol, finished typing them sometime in early December. He immediately sent the manuscript to his agent. As he wrote to Ted Miller:

> The Pastures of Heaven I sent off last Saturday. It should be there by the time you receive this. If the reader will take

> them for what they are, and will not be governed by what a short story should be (for they are not short stories at all, but tiny novels) then they should be charming, but if they are judged by the formal short story, they are lost before they ever start. I am extremely anxious to hear the judgment because of anything I have ever tried, I am fondest of these and more closely tied to them. There is no grand writing nor any grand theme, but I love the stories very much.

The initial reaction from Mavis McIntosh was negative, but she agreed to forward the collection to a publisher for a reading.

That response was immediate and positive. The manuscript had been sent to Robert O. Ballou, an editor at Cape and Smith, and he accepted it for publication within three days. Steinbeck received the news on his thirtieth birthday, February 27, 1932, and it was the most encouraging development of his young career, but the euphoria was not to last. In March he learned that Jonathan Cape had gone bankrupt, and his book was not to be published after all. Then, in a fortuitous development, Robert Ballou, set adrift by the failure of the firm, landed a position at Brewer, Warren, and Putnam, and he brought *The Pastures of Heaven* with him. By May production on the bedeviled volume had resumed under the new imprint, and it appeared in October to very little fanfare, partly because the firm lacked the funds to market it aggressively. Indeed, shortly after publication of Steinbeck's book, this publisher also declared bankruptcy, and Steinbeck made very little money on the project. The Depression, later to figure so importantly in his fiction, had hit him personally.

In the final twist on the matter, two years later, Pascal Covici, head of the publishing firm of Covici-Friede in Chicago, read the stories enthusiastically and decided to buy up the contract and the existing backlog of books and issue the title again under his own imprint, which he did in the fall of 1935. *The Pastures of Heaven* was thus given a second life. However, the curious and convoluted history of the volume's publication is not as important as the role that the book played in Steinbeck's growth as a writer, for it was during the composition of these stories that he found the subject and the mode of artistic expression that were to generate the most important work of his life.

II

If the publication of the volume was encouraging for Steinbeck, the reviews were less so, for many critics did not understand the genre and faulted a collection of interrelated stories for not being a novel. The reactions to *The Pastures of Heaven* varied, but in general they tended to praise Steinbeck's style, to puzzle about his genre, and to marvel at the variety of his characters and scope of his portrait of his fictional valley. Margaret Cheney Dawson, writing at length in the *New York Herald-Tribune Books* (October 23, 1932), remarked on the "author's charming serenity of style" and concluded that "there is a clarity, good humor and delicacy in Mr. Steinbeck's writing that makes the book fine reading." Describing the form of the volume, she observed that "each of the chapters presents an individual or group enacting some small drama against the backdrop of Heaven's Pastures. Short stories they are really." The review in the *Chicago Daily Tribune* (November 19, 1932) concluded that "the novel is well plotted, though, perhaps, the conclusion is of a somewhat obvious type. The characters are as vitally real as your next door neighbor, and the style and presentation of the novel are restrained, compassionate, as well as compelling."

Anita Moffett wrote more extensively in the *New York Times Book Review* for November 20, 1932, praising the prose of the volume: Steinbeck "writes with deep feeling for the tragedy implicit in each situation, yet undeceived by the self-delusion or self-dramatization of the persons involved. Racy, realistically direct and caustically humorous, his writing is noteworthy for originality of phrase and image and a strongly poetic feeling." The commentator for the *Saturday Review of Literature* (November 26, 1932) observed that the "book is . . . a collection of short stories unrelated except by the unity of place and the occasional appearance of one or another character in an episode in which he is not primarily featured," a comment that missed entirely the substantial thematic unity that Steinbeck had given his volume.

A brief comment in *The Nation* on December 7, 1932, called the book a "series of connected sketches" that are obsessed with abnormal character types. Praising Steinbeck's style, the reviewer predicted that "his future work should lead to his recognition as an excellent psychological analyst." Revealing the preoccupation of the age, he added that if Steinbeck "could add social insight to his present equipment he would be a first-rate novelist." Cyrilly Abels, in *The Bookman* for December of 1932, compared *Pastures* to Hilton's *Ill Wind* as another series of linked stories and suggested that in these tales "civilization shows a pathetic gray against the delightful green of Nature, [and] . . . even the Garden of the Hesperides brings disillusion." A brief notice in *The Booklist* (December 1932) observed that "sensitivity, a very human pity, and humor preserve the book from an unwholesome impression that the themes of horror and abnormality might have conveyed in less skillful writing." Helen McAfee praised Steinbeck's characterizations and his description of the valley and remarked that "the author has a sense of motivation, with psychological insight and understanding. The odd and queer people are naturally so. The normal people are normally so. The whole story is plausible, and seemingly historical in its descriptions of places and events."

But to come to terms with the adequacy of these early reviews, and to attempt to understand the literary contributions and context of *The Pastures of Heaven*, it is important to place the book in the context of two important literary traditions that converge in these stories: American Literary Naturalism and the genre of the short-story cycle, both of which had been gaining in importance in American fiction since the 1890s.

III

Growing out of the hard edge of Realism in the last decade of the nineteenth century, Naturalism had become the dominant literary movement in American fiction by the turn of the century, manifesting its influence in the Bowery tales of Stephen Crane, the fight for survival in the work of Jack London, the grim struggle of simple characters against a world they cannot control in Frank Norris's fiction, and the complex inner drives that impel disaster in the novels of Theodore Dreiser. At the ideological heart of this literary tendency is pessimistic Determinism, the notion that the causative factors in human tragedy lie beyond the powers of the individual. The influence of Darwin led to biological determinism and to atavistic scenes in which characters revert to primitive states of animalistic behavior; the influence of Karl Marx, coupled with problems emanating from the urbanization of America and the economic problems at the end of the nineteenth century, engendered the portrayal of socio-economic forces that overwhelm individual lives. These themes came to replace for a time the ethical dilemmas so prevalent in Realism, in which characters struggle, as does Huck Finn, to make morally difficult decisions. Internal struggle is not significant in the context of external determinism, which overwhelms individual prerogatives. Beginning with *The Pastures of Heaven*, these concepts came to play an important role in the fiction of John Steinbeck.

These themes led the Naturalist to focus on the lives of lower-class characters struggling for survival in an alien and often hostile society, one insensitive to their personal needs for fulfillment or self-expression. Often these characters are in some way grotesque, retarded, or misshapen victims of genetic accident, or people obsessed by greed, sexual craving, or a compulsive plan for success that ultimately destroys them. Since the characters themselves are incapable of explaining the complex causal history of the events that sweep them along, the personalized narrative methods of Realism, in which simple characters tell their own stories, is replaced with a dominant, omniscient narrator who can relate deterministic factors far beyond the knowledge of the characters affected by them. Since the underlying assumption of Naturalism is that reality is not only comprehensible but stable and available for detailed, scientific analysis, the tendency is for symbolization, for dominant images that embody determining forces—for example, the variety of gold symbols that pervade Norris's *McTeague*. The plots of Naturalism tend to depict the downward spiral of impending tragedy, and there is normally very little suspense about the final outcome of events. No one emerges triumphant in a Naturalistic novel, since simple survival constitutes a moral victory. The style of Naturalism lacks the grace of Realism, and artistic subtlety and the skillful turn of phrase give way to narrative exposition and the rational explanation of the implications of depicted events.

John Steinbeck was not a dedicated student of American Naturalism, and his fiction does not exhibit an uncompromised utilization of these tendencies, yet in theme and method his work has greater affinity to Naturalism than to any other tradition in American literature. As his letters indicate, he was familiar with the work of Sherwood Anderson, whose *Winesburg, Ohio* is perhaps the greatest influence on *The Pastures of Heaven.* As a college student and aspiring writer in the 1920s, Steinbeck was aware of the growing popularity of such Naturalistic writers as Erskine Caldwell, James T. Farrell, and Edith Summers Kelly, as well as the older generation of Naturalists, Crane, Dreiser, Norris, and London.

The Pastures of Heaven is certainly a compendium of Naturalistic tendencies, dominated by an omniscient narrator who establishes characters through expository comment rather than dramatic revelation. There are no deep mysteries within Steinbeck's characters that are beyond the reach of the narrative intelligence, no background influences that the narrator cannot explain, no events to come that are impossible to predict. Omniscience is a powerful tool in the telling of the story, but it obscures the subtleties of the human personality, subordinates organic development, and tends toward the depiction of static characters who emerge, predictably, as the victims of circumstances beyond their control.

In the stories in *Pastures,* Steinbeck reveals as well the Naturalistic tendency for grotesque characters: Alice Wicks and Manfred Munroe suffer from retardation, Myrtle and John Battle from epilepsy and a form of insanity, Helen Van Deventer from neurosis, and Hilda Van Deventer from schizophrenia. Tularecito, perhaps the most interesting of these personalities, is depicted as a retarded savant, severely restricted in the standard forms of learning but gifted in the artistic re-creation of the nature around him. Other characters suffer from obsessions that impel disaster or humiliation: Shark Wicks, for example, has a compulsive need to appear to be a wealthy and shrewd investor of his mythical fortune; and John Whiteside is driven to create an estate and a dynasty to inhabit it throughout the coming generations, even though every ensuing development thwarts his deepest desires. As Richard Astro has pointed out, the underlying tragedy is that although this rich valley presents the promise of a fulfilling life, the characters within it are either so restricted or so driven by self-deception and obsession that they do not make the most of their abundant opportunities. In narrative method, style, characterization, and theme, *The Pastures of Heaven* owes much to the traditional norms of American Naturalism.

IV

In form, however, its organizational principles derive from another source altogether, from a popular but not widely understood genre customarily called the short-story cycle, a collection of interrelated stories. Distinct in many ways from the more celebrated "novel," a cycle consists of stories that are independent fictional units, with a conflict, a resolution, and a sense of closure in each narrative. These stories are often published individually in magazines prior to being collected as a group, but placed in context with the other stories, each tale is enriched by the presence of the others. Often the stories are linked by a continuing central character, as they are in Sherwood Anderson's *Winesburg, Ohio* and Ernest Hemingway's *In Our Time*; sometimes the unifying feature is the setting for the stories, as it is in Hamlin Garland's *Main-Travelled Roads* or Sarah Orne Jewett's *The Country of the Pointed Firs*; sometimes the unifying element is the narrative voice of the stories, as in Charles Chesnutt's *The Conjure Tales* or Joel Chandler Harris's *Stories of Uncle*

Remus; and sometimes the stories are tied together thematically, with ideas reinforced or presented in counterpoint to the central motifs of the other works.

The short-story cycle is an older form than the novel, having its origins in such works as Boccaccio's *The Decameron* and Chaucer's *Canterbury Tales*, works published centuries before the inception of the novel in English literature in the eighteenth century. In American literature, the story cycle came into prominence in the late nineteenth century, when the demand for short works of fiction was at its highest point. In the late decades of the century, such works as Mary Wilkins Freeman's *Six Trees*, Stephen Crane's *Stories of Whilomville*, and Charles Chesnutt's *The Conjure Tales* gave expression to the form. In the early decades of the twentieth century, the genre emerged as one of the most important forms in literature, and a brief list of important works would include such masterpieces as William Faulkner's *Go Down, Moses*, Eudora Welty's *The Golden Apples*, Jean Toomer's *Cane*, and scores of others.

The artistic challenge of the short-story cycle is always unity, some means of relating one story to another, making the whole greater than the sum of its parts. In *The Pastures of Heaven*, Steinbeck followed a tradition established much earlier by Garland, Crane, and Anderson of developing essentially Naturalistic themes within the form of interrelated stories. Garland had succeeded in *Main-Travelled Roads* by having each story advance the central ideas of democratic Populism, placing in a sympathetic and humane light worthy characters pitted against external forces that overwhelm them. Crane used continuing characters in his tales of Sullivan County and Whilomville, and the growth and development of these characters from story to story enrich the characterizations. Anderson blended several unifying devices in *Winesburg*: a stable location, rich with local personalities and historical conflicts; a continuing protagonist, George Willard, who confronts adult realities and matures through the sequence of stories; and unifying themes that bind one story to the other. Steinbeck was to follow in this tradition in his work on *The Pastures of Heaven.*

V

One of the unifying elements he gave his book was the handling of time, with all the principal stories occurring in the general period of 1928–29. Within that temporal scheme, each succeeding story concludes somewhat later than the preceding one, so that there is a sense of historical progression to the flow of stories, despite the flashbacks that sometimes open the narratives. The volume derives coherence as well from its structural organization, with the framing device of a prologue and an epilogue that provide a thematic "envelope" for ten internal stories, each devoted to a family within a fictional valley. As Steinbeck explained in a letter to his agent,

> I am using the following method. The manuscript is made up of stories, each one complete in itself, having its rise, climax and ending. Each story deals with a family or an individual. They are tied together only by the common locality and by the contact with the Morans.

Although he was to change the name of the unifying family from Moran to Munroe, he conformed to this general plan throughout the writing of the manuscript.

The opening prologue establishes the central unifying location for all of the stories, Las Pasturas del Cielo (The Pastures of Heaven), at the same time suggesting many of the central ideas that are developed later in the stories. The central device of an omniscient narrator who not only relates events and dialogue but comments on the action, often ironically, continues throughout the collection, creating unity of tone and perspective. The motif of religion, beginning with the building of the Carmelo Mission in 1776, serves as a frequent point of reference, always with the suggestion that spirituality in none of its forms provides much solace for the people of the valley. As Joseph Fontenrose points out in his *Steinbeck's Unhappy Valley: A Study of* The Pastures of Heaven, no religion is efficacious:

> The Whitesides failed to establish a family dynasty in the new land. The religions of Maltby and Banks, the foundations of their lives, were shattered by Bert Munroe's suggestions of evil: Junius believed something monstrous about himself and had to leave Eden. There were no gnomes and elves for Tularecito to find. Alice Wicks was not a special gift from heaven. Though Helen Van Deventer, Molly Morgan, and Pat Humbert clung to or lapsed back into the old religion, it gave them no satisfaction.

On the secular level, the Spanish corporal who discovers the valley has a dream of someday having a comfortable house beside a stream, an idea that develops into the repeated concern for the family home, the central issue in the concluding story of John Whiteside and his dreams of a dynasty in the valley. At the core of the Spanish enslavement of the indigenous population to work on the mission is the idea of "civilization" in conflict with a more basic human nature, a motif that recurs in nearly every story. Finally, the prologue concludes with the tragic death of the Spanish corporal, suggesting not only the vanity of human wishes but also that there is a curse associated with the valley, one that is given more direct development in the first full story.

The curse in the opening story functions both historically and dramatically, and the resonance of it lingers throughout the volume. All of the events involve what is known as the Battle farm, founded by George Battle in 1863. He marries an epileptic woman who bears him a son before going insane; the son, John, inherits both proclivities and dies in a religious struggle with a snake. The father having also expired, the farm lies fallow until the Mustrovics move in, an odd family that mysteriously disappears with breakfast left on the table. These bizarre events pave the way for the introduction of the central family in *Pastures*, the Munroes.

In some ways the Munroe patriarch, Bert, is the most important character in *The Pastures of Heaven* in that he appears in a variety of stories, always influencing the action by his presence. By settling on the Battle farm and taming its reversion to wilderness, Bert makes a success of his labors and enjoys the respect of the community. On the surface, there are few problems with the family. His wife is dutiful and fecund, producing three children in short order. The oldest child, Mae, is the satisfied recapitulation of her mother; the son, Jimmie, enjoys extraordinary success in romantic conquest; the youngest child, Manfred, is retarded but obedient, with a submerged tendency for hysteria. But of itself, the opening story is one of financial and social success for the Munroe family, compromised only by reiterations of the curse on the farm. As is soon evident, with the Munroes comes disaster, tragedy not always "caused" by them but somehow precipitated by their presence. Every story that follows contains a Munroe, and the foreboding of the curse provides a motif that pervades all the subsequent action.

The story of Shark Wicks exemplifies the richness with which Steinbeck developed the independent stories while simultaneously linking them to the others in the volume. In the broadest terms, this story chronicles the lives of the Wicks family, newcomers in the valley, but more specifically it is about Edward Wicks, whose nickname, "Shark," results from the pretense that he is a wealthy and sagacious financial investor, despite the homely realities of his daily existence. The irony is that his imaginary world of wealth obscures from him where his real treasures reside: in a loving and understanding wife and a beautiful if simple daughter, Alice. Shark's second obsession is with the virginity of this child, which inspires him to limit her social contacts and restrict her normal development. While he is away on a trip to a family funeral, his wife takes her to a community dance where she meets the wily rake Jimmie Munroe, who later kisses her. When Shark learns of the incident, he seeks revenge with a rifle, is arrested, and, when required to post bond, is forced to confess that he is a poor man, his wealth a ruse to enhance his stature. In a sense, the Munroe curse is his undoing, in that the intervention of Jimmie precipitates his fall. On a deeper level, however, the vulnerability is within Shark from the beginning, in his need to establish his stature on a pretense, in his abnormal insecurity about his daughter's chastity. From this perspective, the collapse of Shark Wicks emerges as the result of obsession and illusion, and the Munroe curse is only the occasion for the fall, not the causal agent. This point was emphasized when Steinbeck revised his manuscript to diminish the role of Jimmie as a predatory seducer and thus transfer the responsibility for the protagonist's humiliation to Shark himself. The fertile promise of the Pastures of Heaven, it would seem, is too precarious to admit of illusion, and all who build on pretense are forced to a painful recognition of reality.

The story of Tularecito, the foundling who is deformed, retarded, and yet gifted with extraordinary physical strength and artistic sensitivity, is perhaps the most remarkable in the collection. This "little frog" senses some affinity for the gnomes, a mythical race of small beings that dwell within the earth, and his desire to return to his own people, and his violence in avenging the destruction of his artistic creations, lead to his incarceration as criminally insane. What links this story to the entire volume is not Tularecito's abnormalities, however, but the application of many of the same themes that inform the surrounding stories. It is again the interaction of the central character with the Munroe family that precipitates the tragic conclusion, when Tularecito attacks Bert Munroe and is arrested. This story introduces another important theme: the conflict between the natural instincts and desires of the individual and the demands for conformity to the norms of "civilization," an idea best understood by the boy's adoptive father, Franklin Gomez, who argues that his son should not go to school but should be allowed to roam free. "He is not crazy," Gomez protests, "but is one of those whom God has not quite finished." The societal restriction on individual prerogatives invests several of the stories that follow, and the fact that Tularecito's teacher is Molly Morgan links this story directly to the later one concerning her life in the valley. In the end, Tularecito has lost his freedom, Gomez has lost a son, and the world has lost the creative potential of one of its extraordinary beings.

The motif of mental instability and violence links the story of Tularecito to that of Helen Van Deventer, a comparatively wealthy woman with a penchant for tragedy in all of its forms. After the death of her husband, Helen gives birth to Hilda, whose pathologies include a violent temper and the creation of imaginative beings of destructive potential. As soon as the widow and her daughter move to the Pastures, Bert Munroe comes to pay an innocent courtesy call, which precipitates a series of events that results in Helen's execution of her daughter, a death interpreted as a suicide by the authorities. Although a Munroe is again involved tangentially in the tragedy, this story differs from the others in the collection in that the dramatic situation is imported into the valley: Hilda is not driven mad by anything inherent in the valley itself, and Helen's proclivity for tragic situations antedates her move. As the family physician says to her, "You love the hair shirt. . . . Your pain is a pleasure. You won't give up any little shred of tragedy."

The events in the life of Junius Maltby also relate to the story of Tularecito in the themes of the child undone by compulsory attendance at school and the destruction of the individual by demands for social conformity. Certainly Junius has his share of tragedy: his father dies in bankruptcy; Junius has a lung condition that forces him out of San Francisco and into the valley of the Pastures of Heaven; his two adopted sons die of influenza; and his wife dies in childbirth, leaving him with an infant son, Robbie—named for Robert Louis Stevenson, who came to Monterey in 1879. If these early tragedies can be attributed to the vagaries of Fate, the final one cannot. Junius, an undisciplined but thoroughly absorbed scholar of a disorganized host of subjects, neglects his farm and domestic responsibilities to give free rein to intellectual interests. Robbie grows to embrace the same free spirit as his father, and they are content and unfettered until the boy is forced to attend school, where he is happy and popular until the inevitable intrusion of yet another Munroe. Mrs. Munroe, appalled at the tattered clothing young Robbie wears to school, presents him with new clothes, highlighting his destitution, and Junius and Robbie leave the valley for San Francisco and a more conventional life. The unwitting gesture of the insensitive Munroes in giving the boy the new clothes, emblems of civilization and conformity, ruins the happiness of the Maltbys. Steinbeck seems to have been particularly intrigued with this story, for he published it independently as *Nothing So Monstrous* in 1936, four years after it was included in *The Pastures of Heaven.*

The most charming and humorous story in the collection features the Lopez sisters, rotund, devout Roman Catholics left to their own devices after the death of their father. Part of the charm results from their attempts at self-deception, at convincing themselves that they run a restaurant and merely "encourage" their customers, the ones who buy three or more enchiladas, with sexual favors. As John H. Timmerman has observed, "Never would the sisters admit that their sex was for sale, a solely commercial venture relegated in their peculiar theology to fallen women." Once they begin this practice, their business booms, and they make a comfortable place for themselves within the valley. It is again the intrusion of the Munroes into the situation that precipitates their demise and compels their admission that they are in fact prostitutes, and they leave the valley, as did the Maltbys, for San Francisco. They find the strength for this recognition in their simple faith and in their love for each other. This story, originally written as part of a manuscript called "The Green Lady" and then incorporated into *Pastures,* provides not only comic relief but another demonstration of the demands of "respectable" society for conformity. Essentially whores with hearts of gold, out of a tradition begun in the stories of Bret Harte, the Lopez sisters are only the first examples of Steinbeck's use of prostitutes in his fiction, which he was to continue most graphically in his next book, *Tortilla Flat,* and later in *East of Eden.*

The story of Molly Morgan is the most artistically complex of all the stories, particularly with regard to the handling of time and motivation. In most of the stories the use of the omniscient narrator simply provides a means of commentary and the establishment of character by exposition rather than dramatic revelation. In this story, however, Steinbeck's skillful juxtaposition of memory with current action allows for the theme of the past living in the present. The great mystery in the background is the whereabouts of Molly's father, an irresponsible parent and absent husband who nevertheless looms as a romantic hero in his daughter's mind. When Molly arrives in the valley to interview for a teaching position with John Whiteside, who heads the school board, their conversation is interspersed with sections recounting Molly's painful memories of her youth. This device also allows for the dramatic irony of the contrast between the tragic memories and the benign personal history she relates to Whiteside. She acquires the position and succeeds until the intrusion of Bert Munroe, who describes the profligacy of his new hired hand, and Molly is forced to confront the conflict between the image of her father as a romantic hero and the awful reality that he may well be the drunken sot sleeping in Bert Munroe's car. It is her fear that her father may have returned, and her desire to sustain the respectability of society, that destroys her happiness.

Respectability is not the issue for Raymond Banks but the confrontation of attitudes. One of the most successful farmers in the valley, Raymond conducts the affairs of his chicken farm in images of purity, with white buildings and chickens and ducks. What does not quite fit the picture is his interest in the hangings at San Quentin, where an old friend serves as warden and allows Raymond to observe the executions, an event he approaches with great detachment, scornful of those who have an emotional reaction. It is the intrusion of Bert Munroe, particularly his graphic depiction of a mutilated and dying chicken, that forces Banks to regard the hangings from a new perspective, and he cancels his trip. This is another of the stories in which the resolution consists of a change of perspective, not the outcome of a physical conflict, and it is a rich psychological study most closely linked to the story of Shark Wicks.

The concluding stories of Pat Humbert and John Whiteside both focus on the family house in the valley and the broken dreams associated with it. For Humbert that house is as stifling as the antiquated attitudes of his parents. When they die he lives for a time with the ghosts of the past, but an accident allows him to see that new possibilities lie open to him. Inadvertently overhearing a conversation between the comely Mae Munroe and her mother, in which Mae expresses an interest in the Humbert house, Pat is inspired to remodel the home as a prelude to beginning their courtship. He finishes the project only to discover that she has just become engaged to young Bill Whiteside. He retreats back to a "dark and unutterably dreary" house, accepting the sterile solitude that had characterized the lives of his parents, his dreams vanquished.

The Munroes are also involved in the destruction of the Whiteside family dreams, although more dramatically so. Mae Munroe is certainly not the cause of Pat Humbert's distress, in the sense that she is not aware that he has overheard her comments about the house, and she has no idea that he is interested in her romantically. Bert Munroe is more directly involved in the Whiteside debacle. The richest story in the collection, the saga of the Whiteside family covers three generations, beginning with Richard's desire to found a dynasty in the Pastures with the family house as its center. His only child, John, carries on the dream, only to have it shattered when his son, Bill, marries Mae Munroe, adopts her values, and moves out of the valley. The burning of the family home is thus emblematic of the destruction of the family dream of dynasty.

The involvement of the Munroe family is complex in this story. In an earlier tale, Bill Whiteside has an opportunity for a romance with Molly Morgan, who might have remained in the valley and helped fulfill the ancient dream of the family. But Bill's insensitive comments to her preclude any development of the relationship. Later, Bert Munroe's hired hand frightens her out of the valley altogether. Mae Munroe might have married Pat Humbert, had the timing of the courtship been more favorable, but she weds Bill and insists on moving to Monterey, violating the objectives of the founding father of the Whitesides. But Bill's parents might have remained in the house had Bert Munroe not assisted in a disastrous attempt to burn the brush in the area, which leads to the immolation of the Whiteside house and the family dream. This event, the simultaneous destruction of the family house and stature, links Steinbeck's story to a rich legacy in American fiction, one that includes Edgar Allan Poe's "The Fall of the House of Usher," George Washington Cable's "Belle Damoiselles Plantation," and William Faulkner's *Absalom, Absalom!*, to name only a few. The collapse of the grand ambitions of the original settlers of the Pastures of Heaven provides a fitting end to the central stories of the volume, one brought to ironic conclusion by the epilogue.

The epilogue provides the enclosing envelope for the ten stories, much as the prologue initiates the central themes of the volume. That it takes place at a temporal and psychological distance from the central action also mirrors the opening sequence, and the irony of the conclusion completes the stories of broken dreams, disillusionment, and painful realizations that awaited the people who moved into the valley. As the opening dramatized the historic beginnings of the settling of the valley, the closing shows a modern bus bringing tourists to the area along the same route the Spanish corporal had taken. But now the valley has been domesticated with homes and farms, and cows wearing bells have replaced the grazing deer of the prologue. The tourists too have their dreams for the valley, but they reflect the mercantile ambitions of the new age: "Some day there'll be big houses in the valley, stone houses and gardens, golf links and big gates and iron work." The grand illusions and dreams of dynasty of the original settlers have been replaced by the commercial interests of the modern age, and the Edenic promise of a verdant nature has drifted back into the past, lost forever in the broken dreams and thwarted ambitions that once belonged to the Pastures of Heaven.

John Steinbeck's reputation as a writer does not rest primarily on *Pastures*, but it is a major work of American fiction, and it was pivotal in his career. In it he discovered the central subject of his greatest work, the simple people of the Salinas Valley, struggling against the odds, against economic deprivation and the legacy of a past that threatens to overwhelm them, ideas that inform *The Grapes of Wrath* and *East of Eden*. His Naturalistic use of characters who are psychologically deformed, or obsessed, or driven by a curse, he was to use again and again, most brilliantly in *Of Mice and Men* and *In Dubious Battle*. Steinbeck went on to write other collections of interrelated stories, containing some of his very best fiction: *Tortilla Flat* and especially *The Long Valley*, which features perhaps his best known story, "The Red Pony." Many of the themes of *Pastures*—the destructive potential of conformity, the dangers of self-delusion and false social values—he continued to explore throughout his career, even through *The Winter of Our Discontent* in 1961. Perhaps it is not too much to claim that the central components of the greatness of Steinbeck's work, his basic style and subject and fundamental themes, have their origin not in his most celebrated novels but in an often ignored collection of stories that appeared, unceremoniously, in 1932, *The Pastures of Heaven*.

SUGGESTIONS FOR FURTHER READING

Astro, Richard. *John Steinbeck and Edward F. Ricketts: The Shaping of a Novelist.* Minneapolis: University of Minnesota Press, 1973.

Benson, Jackson J. *The True Adventures of John Steinbeck, Writer.* New York: Viking, 1984.

Ferrell, Keith. *John Steinbeck: The Voice of the Land.* New York: M. Evans, 1986.

Fontenrose, Joseph. *John Steinbeck: An Introduction and Interpretation.* New York: Holt, Rinehart and Winston, Inc., 1963.

———. *Steinbeck's Unhappy Valley: A Study of* The Pastures of Heaven. Berkeley: Joseph Fontenrose, 1981.

French, Warren. *John Steinbeck.* New York: Twayne, 1961.

Gladstein, Mimi Reisel. "Female Characters in Steinbeck: Minor Characters of Major Importance?" *Steinbeck's Women: Essays in Criticism*, ed. Tetsumaro Hayashi. Steinbeck Monograph Series No. 9. Muncie: Steinbeck Society, 1979, pp. 17–25.

Hearle, Kevin. "The Pastures of Contested Pastoral Discourse." *Steinbeck Quarterly*, 26, No. 1–2 (1993): 38–45.

Hughes, R. S. *Beyond The Red Pony: A Reader's Companion to Steinbeck's Complete Short Stories.* Metuchen: Scarecrow, 1987.

———. *John Steinbeck: A Study of the Short Fiction.* Boston: Twayne, 1989.

Ingram, Forrest L. *Representative Short Story Cycles of the Twentieth Century: Studies in a Literary Genre.* The Hague: Mouton, 1971.

Levant, Howard. *The Novels of John Steinbeck: A Critical Study.* Columbia: University of Missouri Press, 1974.

Lisca, Peter. *The Wide World of John Steinbeck.* New York: Gordian Press, 1981.

Mann, Susan Garland. *The Short Story Cycle: A Genre Companion and Reference Guide.* Westport: Greenwood, 1989.

Mawer, Randall R. "Takashi Kato, 'Good American': The Central Episode in Steinbeck's *The Pastures of Heaven.*" *Steinbeck Quarterly* 13 (Winter–Spring 1980): 23–31.

Mortlock, Melanie. "The Eden Myth as Paradox: An Allegorical Reading of *The Pastures of Heaven*." *Steinbeck Quarterly* 11 (Winter 1978): 6–15.

Owens, Louis. *John Steinbeck's Re-Vision of America*. Athens: University of Georgia Press, 1985.

Peterson, Richard. "The Turning Point: *The Pastures of Heaven* (1932)." *A Study Guide to Steinbeck: A Handbook to His Major Works*, ed. Tetsumaro Hayashi. Metuchen: Scarecrow, 1974, pp. 87–106.

Steinbeck, Elaine, and Robert Wallsten, eds. *Steinbeck: A Life in Letters*. New York: Viking, 1975.

Timmerman, John H. *The Dramatic Landscape of Steinbeck's Short Stories*. Norman: University of Oklahoma Press, 1990.

———. *John Steinbeck's Fiction: The Aesthetics of the Road Taken*. Norman: University of Oklahoma Press, 1986.

A NOTE ON THE TEXT

The text of this volume reproduces that issued by the Viking Press in 1963, which was based on the original Brewer, Warren, and Putnam edition of 1932. The first edition was reprinted under the Covici-Friede imprint in 1935.

THE PASTURES
OF HEAVEN

TO MY FATHER AND MOTHER

I

When the Carmelo Mission of Alta California was being built, some time around 1776, a group of twenty converted Indians abandoned religion during a night, and in the morning they were gone from their huts. Besides being a bad precedent, this minor schism crippled the work in the clay pits where adobe bricks were being molded.

After a short council of the religious and civil authorities, a Spanish corporal with a squad of horsemen set out to restore these erring children to the bosom of Mother Church. The troop made a difficult journey up the Carmel Valley and into the mountains beyond, a trip not the less bewildering because the fleeing dissenters had proved themselves masters of a diabolic guile in concealing traces of their journey. It was a week before the soldiery found them, but they were discovered at last practicing abominations in the bottom of a ferny canyon in which a stream flowed; that is, the twenty heretics were fast asleep in attitudes of abandon.

The outraged military seized them and in spite of their howlings attached them to a long slender chain. Then the column turned about and headed for Carmel again to give the poor neophytes a chance at repentance in the clay pits.

In the late afternoon of the second day a small deer started up before the troop and popped out of sight over a ridge. The corporal disengaged himself from his column and rode in its pursuit. His heavy horse scrambled and floundered up the steep slope; the manzanita reached sharp claws for the corporal's face, but he plunged on after his dinner. In a few minutes he arrived at the top of the ridge, and there he stopped, stricken with wonder at what he saw—a long valley floored with green pasturage on which a herd of deer browsed. Perfect live oaks grew in the meadow of the lovely place, and the hills hugged it jealously against the fog and the wind.

The disciplinarian corporal felt weak in the face of so serene a beauty. He who had whipped brown backs to tatters, he whose rapacious manhood was building a new race for California, this bearded, savage bearer of civilization slipped from his saddle and took off his steel hat.

"Holy Mother!" he whispered. "Here are the green pastures of Heaven to which our Lord leadeth us."

His descendants are almost white now. We can only reconstruct his holy emotion of discovery, but the name he gave to the sweet valley in the hills remains there. It is known to this day as *Las Pasturas del Cielo.*

By some regal accident the section came under no great land grant. No Spanish nobleman became its possessor through the loan of his money or his wife. For a long time it lay forgotten in its embracing hills. The Spanish corporal, the discoverer, always intended to go back. Like most violent men he looked forward with sentimental wistfulness to a little time of peace before he died, to an adobe house beside a stream, and cattle nuzzling the walls at night.

An Indian woman presented him with the pox, and, when his face began to fall away, good friends locked him in an old barn to prevent the infection of others, and there he died peacefully, for the pox, although horrible to look at, is no bad friend to its host.

After a long time a few families of squatters moved into the Pastures of Heaven and built fences and planted fruit trees. Since no one owned the land, they squabbled a great deal over its possession. After a hundred years there were twenty families on twenty little farms in the Pastures of Heaven. Near the center of the valley stood a general store and post office, and half a mile above, beside the stream, a hacked and much initialed schoolhouse.

The families at last lived prosperously and at peace. Their land was rich and easy to work. The fruits of their gardens were the finest produced in central California.

II

To the people of the Pastures of Heaven the Battle farm was cursed, and to their children it was haunted. Good land although it was, well watered and fertile, no one in the valley coveted the place, no one would live in the house, for land and houses that have been tended, loved and labored with and finally deserted, seem always sodden with gloom and with threatening. The trees which grow up around a deserted house are dark trees, and the shadows they throw on the ground have suggestive shapes.

For five years now the old Battle farm had stood vacant. The weeds, with a holiday energy, free of fear of the hoe, grew as large as small trees. In the orchard the fruit trees were knotty and strong and tangled. They increased the quantity of their fruit, and diminished its size. The brambles grew about their roots and swallowed up the windfalls.

The house itself, a square, well-built, two-story place, had been dignified and handsome when its white paint was fresh, but a singular latter history had left about it an air unbearably lonely. Weeds warped up the boards of the porches, the walls were grey with weathering. Small boys, those lieutenants of time in its warfare against the works of man, had broken out all the windows and carted away every movable thing. Boys believe that all kinds of portable articles which have no obvious owner, if taken home, can be put to some joyous use. The boys had gutted the house, had filled the wells with various kinds of refuse, and, quite by accident, while secretly smoking real tobacco in the hayloft, had burned the old barn to the ground. The fire was universally attributed to tramps.

The deserted farm was situated not far from the middle

of the narrow valley. On both sides it was bounded by the best and most prosperous farms in the Pastures of Heaven. It was a weedy blot between two finely cultivated, contented pieces of land. The people of the valley considered it a place of curious evil, for one horrible event and one impenetrable mystery had taken place there.

Two generations of Battles had lived on the farm. George Battle came west in 1863 from upper New York State; he was quite young when he arrived, just draft age. His mother supplied the money to buy the farm and to build the big square house upon it. When the house was completed, George Battle sent for his mother to come to live with him. She tried to come, that old woman who thought that space stopped ten miles from her village. She saw mythological places, New York and Rio and Buenos Aires. Off Patagonia she died, and a ship's watch buried her in a grey ocean with a piece of canvas for her coffin and three links of anchor chain sewn in between her feet; and she had wanted the crowded company of her home graveyard.

George Battle looked about for a good investment in a woman. In Salinas he found Miss Myrtle Cameron, a spinster of thirty-five, with a small fortune. Miss Myrtle had been neglected because of a mild tendency to epilepsy, a disease then called "fits" and generally ascribed to animosity on the part of the deity. George did not mind the epilepsy. He knew he couldn't have everything he wanted. Myrtle became his wife and bore him a son, and, after twice trying to burn the house, was confined in a little private prison called the Lippman Sanitarium, in San Jose. She spent the rest of her existence crocheting a symbolic life of Christ in cotton thread.

Thereafter the big house on the Battle farm was governed by a series of evil-tempered housekeepers of that kind who advertise: "Widow, 45, wants position housekeeper on farm.

Good cook. Obj. Mat." One by one they came and were sweet and sad for a few days until they found out about Myrtle. After that they tramped through the house with flashing eyes, feeling that they had been abstractly raped.

George Battle was old at fifty, bent with work, pleasureless and dour. His eyes never left the ground he worked with so patiently. His hands were hard and black and covered with little crevices, like the pads of a bear. And his farm was beautiful. The trees in the orchard were trim and groomed, each one a counterpart of its fellows. The vegetables grew crisp and green in their line-straight rows. George cared for his house and kept a flower garden in front of it. The upper story of the house had never been lived in. This farm was a poem by the inarticulate man. Patiently he built his scene and waited for a Sylvia. No Sylvia ever came, but he kept the garden waiting for her just the same. In all the years when his son was growing up, George Battle paid very little attention to him. Only the fruit trees and the fresh green rows of vegetables were vital. When John, his son, went missionarying in a caravan, George didn't even miss him. He went on with the work, yearly bending his body lower over his earth. His neighbors never talked to him because he did not listen to talk. His hands were permanently hooked, had become sockets into which the handles of tools fitted tightly. At sixty-five he died of old age and a cough.

John Battle came home in his caravan to claim the farm. From his mother he had inherited both the epilepsy and the mad knowledge of God. John's life was devoted to a struggle with devils. From camp meeting to camp meeting he had gone, hurling his hands about, invoking devils and then confounding them, exorcising and flaying incarnate evil. When he arrived at home the devils still claimed attention. The lines of vegetables went to seed, volunteered a few times, and succumbed to the weeds. The farm slipped back to nature, but the devils grew stronger and more importunate.

As a protection John Battle covered his clothes and his hat with tiny cross-stitches in white thread, and, thus armored, made war on the dark legions. In the grey dusk he sneaked about the farm armed with a heavy stick. He charged into the underbrush, thrashed about with his stick and shouted maledictions until the devils were driven from cover. At night he crept through the thickets upon a congregation of the demons, then fearlessly rushed forward, striking viciously with his weapon. In the daytime he went into his house and slept, for the devils did not work in the light.

One day in the deepening twilight John crept carefully upon a lilac bush in his own yard. He knew the bush sheltered a secret gathering of fiends. When he was so close that they could not escape, he jumped to his feet and lunged toward the lilac, flailing his stick and screaming. Aroused by the slashing blows, a snake rattled sleepily and raised its flat, hard head. John dropped his stick and shuddered, for the dry sharp warning of a snake is a terrifying sound. He fell upon his knees and prayed for a moment. Suddenly he shouted, "This is the damned serpent. Out, devil," and sprang forward with clutching fingers. The snake struck him three times in the throat where there were no crosses to protect him. He struggled very little, and died in a few minutes.

His neighbors only found him when the buzzards began to drop out of the sky, and the thing they found made them dread the Battle farm after that.

For ten years the farm lay fallow. The children said the house was haunted and made night excursions to it to frighten themselves. There was something fearsome about the gaunt old house with its staring vacant windows. The white paint fell off in long scales; the shingles curled up shaggily. The farm itself went completely wild. It was owned by a distant cousin of George Battle's, who had never seen it.

In 1921 the Mustrovics took possession of the Battle farm. Their coming was sudden and mysterious. One morning they were there, an old man and his old wife, skeleton people with tight yellow skin stretched and shiny over their high cheek bones. Neither of them spoke English. Communication with the valley was carried on by their son, a tall man with the same high cheek bones, with coarse-cropped black hair growing halfway down his forehead, and with soft, sullen black eyes. He spoke English with an accent, and he only spoke his wants.

At the store the people gently questioned him, but they received no information.

"We always thought that place was haunted. Seen any ghosts yet?" T. B. Allen, the storekeeper, asked.

"No," said young Mustrovic.

"It's a good farm all right when you get the weeds off."

Mustrovic turned and walked out of the store.

"There's something about that place," said Allen. "Everybody who lives there hates to talk."

The old Mustrovics were rarely seen, but the young man worked every daylight hour on the farm. All by himself he cleared the land and planted it, pruned the trees and sprayed them. At any hour he could be seen working feverishly, half running about his tasks, with a look on his face as though he expected time to stop before a crop was in.

The family lived and slept in the kitchen of the big house. All the other rooms were shut up and vacant, the broken windows unmended. They had stuck fly-paper over the holes in the kitchen windows to keep out the air. They did not paint the house nor take care of it in any way, but under the frantic efforts of the young man, the land began to grow beautiful again. For two years he slaved on the soil. In the grey of the dawn he emerged from the house, and the last of the dusk was gone before he went back into it.

One morning, Pat Humbert, driving to the store, noticed that no smoke came from the Mustrovic chimney. "The place looks deserted again," he said to Allen. " 'Course we never saw anybody but that young fellow around there, but something's wrong. What I mean is, the place kind of *feels* deserted."

For three days the neighbors watched the chimney apprehensively. They hated to investigate and make fools of themselves. On the fourth day Pat Humbert and T. B. Allen and John Whiteside walked up to the house. It was rustlingly still. It really did seem deserted. John Whiteside knocked at the kitchen door. When there was no answer and no movement, he turned the knob. The door swung open. The kitchen was immaculately clean, and the table set; there were dishes on the table, saucers of porridge, and fried eggs and sliced bread. On the food a little mold was forming. A few flies wandered aimlessly about in the sunshine that came through the open door. Pat Humbert shouted, "Anybody here?" He knew he was silly to do it.

They searched the house thoroughly, but it was vacant. There was no furniture in any rooms except the kitchen. The farm was completely deserted—had been deserted at a moment's notice.

Later, when the sheriff was informed, he found out nothing revealing. The Mustrovics had paid cash for the farm, and in going away had left no trace. No one saw them go, and no one ever saw them again. There was not even any crime in that part of the country that they might have taken part in. Suddenly, just as they were about to sit down to breakfast one morning, the Mustrovics had disappeared. Many, many times the case was discussed at the store, but no one could advance a tenable solution.

The weeds sprang up on the land again, and the wild berry vines climbed into the branches of the fruit trees. As though practice had made it adept, the farm fell quickly back to wildness. It was sold for taxes to a Monterey realty company, and the people of the Pastures of Heaven, whether they admitted it or not, were convinced that the Battle farm bore a curse. "It's good land," they said, "but I wouldn't own it if you gave it to me. I don't know what's the matter, but there's sure something funny about that place, almost creepy. Wouldn't be hard for a fellow to believe in haunts."

A pleasant shudder went through the people of the Pastures of Heaven when they heard that the old Battle farm was again to be occupied. The rumor was brought in to the General Store by Pat Humbert who had seen automobiles in front of the old house, and T. B. Allen, the store proprietor, widely circulated the story. Allen imagined all the circumstances surrounding the new ownership and told them to his customers, beginning all his confidences with "They say." "They say the fellow who's bought the Battle place is one of those people that goes about looking for ghosts and writing about them." T. B. Allen's "they say" was his protection. He used it as newspapers use the word "alleged."

Before Bert Munroe took possession of his new property, there were a dozen stories about him circulating through the Pastures of Heaven. He knew that the people who were to be his new neighbors were staring at him although he could never catch them at it. This secret staring is developed to a high art among country people. They have seen every uncovered bit of you, have tabulated and memorized the clothes you are wearing, have noticed the color of your eyes and the shape of your nose, and, finally, have reduced your figure and personality to three or four adjectives, and all the time you thought they were oblivious to your presence.

After he had bought the old place, Bert Munroe went to

work in the overgrown yard while a crew of carpenters made over the house. Every stick of furniture was taken out and burned in the yard. Partitions were torn down and other partitions put in. The walls were repapered and the house reroofed with asbestos shingles. Finally a new coat of pale yellow paint was applied to the outside.

Bert himself cut down all the vines, and all the trees in the yard, to let in the light. Within three weeks the old house had lost every vestige of its deserted, haunted look. By stroke after stroke of genius it had been made to look like a hundred thousand other country houses in the West.

As soon as the paint inside and out was dry, the new furniture arrived, overstuffed chairs and a davenport, an enameled stove, steel beds painted to look like wood and guaranteed to provide a mathematical comfort. There were mirrors with scalloped frames, Wilton rugs and prints of pictures by a modern artist who has made blue popular.

With the furniture came Mrs. Munroe and the three younger Munroes. Mrs. Munroe was a plump woman who wore a rimless pince nez on a ribbon. She was a good house manager. Again and again she had the new furniture moved about until she was satisfied, but once satisfied, once she had regarded the piece with a concentrated gaze and then nodded and smiled, that piece was fixed forever, only to be moved for cleaning.

Her daughter Mae was a pretty girl with round smooth cheeks and ripe lips. She was voluptuous of figure, but under her chin there was a soft, pretty curve which indicated a future plumpness like her mother's. Mae's eyes were friendly and candid, not intelligent, but by no means stupid. Imperceptibly she would grow to be her mother's double, a good manager, a mother of healthy children, a good wife with no regrets.

In her own new room, Mae stuck dance programs between the glass and the frame of the mirror. On the walls she hung framed photographs of her friends in Monterey, and laid out her photograph album and her locked diary on the little bedside table. In the diary she concealed from prying eyes a completely uninteresting record of dances, of parties, of recipes for candy and of mild preferences for certain boys. Mae bought and made her own room curtains, pale pink theatrical gauze to strain the light, and a valance of flowered cretonne. On her bedspread of gathered satin, she arranged five boudoir pillows in positions of abandon, and against them leaned a long-legged French doll with clipped blonde hair and with a cloth cigarette dangling from languid lips. Mae considered that this doll proved her openness of mind, her tolerance of things she did not quite approve. She liked to have friends who had pasts, for, having such friends and listening to them, destroyed in her any regret that her own life had been blameless. She was nineteen; she thought of marriage most of the time. When she was out with boys she talked of ideals with some emotion. Mae had very little conception of what ideals were except that in some manner they governed the kind of kisses one received while driving home from dances.

Jimmie Munroe was seventeen, just out of high school and enormously cynical. In the presence of his parents, Jimmie's manner was usually sullen and secretive. He knew he couldn't trust them with his knowledge of the world, for they would not understand. They belonged to a generation which had no knowledge of sin nor of heroism. A firm intention to give over one's life to science after gutting it of emotional possibilities would not be tenderly received by his parents. By science, Jimmie meant radios, archaeology and airplanes. He pictured himself digging up golden vases in Peru. He dreamed of shutting himself up in a cell-like workshop, and, after years of agony and ridicule, of emerging with an airplane new in design and devastating in speed.

Jimmie's room in the new house became a clutter of small machines as soon as he was settled. There was a radio crystal set with ear phones, a hand-powered magneto which operated a telegraph key, a brass telescope and innumerable machines partly taken to pieces. Jimmie, too, had a secret repository, an oaken box fastened with a heavy padlock. In the box were: half a can of dynamite caps, an old revolver, a package of Melachrino cigarettes, three contraptions known as Merry Widows, a small flask of peach brandy, a paper knife shaped like a dagger, four bundles of letters from four different girls, sixteen lipsticks pilfered from dance partners, a box containing mementos of current loves—dried flowers, handkerchiefs and buttons, and most prized of all, a round garter covered with black lace. Jimmie had forgotten how he really got the garter. What he *did* remember was far more satisfactory anyway. He always locked his bedroom door before he unlocked the box.

In high school Jimmie's score of sinfulness had been equaled by many of his friends and easily passed by some. Soon after moving to the Pastures of Heaven, he found that his iniquities were unique. He came to regard himself as a reformed rake, but one not reformed beyond possible outbreak. It gave him a powerful advantage with the younger girls of the valley to have lived so fully. Jimmy was rather a handsome boy, lean and well made, dark of hair and eyes.

Manfred, the youngest boy, ordinarily called Manny, was a serious child of seven, whose face was pinched and drawn by adenoids. His parents knew about the adenoids; they had even talked of having them removed. Manny became terrified of the operation, and his mother, seeing this, had used it as a deterrent threat when he was bad. Now, a mention of having his adenoids removed made Manny hysterical with terror. Mr. and Mrs. Munroe considered him a thoughtful child, perhaps a genius. He played usually by himself, or sat for hours staring into space, "dreaming," his mother said. They would not know for some years that he was subnormal, his brain development arrested by his adenoidal condition. Ordinarily Manny was a good child, tractable and easily terrified into obedience, but, if he were terrified a little too much, a hysteria resulted that robbed him of his self-control and even of a sense of self-preservation. He had been known to beat his forehead on the floor until the blood ran into his eyes.

Bert Munroe came to the Pastures of Heaven because he was tired of battling with a force which invariably defeated him. He had engaged in many enterprises and every one had failed, not through any shortcoming on Bert's part, but through mishaps, which, if taken alone, were accidents. Bert saw all the accidents together and they seemed to him the acts of a Fate malignant to his success. He was tired of fighting the nameless thing that stopped every avenue to success. Bert was only fifty-five, but he wanted to rest; he was half convinced that a curse rested upon him.

Years ago he opened a garage on the edge of a town. Business was good; money began to roll in. When he considered himself safe, the state highway came through on another street and left him stranded without business. He sold the garage a year or so later and opened a grocery store. Again he was successful. He paid off his indebtedness and began to put money in the bank. A chain grocery crowded up against him, opened a price war and forced him from business. Bert was a sensitive man. Such things as these had happened to him a dozen times. Just when his success seemed permanent, the curse struck him. His self-confidence dwindled. When the war broke out his spirit was nearly gone. He knew there was money to be made from the war, but he was afraid, after having been beaten so often.

He had to reassure himself a great deal before he made his first contract for beans in the field. In the first year of business, he made fifty thousand dollars, the second year two hundred thousand. The third year he contracted for thousands of acres of beans before they were even planted. By his contracts, he guaranteed to pay ten cents a pound for the crops. He could sell all the beans he could get for eighteen cents a pound. The war ended in November, and he sold his crop for four cents a pound. He had a little less money than when he started.

This time he was sure of the curse. His spirit was so badly broken that he didn't leave his house very often. He worked in the garden, planted a few vegetables and brooded over the enmity of his fate. Slowly, over a period of stagnant years, a nostalgia for the soil grew in him. In farming, he thought, lay the only line of endeavor that did not cross with his fate. He thought perhaps he could find rest and security on a little farm.

The Battle place was offered for sale by a Monterey realty company. Bert looked at the farm, saw the changes that could be made, and bought it. At first his family opposed the move, but, when he had cleaned the yard, installed electricity and a telephone in the house, and made it comfortable with new furniture, they were almost enthusiastic about it. Mrs. Munroe thought any change desirable that would stop Bert's moping in the yard in Monterey.

The moment he had bought the farm, Bert felt free. The doom was gone. He knew he was safe from his curse. Within a month his shoulders straightened, and his face lost its haunted look. He became an enthusiastic farmer; he read exhaustively on farming methods, hired a helper and worked from morning until night. Every day was a new excitement to him. Every seed sprouting out of the ground seemed to renew a promise of immunity to him. He was happy, and because he was confident again, he began to make friends in the valley and to entrench his position.

It is a difficult thing and one requiring great tact quickly to become accepted in a rural community. The people of the valley had watched the advent of the Munroe family with a little animosity. The Battle farm was haunted. They had always considered it so, even those who laughed at the idea. Now a man came along and proved them wrong. More than that, he changed the face of the countryside by removing the accursed farm and substituting a harmless and fertile farm. The people were used to the Battle place as it was. Secretly they resented the change.

That Bert could remove this animosity was remarkable. Within three months he had become a part of the valley, a solid man, a neighbor. He borrowed tools and had tools borrowed from him. At the end of six months he was elected a member of the school board. To a large extent Bert's own happiness at being free of his Furies made the people like him. In addition he was a kindly man; he enjoyed doing favors for his friends, and, more important, he had no hesitancy in asking favors.

At the store he explained his position to a group of farmers, and they admired the honesty of his explanation. It was soon after he had come to the valley. T. B. Allen asked his old question.

"We always kind of thought that place was cursed. Lots of funny things have happened there. Seen any ghosts yet?"

Bert laughed. "If you take away all the food from a place, the rats will leave," he said. "I took all the oldness and darkness away from that place. That's what ghosts live on."

"You sure made a nice looking place of it," Allen admitted. "There ain't a better place in the Pastures when it's kept up."

Bert had been frowning soberly as a new thought began to work in his mind. "I've had a lot of bad luck," he said. "I've been in a lot of businesses and every one turned out bad. When I came down here, I had a kind of an idea that I was under a curse." Suddenly he laughed delightedly at the thought that had come to him. "And what do I do? First thing out of the box, I buy a place that's supposed to be under a curse. Well, I just happened to think, maybe my curse and the farm's curse got to fighting and killed each other off. I'm dead certain they've gone, anyway."

The men laughed with him. T. B. Allen whacked his hand down on the counter. "That's a good one," he cried. "But here's a better one. Maybe your curse and the farm's curse has mated and gone into a gopher hole like a pair of rattlesnakes. Maybe there'll be a lot of baby curses crawling around the Pastures the first thing we know."

The gathered men roared with laughter at that, and T. B. Allen memorized the whole scene so he could repeat it. It was almost like the talk in a play, he thought.

III

Edward Wicks lived in a small, gloomy house on the edge of the country road in the Pastures of Heaven. Behind the house there was a peach orchard and a large vegetable garden. While Edward Wicks took care of the peaches, his wife and beautiful daughter cultivated the garden and got the peas and string beans and early strawberries ready to be sold in Monterey.

Edward Wicks had a blunt, brown face and small, cold eyes almost devoid of lashes. He was known as the trickiest man in the valley. He drove hard deals and was never so happy as when he could force a few cents more out of his peaches than his neighbors did. When he could, he cheated ethically in horse trades, and because of his acuteness he gained the respect of the community, but strangely became no richer. However, he liked to pretend that he was laying away money in securities. At school board meetings he asked the advice of the other members about various bonds, and in this way managed to give them the impression that his savings were considerable. The people of the valley called him "Shark" Wicks.

"Shark?" they said. "Oh, I'd guess he was worth around twenty thousand, maybe more. He's nobody's fool."

And the truth was that Shark had never had more than five hundred dollars at one time in his life.

Shark's greatest pleasure came of being considered a wealthy man. Indeed, he enjoyed it so much that the wealth itself became real to him. Setting his imaginary fortune at fifty thousand dollars, he kept a ledger in which he calculated his interest and entered records of his various investments. These manipulations were the first joy of his life.

An oil company was formed in Salinas with the purpose of boring a well in the southern part of Monterey county. When he heard of it, Shark walked over to the farm of John Whiteside to discuss the value of its stock. "I been wondering about that South County Oil Company," he said.

"Well, the geologist's report sounds good," said John Whiteside. "I have always heard that there was oil in that section. I heard it years ago." John Whiteside was often consulted in such matters. "Of course I wouldn't put too much into it."

Shark creased his lower lip with his fingers and pondered for a moment. "I been turning it over in my mind," he said. "It looks like a pretty good proposition to me. I got about ten thousand lying around that ain't bringing in what it should. I guess I'd better look into it pretty carefully. Just thought I'd see what your opinion was."

But Shark's mind was already made up. When he got home, he took down the ledger and withdrew ten thousand dollars from his imaginary bank account. Then he entered one thousand shares of Southern County Oil Company stock to his list of securities. From that day on he watched the stock lists feverishly. When the price rose a little, he went about whistling monotonously, and when the price dropped, he felt a lump of apprehension forming in his throat. At length, when there came a quick rise in the price of South County, Shark was so elated that he went to the Pastures of Heaven General Store and bought a black marble mantel clock with onyx columns on either side of the dial and a bronze horse to go on top of it. The men in the store looked wise and whispered that Shark was about to make a killing.

A week later the stock dropped out of sight and the company disappeared. The moment he heard the news, Shark dragged out his ledger and entered the fact that he had sold his shares the day before the break, had sold with a two thousand dollar profit.

Pat Humbert, driving back from Monterey, stopped his car on the county road in front of Shark's house. "I heard you got washed out in that South County stock," he observed.

Shark smiled contentedly. "What do you think I am, Pat? I sold out two days ago. You ought to know as well as the next man that I ain't a sucker. I knew that stock was bum, but I also knew it would take a rise so the backers could get out whole. When they unloaded, I did too."

"The hell you did!" said Pat admiringly. And when he went into the General Store he passed the information on. Men nodded their heads and made new guesses at the amount of Shark's money. They admitted they'd hate to come up against him in a business deal.

At this time Shark borrowed four hundred dollars from a Monterey bank and bought a second-hand Fordson tractor.

Gradually his reputation for good judgment and foresight became so great that no man in the Pastures of Heaven thought of buying a bond or a piece of land or even a horse without first consulting Shark Wicks. With each of his admirers Shark went carefully into the problem and ended by giving startlingly good advice.

In a few years his ledger showed that he had accumulated one hundred and twenty-five thousand dollars through sagacious investing. When his neighbors saw that he lived like a poor man, they respected him the more because his riches did not turn his head. He was nobody's fool. His wife and beautiful daughter still cared for the vegetables and prepared them for sale in Monterey, while Shark attended to the thousand duties of the orchard.

In Shark's life there had been no literary romance. At nineteen he took Katherine Mullock to three dances because she was available. This started the machine of precedent and he married her because her family and all of the neighbors expected it. Katherine was not pretty, but she had the firm freshness of a new weed, and the bridling vigor of a young mare. After her marriage she lost her vigor and her freshness as a flower does once it has received pollen. Her face sagged, her hips broadened, and she entered into her second destiny, that of work.

In his treatment of her, Shark was neither tender nor cruel. He governed her with the same gentle inflexibility he used on horses. Cruelty would have seemed to him as foolish as indulgence. He never talked to her as to human, never spoke of his hopes or thoughts or failures, of his paper wealth nor of the peach crop. Katherine would have been puzzled and worried if he had. Her life was sufficiently complicated without the added burden of another's thoughts and problems.

The brown Wicks house was the only unbeautiful thing on the farm. The trash and litter of nature disappears into the ground with the passing of each year, but man's litter has more permanence. The yard was strewn with old sacks, with papers, bits of broken glass and tangles of baling wire. The only place on the farm where grass and flowers would not grow was the hard-packed dirt around the house, dirt made sterile and unfriendly by emptied tubs of soapy water. Shark irrigated his orchard, but he could see no reason for wasting good water around the house.

When Alice was born, the women of the Pastures of Heaven came herding into Shark's house prepared to exclaim that it was a pretty baby. When they saw it was a beautiful baby, they did not know what to say. Those feminine exclamations of delight designed to reassure young mothers that the horrible reptilian creatures in their arms are human and will not grow up to be monstrosities, lost their meaning. Furthermore, Katherine had looked at her child with eyes untainted by the artificial enthusiasm with which most women smother their disappointments. When Katherine had seen that the baby was beautiful, she was filled with wonder and with awe and misgiving. The fact of Alice's beauty was too marvelous to be without retribution. Pretty babies, Katherine said to herself, usually turned out ugly men and women. By saying it, she beat off some of the misgiving as though she had apprehended Fate at its tricks and robbed it of potency by her foreknowledge.

On that first day of visiting, Shark heard one of the women say to another in a tone of unbelief, "But it really is a pretty baby. How do you suppose it *could* be so pretty?"

Shark went back to the bedroom and looked long at his little daughter. Out in the orchard he pondered over the matter. The baby really was beautiful. It was foolish to think that he or Katherine or any of their relatives had anything to do with it for they were all homely even as ordinary people go. Clearly a very precious thing had been given to him, and, since precious things were universally coveted, Alice must be protected. Shark believed in God when he thought of it, of course, as that shadowy being who did everything he could not understand.

Alice grew and became more and more beautiful. Her skin was as lucent and rich as poppies; her black hair had the soft crispness of fern stems, her eyes were misty skies of promise. One looked into the child's serious eyes and started forward thinking—"Something is in there that I know, something I seem to remember sharply, or something I have spent all my life searching for." Then Alice turned her head. "Why! It is only a lovely little girl."

Shark saw this recognition take place in many people. He

saw men blush when they looked at her, saw little boys fight like tigers when she was about.

He thought he read covetousness in every male face. Often when he was working in the orchard he tortured himself by imagining scenes wherein gypsies stole the little girl. A dozen times a day he cautioned her against dangerous things: the hind heels of horses, the highness of fences, the danger that lurked in gullies and the absolute suicide of crossing a road without carefully looking for approaching automobiles. Every neighbor, every pedlar, and worst of all, every stranger he looked upon as a possible kidnapper. When tramps were reported in the Pastures of Heaven he never let the little girl out of his sight. Picnickers wondered at Shark's ferocity in ordering them off his land.

As for Katherine, the constantly increasing beauty of Alice augmented her misgiving. Destiny was waiting to strike, and that could only mean that destiny was storing strength for a more violent blow. She became the slave of her daughter, hovered about and did little services such as one might accord an invalid who is soon to die.

In spite of the worship of the Wickses for their child and their fears for her safety and their miser-like gloating over her beauty, they both knew that their lovely daughter was an incredibly stupid, dull and backward little girl. In Shark, this knowledge only added to his fears, for he was convinced that she could not take care of herself and would become an easy prey to anyone who wished to make off with her. But to Katherine, Alice's stupidity was a pleasant thing since it presented so many means by which her mother could help her. By helping, Katherine proved a superiority, and cut down to some extent the great gap between them. Katherine was glad of every weakness in her daughter since each one made her feel closer and more worthy.

When Alice turned fourteen a new responsibility was added to the many her father felt concerning her. Before that time Shark had only feared her loss or disfigurement, but after that he was terrified at the thought of her loss of chastity. Little by little, through much dwelling on the subject, this last fear absorbed the other two. He came to regard the possible defloration of his daughter as both loss and disfigurement. From that time on he was uncomfortable and suspicious when any man or boy was near the farm.

The subject became a nightmare to him. Over and over he cautioned his wife never to let Alice out of her sight. "You just can't tell what might happen," he repeated, his pale eyes flaring with suspicions. "You just can't tell what might happen." His daughter's mental inadequateness greatly increased his fear. Anyone, he thought, might ruin her. Anyone at all who was left alone with her might misuse her. And she couldn't protect herself, because she was so stupid. No man ever guarded his prize bitch when she was in heat more closely than Shark watched his daughter.

After a time Shark was no longer satisfied with her purity unless he had been assured of it. Each month he pestered his wife. He knew the dates better than she did. "Is she all right?" he asked wolfishly.

Katherine answered contemptuously, "Not yet."

A few hours later—"Is she all right?"

He kept this up until at last Katherine answered, "Of course she's all right. What did you think?"

This answer satisfied Shark for a month, but it did not decrease his watchfulness. The chastity was intact, therefore it was still to be guarded.

Shark knew that some time Alice would want to be married, but, often as the thought came to him, he put it away and tried to forget it, for he regarded her marriage with no less repugnance than her seduction. She was a precious thing, to be watched and preserved. To him it was not a moral problem, but an aesthetic one. Once she was deflorated, she would no longer be the precious thing he treasured so. He did not love her as a father loves a child. Rather he hoarded her, and gloated over the possession of a fine, unique thing. Gradually, as he asked his question—"Is she all right?"—month by month, this chastity came to symbolize her health, her preservation, her intactness.

One day when Alice was sixteen, Shark went to his wife with a worried look on his face. "You know we really can't tell if she's all right—that is—we couldn't really be sure unless we took her to a doctor."

For a moment Katherine stared at him, trying to realize what the words meant. Then she lost her temper for the first time in her life. "You're a dirty, suspicious skunk," she told him. "You get out of here! And if you ever talk about it again, I'll—I'll go away."

Shark was a little astonished, but not frightened, at her outburst. He did, however, give up the idea of a medical examination, and merely contented himself with his monthly question.

Meanwhile, Shark's ledger fortune continued to grow. Every night, after Katherine and Alice had gone to bed, he took down the thick book and opened it under the hanging lamp. Then his pale eyes narrowed and his blunt face took on a crafty look while he planned his investments and calculated his interest. His lips moved slightly, for now he was telephoning an order for stock. A stern and yet sorrowful look crossed his face when he foreclosed a mortgage on a good farm. "I hate to do this," he whispered. "You folks got to realize it's just business."

Shark wetted his pen in the ink bottle and entered the fact of the foreclosure in his ledger. "Lettuce," he mused. "Everybody's putting in lettuce. The market's going to be flooded. Seems to me I might put in potatoes and make some money. That's fine bottom land." He noted in the book the planting of three hundred acres of potatoes. His eye traveled along the line. Thirty thousands dollars lay in the bank just drawing bank interest. It seemed a shame. The money was practically idle. A frown of concentration settled over his eyes. He wondered how San Jose Building and Loan was. It paid six per cent. It wouldn't do to rush into it blindly without investigating the company. As he closed the ledger for the night, Shark determined to talk to John Whiteside about it. Sometimes those companies went broke, the officers absconded, he thought uneasily.

Before the Munroe family moved into the valley, Shark suspected all men and boys of evil intent toward Alice, but when once he had set eyes on young Jimmie Munroe, his fear and suspicion narrowed until it had all settled upon the sophisticated Jimmie. The boy was lean and handsome of face, his mouth was well developed and sensual, and his eyes shone with that insulting cockiness high school boys assume. Jimmie was said to drink gin; he wore town clothes of wool—never overalls. His hair shone with oil, and his whole manner and posture were of a rakishness that set the girls of the Pastures of Heaven giggling and squirming with admiration and embarrassment. Jimmie watched the girls with quiet, cynical eyes, and tried to appear dissipated for their benefit. He knew that young girls are vastly attracted to young men with pasts. Jimmie had a past. He had been drunk several times at the Riverside Dance Palace; he had kissed at least a hundred girls, and, on three occasions, he had sinful adventures in the willows by the Salinas River. Jimmie tried to make his face confess his vicious life, but, fearing that his appearance was not enough, he set free a number of mischievous little rumors that darted about the Pastures of Heaven with flattering speed.

Shark Wicks heard the rumors. In Shark there grew up a hatred of Jimmie Munroe that was born of fear of Jimmie's way with women. What chance, Shark thought, would beautiful, stupid Alice have against one so steeped in knowledge of wordliness?

Before Alice had ever seen the boy, Shark forbade her to see him. He spoke with such vehemence that a mild interest was aroused in the dull brain of the girl.

"Don't you ever let me catch you talking to that Jimmie Munroe," he told her.

"Who's Jimmie Munroe, Papa?"

"Never you mind who he is. Just don't let me catch you talking to him. You hear me! Why! I'll skin you alive if you even look at him."

Shark had never laid a hand on Alice for the same reason that he would not have whipped a Dresden vase. He even hesitated to caress her for fear of leaving a mark. Punishment was never necessary. Alice had always been a good and tractable child. Badness must originate in an idea or an ambition. She had never experienced either.

And again—"You haven't been talking to that Jimmie Munroe, have you?"

"No, Papa."

"Well just don't let me catch you at it."

After a number of repetitions of this order, a conviction crept into the thickened cells of Alice's brain that she would really like to see Jimmie Munroe. She even had a dream about him, which shows how deeply she was stirred. Alice very rarely dreamed about anything. In her dream, a man who looked like the Indian on her room calendar, and whose name was Jimmie, drove up in a shiny automobile and gave her a large juicy peach. When she bit into the peach, the juice ran down her chin and embarrassed her. Then her mother awakened her for she was snoring. Katherine was glad her daughter snored. It was one of the equaling imperfections. But at the same time it was not ladylike.

Shark Wicks received a telegram. "Aunt Nellie passed away last night. Funeral Saturday." He got into his Ford and drove to the farm of John Whiteside to say he couldn't attend the school board meeting. John Whiteside was clerk of the board. Before he left, Shark looked worried for a moment and then said, "I been wanting to ask you what you thought about that San Jose Building and Loan Company."

John Whiteside smiled. "I don't know much about that particular company," he said.

"Well, I've got thirty thousand lying in the bank drawing three per cent. I thought I could turn a little more interest than that if I looked around."

John Whiteside pursed his lips and blew softly and tapped the stream of air with his forefinger. "Offhand, I'd say Building and Loan was your best bet."

"Oh, that ain't my way of doing business. I don't want bets," Shark cut in. "If I can't see a sure profit in a thing, I won't go into it. Too many people bet."

"That was only a manner of speaking, Mr. Wicks. Few Building and Loan Companies go under. And they pay good interest."

"I'll look into it anyway," Shark decided. "I'm going up to Oakland for Aunt Nellie's funeral, and I'll just stop off a few hours in San Jose and look into this company."

At the Pastures of Heaven General Store that night there were new guesses made at the amount of Shark's wealth, for Shark had asked the advice of several men.

"Well anyway, there's one thing you can say," T. B. Allen concluded, "Shark Wicks is nobody's fool. He'll ask a man's advice as well as the next one, but he's not going to take anybody's say-so until he looks into it himself."

"Oh, he's nobody's fool," the gathering concurred.

Shark went to Oakland on Saturday morning, leaving his wife and daughter alone for the first time in his life. On Saturday evening Tom Breman called by to take Katherine and Alice to a dance at the schoolhouse.

"Oh, I don't think Mr. Wicks would like it," Katherine said, in a thrilled, frightened tone.

"He didn't tell you not to go, did he?"

"No, but—he's never been away before. I don't think he'd like it."

"He just never thought of it," Tom Breman assured her. "Come on! Get your things on."

"Let's go, Ma," said Alice.

Katherine knew her daughter could make such an easy decision because she was too stupid to be afraid. Alice was no judge of consequences. She couldn't think of the weeks of torturing conversation that would follow when Shark returned. Katherine could hear him already. "I don't see why you'd *want* to go when I wasn't here. When I left, I kind of thought you two would look after the place, and the first thing you did was run off to a dance." And then the questions—"Who did Alice dance with? Well—what did he say? Why didn't you hear it? You ought to of heard." There would be no anger on Shark's part, but for weeks and weeks he would talk about it, just keep talking about it until she hated the whole subject of dances. And when the right time of the month came around, his questions would buzz like mosquitoes, until he was sure Alice wasn't going to have a baby. Katherine didn't think it worth the fun of going to the dance if she had to listen to all the fuss afterwards.

"Let's go, Ma," Alice begged her. "We never went any place alone in our lives."

A wave of pity arose in Katherine. The poor girl had never had a moment of privacy in her life. She had never talked nonsense with a boy because her father would not let her out of earshot.

"All right," she decided breathlessly. "If Mr. Breman will wait 'til we get ready, we *will* go." She felt very brave to be encouraging Shark's unease.

Too great beauty is almost as great a disadvantage to a country girl as ugliness is. When the country boys looked at Alice, their throats tightened, their hands and feet grew restless and huge, and their necks turned red. Nothing could force them to talk to her nor to dance with her. Instead, they danced furiously with less beautiful girls, became as noisy as self-conscious children and showed off frantically. When her head was turned, they peeked at Alice, but when she looked at them, they strove to give an impression of unawareness of her presence. Alice, who had always been treated in this way, was fairly unconscious of her beauty. She was almost resigned to the status of a wall flower at the dances.

Jimmie Munroe was leaning against a wall with elegant nonchalance and superb ennui when Katherine and Alice entered the schoolhouse door. Jimmie's trousers had twenty-seven inch bottoms, his patent leather shoes were as square across the toes as bricks. A black jazzbow tie fluttered at the neck of a white silk shirt, and his hair lay glitteringly on his head. Jimmie was a town boy. He swooped like a lazy hawk. Before Alice had taken off her coat he was beside her. In the tired voice he had acquired in high school he demanded, "Dancing, baby?"

"Huh?" said Alice.

"How'd you like to dance with me?"

"Dance, you mean?" Alice turned her smoky, promiseful eyes on him, and the stupid question became humorous and delightful, and at the same time it hinted at other things which moved and excited even the cynical Jimmie.

"Dance?" he thought she asked. "Only dance?" And in spite of his high school training, Jimmie's throat tightened, his feet and hands shifted nervously and the blood rose to his neck.

Alice turned to her mother who was already talking with Mrs. Breman that peculiar culinary gabble of housekeepers. "Ma," said Alice, "can I dance?"

Katherine smiled. "Go on," she said, and then, "Enjoy yourself for once."

Jimmie found that Alice danced badly. When the music stopped, "It's hot in here, isn't it? Let's stroll outside," he suggested. And he led her out under the willow trees in the schoolhouse yard.

Meanwhile a woman who had been standing on the porch of the schoolhouse went inside and whispered in Katherine's ear. Katherine stared up and hurried outside. "Alice!" she called wildly. "Alice, you come right here!"

When the wayward two appeared out of the shadows, Katherine turned on Jimmie. "You keep away, do you hear me? You keep away from this girl or you'll get into trouble."

Jimmie's manhood melted. He felt like a sent-home child. He hated it, but he couldn't override it.

Katherine led her daughter into the schoolhouse again. "Didn't your father tell you to keep away from Jimmie Munroe? Didn't he?" she demanded. Katherine was terrified.

"Was that him?" Alice whispered.

"Sure it was. What were you two doing out there?"

"Kissing," said Alice in an awed voice.

Katherine's mouth dropped open. "Oh, Lord!" she said. "Oh, Lord, what shall I do?"

"Is it bad, Ma?"

Katherine frowned. "No—no, of course it's not bad," she cried. "It's—good. But don't you ever let your father know about it. Don't you tell him even if he asks you! He—why, he'd go crazy. And you sit here beside me the rest of the evening, and don't you see Jimmie Munroe any more, will you? Maybe your father won't hear about it. Oh, Lord, I hope he don't hear about it!"

On Monday Shark Wicks got off the evening train in Salinas, and took a bus to the cross-road which ran from the highway into the Pastures of Heaven. Shark clutched his bag and began the four mile walk home.

The night was clear and sweet and heavy with stars. The faint mysterious sounds of the hills welcomed him home and set up reveries in his head so that he forgot his footsteps.

He had been pleased with the funeral. The flowers were nice, and there were so many of them. The weeping of the women and the solemn tip-toeing of the men had set up a gentle sorrow in Shark which was far from unpleasant. Even the profound ritual of the church, which no one understands nor listens to, had been a drug which poured sweet mysterious juices into his body and his brain. The church opened and closed over him for an hour, and out of his contact he had brought the drowsy peace of strong flowers and drifting incense, and the glow of relationship with eternity. These things were wrought in him by the huge simplicity of the burial.

Shark had never known his Aunt Nellie very well, but he had thoroughly enjoyed her funeral. In some way his relatives had heard of his wealth, for they treated him with deference and dignity. Now, as he walked home, he thought of these things again and his pleasure speeded up the time, shortened the road and brought him quickly to the Pastures of Heaven General Store. Shark went in, for he knew he could find someone in the store who would report on the valley and its affairs during his absence.

T. B. Allen, the proprietor, knew everything that happened, and also he enhanced the interest of every bit of news by simulating a reluctance to tell it. The most stupid piece of gossip became exciting when old T. B. had it to tell.

No one but the owner was in the store when Shark entered. T. B. let down his chair-back from the wall, and his eyes sparkled with interest.

"Hear you been away," he suggested in a tone that invited confidence.

"Been up to Oakland," said Shark. "I had to go to a funeral. Thought I might as well do some business at the same time."

T. B. waited as long for elaboration as he thought decent. "Anything happen, Shark?"

"Well, I don't know if you'd call it that. I was looking into a company."

"Put any money in?" T. B. asked respectfully.

"Some."

Both men looked at the floor.

"Anything happen while I was gone?"

Immediately a look of reluctance came over the face of the old man. One read a dislike for saying just what had happened, a natural aversion for scandal. "Dance at the schoolhouse," he admitted at last.

"Yes, I knew about that."

T. B. squirmed. Apparently there was a struggle going on in his mind. Should he tell Shark what he knew, for Shark's own good, or should he keep all knowledge to himself. Shark watched the struggle with interest. He had seen others like it many times before.

"Well, what is it?" he prodded.

"Hear there might be a wedding pretty soon."

"Yeah? Who?"

"Well, pretty close to home, I guess."

"Who?" Shark asked again.

T. B. struggled vainly and lost. "You," he admitted.

Shark chuckled. "Me?"

"Alice."

Shark stiffened and stared at the old man. Then he stepped forward and stood over him threateningly. "What do you mean? Tell me what you mean—you!"

T. B. knew he had overstepped. He cowered away from Shark. "Now don't, Mr. Wicks! Don't you do nothing!"

"Tell me what you mean! Tell me everything." Shark grasped T. B. by the shoulder and shook him fiercely.

"Well, it was only at the dance—just at the dance."

"Alice was at the dance?"

"Uh-huh."

"What was she doing there?"

"I don't know. I mean, nothing."

Shark pulled him out of his chair and stood him roughly on his fumbling feet. "Tell me!" he demanded.

The old man whimpered. "She just walked out in the yard with Jimmie Munroe."

Shark had both of the shoulders now. He shook the terrified storekeeper like a sack. "Tell me! What did they do?"

"I don't know, Mr. Wicks."

"Tell me."

"Well, Miss Burke—Miss Burke said—they were kissing."

Shark dropped the sack and sat down. He was appalled with a sense of loss. While he glared at T. B. Allen, his brain fought with the problem of his daughter's impurity. It did not occur to him that the passage had stopped with a kiss.

Shark moved his head and his eyes roved helplessly around the store. T. B. saw his eyes pass over the glass-fronted gun case.

"Don't you do nothing, Shark," he cried. "Them guns ain't yours."

Shark hadn't seen the guns at all, but now that his attention was directed toward them, he leaped up, threw open the sliding glass door and took out a heavy rifle. He tore off the price tag and tossed a box of cartridges into his pocket. Then, without a glance at the storekeeper, he strode out into the dark. And old T. B. was at the telephone before Shark's quick footsteps had died away into the night.

As Shark walked quickly along toward the Munroe place, his thoughts raced hopelessly. He was sure of one thing, though, now that he had walked a little; he didn't want to kill Jimmie Munroe. He hadn't even been thinking about shooting him until the storekeeper suggested the idea. Then he had acted upon it without thinking. What could he do now? He tried to picture what he would do when he came to the Munroe house. Perhaps he would have to shoot Jimmie Munroe. Maybe things would fall out in a way that would force him to commit murder to maintain his dignity in the Pastures of Heaven.

Shark heard a car coming and stepped into the brush while it roared by, with a wide open throttle. He would be getting there pretty soon, and he didn't hate Jimmie Munroe. He didn't hate anything except the hollow feeling that had entered him when he heard of Alice's loss of virtue. Now he could only think of his daughter as one who was dead.

Ahead of him, he could see the lights of the Munroe house now. And Shark knew that he couldn't shoot Jimmie. Even if he were laughed at he couldn't shoot the boy. There was no murder in him. He decided that he would look in at the gate and then go along home. Maybe people would laugh at him, but he simply could not shoot anybody.

Suddenly a man stepped from the shadow of a bush and shouted at him. "Put down that gun, Wicks, and put up your hands."

Shark laid the rifle on the ground with a kind of tired obedience. He recognized the voice of the deputy sheriff. "Hello Jack," he said.

Then there were people all around him. Shark saw Jimmie's frightened face in the background. Bert Munroe was frightened too. He said, "What did you want to shoot Jimmie for? He didn't hurt you. Old T. B. phoned me. I've got to put you where you can't do any harm."

"You can't jail him," the deputy said. "He hasn't done anything. Only thing you can do is put him under bond to keep the peace."

"Is that so? I guess I have to do that then." Bert's voice was trembling.

"You better ask for a big bond," the deputy went on. "Shark's a pretty rich man. Come on! We'll take him into Salinas now, and you can make your complaint."

The next morning Shark Wicks walked listlessly into his house and lay down on his bed. His eyes were dull and tired but he kept them open. His arms lay as loosely as a corpse's arms beside him. Hour after hour he lay there.

Katherine, from the vegetable garden, saw him go into the house. She was bitterly glad of the slump of his shoulders and of his head's weak carriage, but when she went in to get luncheon ready, she walked on her toes and cautioned Alice to move quietly.

At three o'clock Katherine looked in at the bedroom door. "Alice was all right," she said. "You should have asked me before you did anything."

Shark did not answer her nor change his position.

"Don't you believe me?" The loss of vitality in her husband frightened her. "If you don't believe me, we can get a doctor. I'll send for one right now if you don't believe me."

Shark's head did not turn. "I believe you," he said lifelessly.

As Katherine stood in the doorway, a feeling she had never experienced crept into her. She did a thing she had never contemplated in her life. A warm genius moved in her. Katherine sat down on the edge of the bed and with a sure hand, took Shark's head on her lap. This was instinct, and the same sure, strong instinct set her hand to stroking Shark's forehead. His body seemed boneless with defeat.

Shark's eyes did not move from the ceiling, but under the stroking, he began to talk brokenly. "I haven't any money," his monotonous voice said. "They took me in and asked for a ten thousand dollar bond. I had to tell the judge. They all heard. They all know—I haven't any money. I never had any. Do you understand? That ledger was nothing but a lie. Every bit of it was lies. I made it all up. Now everybody knows. I had to tell the judge."

Katherine stroked his head gently and the great genius continued to grow in her. She felt larger than the world. The whole world lay in her lap and she comforted it. Pity seemed to make her huge in stature. Her soothing breasts yearned toward the woe of the world.

"I didn't mean to hurt anyone," Shark went on. "I wouldn't have shot Jimmie. They caught me before I could turn back. They thought I meant to kill him. And now everybody knows. I haven't any money." He lay limply and stared upward.

Suddenly the genius in Katherine became power and the power gushed in her body and flooded her. In a moment she knew what she was and what she could do. She was exultantly happy and very beautiful. "You've had no chance," she said softly. "All of your life you've been out on this old farm and there's been no chance for you. How do you know you can't make money? I think you can. I know you can."

She had known she could do this. As she sat there the knowledge of her power had been born in her, and she knew that all of her life was directed at this one moment. In this moment she was a goddess, a singer of destiny. It did not surprise her when his body gradually stiffened. She continued to stroke his forehead.

"We'll go out of here," she chanted. "We'll sell this ranch and go away from here. Then you'll get the chance you never had. You'll see. I know what you are. I believe in you."

Shark's eyes lost their awful lifelessness. His body found strength to turn itself. He looked at Katherine and saw how beautiful she was in this moment, and, as he looked, her genius passed into him. Shark pressed his head tightly against her knees.

She lowered her head and looked at him. She was frightened now the power was leaving her. Suddenly Shark sat up on the bed. He had forgotten Katherine, but his eyes shone with the energy she had given him.

"I'll go soon," he cried. "I'll go just as soon as I can sell the ranch. Then I'll get in a few licks. I'll get my chance then. I'll show people what I am."

IV

The origin of Tularecito is cast in obscurity, while his discovery is a myth which the folks of the Pastures of Heaven refuse to believe, just as they refuse to believe in ghosts.

Franklin Gomez had a hired man, a Mexican Indian named Pancho, and nothing else. Once every three months, Pancho took his savings and drove into Monterey to confess his sins, to do his penance, and be shriven and to get drunk, in the order named. If he managed to stay out of jail, Pancho got into his buggy and went to sleep when the saloons closed. The horse pulled him home, arriving just before daylight, and in time for Pancho to have breakfast and go to work. Pancho was always asleep when he arrived; that is why he created so much interest on the ranch when, one morning, he drove into the corral at a gallop, not only awake, but shouting at the top of his voice.

Franklin Gomez put on his clothes and went out to interview his ranch hand. The story, when it was stretched out of its tangle of incoherencies, was this: Pancho had been driving home, very sober as always. Up near the Blake place, he heard a baby crying in the sage brush beside the road. He stopped the horse and went to investigate, for one did not often come upon babies like that. And sure enough he found a tiny child lying in a clear place in the sage. It was about three months old by the size of it, Pancho thought. He picked it up and lighted a match to see just what kind of a thing he had found, when—horror of horrors!—the baby winked maliciously and said in a deep voice, "Look! I have very sharp teeth." Pancho did not look. He flung the thing from him, leaped into his buggy and galloped for home, beating the old horse with the butt end of the whip and howling like a dog.

Franklin Gomez pulled his whiskers a good deal. Pancho's nature, he considered, was not hysterical even under the influence of liquor. The fact that he had awakened at all rather proved there must be something in the brush. In the end, Franklin Gomez had a horse saddled, rode out and brought in the baby. It did not speak again for nearly three years; nor, on inspection, did it have any teeth, but neither of these facts convinced Pancho that it did not make that first ferocious remark.

The baby had short, chubby arms, and long, loose-jointed legs. Its large head sat without interval of neck between deformedly broad shoulders. The baby's flat face, together with its peculiar body, caused it automatically to be named Tularecito, Little Frog, although Franklin Gomez often called it Coyote, "for," he said, "there is in this boy's face that ancient wisdom one finds in the face of a coyote."

"But surely the legs, the arms, the shoulders, Señor," Pancho reminded him. And so Tularecito the name remained. It was never discovered who abandoned the misshapen little creature. Franklin Gomez accepted him into the patriarchate of his ranch, and Pancho took care of him. Pancho, however, could never lose a little fear of the boy. Neither the years nor a rigorous penance eradicated the effect of Tularecito's first utterance.

The boy grew rapidly, but after the fifth year his brain did not grow any more. At six Tularecito could do the work of a grown man. The long fingers of his hands were more dexterous and stronger than most men's fingers. On the ranch, they made use of the fingers of Tularecito. Hard knots could not long defy him. He had planting hands, tender fingers that never injured a young plant nor bruised the surfaces of a grafting limb. His merciless fingers could wring the head from a turkey gobbler without effort. Also Tularecito had an amusing gift. With his thumbnail he could carve remarkably correct animals from sandstone. Franklin Gomez kept many little effigies of coyotes and mountain lions, of chickens and squirrels, about the house. A two-foot image of a hovering hawk hung by wires from the ceiling of the dining room. Pancho, who had never quite considered the boy human, put his gift for carving in a growing category of diabolical traits definitely traceable to his supernatural origin.

While the people of the Pastures of Heaven did not believe in the diabolic origin of Tularecito, nevertheless they were uncomfortable in his presence. His eyes were ancient and dry; there was something troglodytic about his face. The great strength of his body and his strange and obscure gifts set him apart from other children and made men and women uneasy.

Only one thing could provoke anger in Tularecito. If any person, man, woman or child, handled carelessly or broke one of the products of his hands, he became furious. His eyes shone and he attacked the desecrator murderously. On three occasions when this had happened, Franklin Gomez tied his hands and feet and left him alone until his ordinary good nature returned.

Tularecito did not go to school when he was six. For five years thereafter, the county truant officer and the school superintendent sporadically worked on the case. Franklin Gomez agreed that he should go to school and even went so far as to start him off several times, but Tularecito never got there. He was afraid that school might prove unpleasant, so he simply disappeared for a day or so. It was not until the boy was eleven, with the shoulders of a weight lifter and the hands and forearms of a strangler that the concerted forces of the law gathered him in and put him in school.

As Franklin Gomez had known, Tularecito learned nothing at all, but immediately he gave evidence of a new gift. He could draw as well as he could carve in sandstone. When Miss Martin, the teacher, discovered his ability, she gave him a piece of chalk and told him to make a procession of animals around the blackboard. Tularecito worked long after school was dismissed, and the next morning an astounding parade was shown on the walls. All of the animals Tularecito had ever seen were there; all the birds of the hills flew above them. A rattlesnake crawled behind a cow; a coyote, his brush proudly aloft, sniffed at the heels of a pig. There were tomcats and goats, turtles and gophers, every one of them drawn with astonishing detail and veracity.

Miss Martin was overcome with the genius of Tularecito. She praised him before the class and gave a short lecture about each one of the creatures he had drawn. In her own mind she considered the glory that would come to her for discovering and fostering this genius.

"I can make lots more," Tularecito informed her.

Miss Martin patted his broad shoulder. "So you shall," she said. "You shall draw every day. It is a great gift that God has given you." Then she realized the importance of what she had just said. She leaned over and looked searchingly into his hard eyes while she repeated slowly, "It is a *great gift* that God has given you." Miss Martin glanced up at the clock and announced crisply, "Fourth grade arithmetic—at the board."

The fourth grade struggled out, seized erasers and began to remove the animals to make room for their numbers. They had not made two sweeps when Tularecito charged. It was a great day. Miss Martin, aided by the whole school, could not hold him down, for the enraged Tularecito had the strength of a man, and a madman at that. The ensuing battle wrecked the schoolroom, tipped over the desks, spilled rivers of ink, hurled bouquets of Teacher's flowers about the room. Miss Martin's clothes were torn to streamers, and the big boys, on whom the burden of the battle fell, were bruised and battered cruelly. Tularecito fought with hands, feet, teeth and head. He admitted no honorable rules and in the end he won. The whole school, with Miss Martin guarding its rear, fled from the building, leaving the enraged Tularecito in possession. When they were gone, he locked the door, wiped the blood out of his eyes and set to work to repair the animals that had been destroyed.

That night Miss Martin called on Franklin Gomez and demanded that the boy be whipped.

Gomez shrugged. "You really wish me to whip him, Miss Martin?"

The teacher's face was scratched; her mouth was bitter. "I certainly do," she said. "If you had seen what he did today, you wouldn't blame me. I tell you he needs a lesson."

Gomez shrugged again and called Tularecito from the bunk house. He took a heavy quirt down from the wall. Then, while Tularecito smiled blandly at Miss Martin, Franklin Gomez beat him severely across the back. Miss Martin's hand made involuntary motions of beating. When it was done, Tularecito felt himself over with long, exploring fingers, and still smiling, went back to the bunk house.

Miss Martin had watched the end of the punishment with horror. "Why, he's an animal," she cried. "It was just like whipping a dog."

Franklin Gomez permitted a slight trace of his contempt for her to show on his face. "A dog would have cringed," he said. "Now you have seen, Miss Martin. You say he is an animal, but surely he is a good animal. You told him to make pictures and then you destroyed his pictures. Tularecito does not like that—"

Miss Martin tried to break in, but he hurried on.

"This Little Frog should not be going to school. He can work; he can do marvelous things with his hands, but he cannot learn to do the simple little things of the school. He is not crazy; he is one of those whom God has not quite finished.

"I told the superintendent these things, and he said the law required Tularecito to go to school until he is eighteen years old. That is seven years from now. For seven years my Little Frog will sit in the first grade because the law says he must. It is out of my hands."

"He ought to be locked up," Miss Martin broke in. "This creature is dangerous. You should have seen him today."

"No, Miss Martin, he should be allowed to go free. He is not dangerous. No one can make a garden as he can. No one can milk so swiftly nor so gently. He is a good boy. He can break a mad horse without riding it; he can train a dog without whipping it, but the law says he must sit in the first grade repeating 'C-A-T, cat,' for seven years. If he had been dangerous he could easily have killed me when I whipped him."

Miss Martin felt that there were things she did not understand and she hated Franklin Gomez because of them. She felt that she had been mean and he generous. When she got to school the next morning, she found Tularecito before her. Every possible space on the wall was covered with animals.

"You see?" he said, beaming over his shoulder at her. "Lots more. And I have a book with others yet, but there is no room for them on the wall."

Miss Martin did not erase the animals. Class work was done on paper, but at the end of the term she resigned her position, giving ill health as her reason.

Miss Morgan, the new teacher, was very young and very pretty; too young and dangerously pretty, the aged men of the valley thought. Some of the boys in the upper grades were seventeen years old. It was seriously doubted that a teacher so young and so pretty could keep any kind of order in the school.

She brought with her a breathless enthusiasm for her trade. The school was astounded, for it had been used to ageing spinsters whose faces seemed to reflect consistently tired feet. Miss Morgan enjoyed teaching and made school an exciting place where unusual things happened.

From the first Miss Morgan was vastly impressed with Tularecito. She knew all about him, had read books and taken courses about him. Having heard about the fight, she laid off a border around the top of the blackboards for him to fill with animals, and, when he had completed his parade, she bought with her own money a huge drawing pad and a soft pencil. After that he did not bother with spelling. Every day he labored over his drawing board, and every afternoon presented the teacher with a marvelously wrought animal. She pinned his drawings to the schoolroom wall above the blackboards.

The pupils received Miss Morgan's innovations with enthusiasm. Classes became exciting, and even the boys who had made enviable reputations through teacher-baiting, grew less interested in the possible burning of the schoolhouse.

Miss Morgan introduced a practice that made the pupils adore her. Every afternoon she read to them for half an hour. She read by installments, *Ivanhoe* and *The Talisman*; fishing stories by Zane Grey, hunting stories of James Oliver Curwood; *The Sea Wolf, The Call of the Wild*—not baby stories about the little red hen and the fox and geese, but exciting, grown-up stories.

Miss Morgan read well. Even the tougher boys were won over until they never played hookey for fear of missing an installment, until they leaned forward gasping with interest.

But Tularecito continued his careful drawing, only pausing now and then to blink at the teacher and to try to understand how these distant accounts of the actions of strangers could be of interest to anyone. To him they were chronicles of actual events—else why were they written down. The stories were like the lessons. Tularecito did not listen to them.

After a time Miss Morgan felt that she had been humoring the older children too much. She herself liked fairy tales, liked to think of whole populations who believed in fairies and consequently saw them. Within the safe circle of her tried and erudite acquaintance, she often said that "part of America's cultural starvation was due to its boorish and superstitious denial of the existence of fairies." For a time she devoted the afternoon half hour to fairy tales.

Now a change came over Tularecito. Gradually, as Miss Morgan read about elves and brownies, fairies, pixies, and changelings, his interest centered and his busy pencil lay idly in his hand. Then she read about gnomes, and their lives and habits, and he dropped his pencil altogether and leaned toward the teacher to intercept her words.

After school Miss Morgan walked half a mile to the farm where she boarded. She liked to walk the way alone, cutting off thistle heads with a switch, or throwing stones into the brush to make the quail roar up. She thought she should get a bounding, inquisitive dog that could share her excitements, could understand the glamour of holes in the ground, and scattering pawsteps on dry leaves, of strange melancholy bird whistles and the gay smells that came secretly out of the earth.

One afternoon Miss Morgan scrambled high up the side of a chalk cliff to carve her initials on the white plane. On the way up she tore her finger on a thorn, and, instead of initials, she scratched: "Here I have been and left this part of me," and pressed her bloody finger against the absorbent chalk rock.

That night, in a letter, she wrote: "After the bare requisites to living and reproducing, man wants most to leave some record of himself, a proof, perhaps, that he has really existed. He leaves his proof on wood, on stone or on the lives of other people. This deep desire exists in everyone, from the boy who writes dirty words in a public toilet to the Buddha who etches his image in the race mind. Life is so unreal. I think that we seriously doubt that we exist and go about trying to prove that we do." She kept a copy of the letter.

On the afternoon when she had read about the gnomes, as she walked home, the grasses beside the road threshed about for a moment and the ugly head of Tularecito appeared.

"Oh! You frightened me," Miss Morgan cried. "You shouldn't pop up like that."

Tularecito stood up and smiled bashfully while he whipped his hat against his thigh. Suddenly Miss Morgan felt fear rising in her. The road was deserted—she had read stories of half-wits. With difficulty she mastered her trembling voice.

"What—what is it you want?"

Tularecito smiled more broadly and whipped harder with his hat.

"Were you just lying there, or do you want something?"

The boy struggled to speak, and then relapsed into his protective smile.

"Well, if you don't want anything, I'll go on." She was really prepared for flight.

Tularecito struggled again. "About those people—"

"What people?" she demanded shrilly. "What about people?"

"About those people in the book—"

Miss Morgan laughed with relief until she felt that her hair was coming loose on the back of her head. "You mean—you mean—gnomes?"

Tularecito nodded.

"What do you want to know about them?"

"I never saw any," said Tularecito. His voice neither rose nor fell, but continued on one low note.

"Why, few people do see them, I think."

"But I knew about them."

Miss Morgan's eyes squinted with interest. "You did? Who told you about them?"

"Nobody."

"You never saw them, and no one told you? How could you know about them then?"

"I just knew. Heard them, maybe. I knew them in the book all right."

Miss Morgan thought: "Why should I deny gnomes to this queer, unfinished child? Wouldn't his life be richer and happier if he did believe in them? And what harm could it possibly do?"

"Have you ever looked for them?" she asked.

"No, I never looked. I just knew. But I will look now."

Miss Morgan found herself charmed with the situation. Here was paper on which to write, here was a cliff on which to carve. She could carve a lovely story that would be far more real than a book story ever could. "Where will you look?" she asked.

"I'll dig in holes," said Tularecito soberly.

"But the gnomes only come out at night, Tularecito. You must watch for them in the night. And you must come and tell me if you find any. Will you do that?"

"I'll come," he agreed.

She left him staring after her. All the way home she pictured him searching in the night. The picture pleased her. He might even find the gnomes, might live with them and talk to them. With a few suggestive words she had been able to make his life unreal and very wonderful, and separated from the stupid lives about him. She deeply envied him his searching.

In the evening Tularecito put on his coat and took up a shovel. Old Pancho came upon him as he was leaving the tool shed. "Where goest thou, Little Frog?" he asked.

Tularecito shifted his feet restlessly at the delay. "I go out into the dark. Is that a new thing?"

"But why takest thou the shovel? Is there gold, perhaps?"

The boy's face grew hard with the seriousness of his purpose. "I go to dig for the little people who live in the earth."

Now Pancho was filled with horrified excitement. "Do not go, Little Frog! Listen to your old friend, your father in God, and do not go! Out in the sage I found thee and saved thee from the devils, thy relatives. Thou art a little brother of Jesus now. Go not back to thine own people! Listen to an old man, Little Frog!"

Tularecito stared hard at the ground and drilled his old thoughts with this new information. "Thou hast said they are my people," he exclaimed. "I am not like the others at the school or here. I know that. I have loneliness for my own people who live deep in the cool earth. When I pass a squirrel hole, I wish to crawl into it and hide myself. My own people are like me, and they have called me. I must go home to them, Pancho."

Pancho stepped back and held up crossed fingers. "Go back to the devil, thy father, then. I am not good enough to fight this evil. It would take a saint. But see! At least I make the sign against thee and against all thy race." He drew the cross of protection in the air in front of him.

Tularecito smiled sadly, and turning, trudged off into the hills.

The heart of Tularecito gushed with joy at his homecoming. All his life he had been an alien, a lonely outcast, and now he was going home. As always, he heard the voices of the earth—the far-off clang of cow bells, the muttering of disturbed quail, the little whine of a coyote who would not sing this night, the nocturnes of a million insects. But Tularecito was listening for another sound, the movement of two-footed creatures, and the hushed voices of the hidden people.

Once he stopped and called, "My father, I have come home," and he heard no answer. Into squirrel holes he whispered, "Where are you, my people? It is only Tularecito come home." But there was no reply. Worse, he had no feeling that the gnomes were near. He knew that a doe and fawn were feeding near him; he knew a wildcat was stalking a rabbit behind a bush, although he could not see them, but from the gnomes he had no message.

A sugar-moon arose out of the hills.

"Now the animals will come out to feed," Tularecito said in the papery whisper of the half witless. "Now the people will come out, too."

The brush stopped at the edge of a little valley and an orchard took its place. The trees were thick with leaves, and the land finely cultivated. It was Bert Munroe's orchard. Often, when the land was deserted and ghost-ridden, Tularecito had come here in the night to lie on the ground under the trees and pick the stars with gentle fingers.

The moment he walked into the orchard he knew he was nearing home. He could not hear them, but he knew the gnomes were near. Over and over he called to them, but they did not come.

"Perhaps they do not like the moonlight," he said.

At the foot of a large peach tree he dug his hole—three feet across and very deep. All night he worked on it, stopping to listen awhile and then digging deeper and deeper into the cool earth. Although he heard nothing, he was positive that he was nearing them. Only when the daylight came did he give up and retire into the bushes to sleep.

In midmorning Bert Munroe walked out to look at a coyote trap and found the hole at the foot of the tree. "What the devil!" he said. "Some kids must have been digging a tunnel. That's dangerous! It'll cave in on them, or somebody will fall into it and get hurt." He walked back to the house, got a shovel and filled up the hole.

"Manny," he said to his youngest boy, "you haven't been digging in the orchard, have you?"

"Uh-uh!" said Manny.

"Well, do you know who has?"

"Uh-uh!" said Manny.

"Well, somebody dug a deep hole out there. It's dangerous. You tell the boys not to dig or they'll get caved in."

The dark came and Tularecito walked out of the brush to dig in his hole again. When he found it filled up, he growled savagely, but then his thought changed and he laughed. "The people were here," he said happily. "They didn't know who it was, and they were frightened. They filled up the hole the way a gopher does. This time I'll hide, and when they come to fill the hole, I'll tell them who I am. Then they will love me."

And Tularecito dug out the hole and made it much deeper than before, because much of the dirt was loose. Just before daylight, he retired into the brush at the edge of the orchard and lay down to watch.

Bert Munroe walked out before breakfast to look at his

trap again, and again he found the open hole. "The little devils!" he cried. "They're keeping it up, are they? I'll bet Manny is in it after all."

He studied the hole for a moment and then began to push dirt into it with the side of his foot. A savage growl spun him around. Tularecito came charging down upon him, leaping like a frog on his long legs, and swinging his shovel like a club.

When Jimmie Munroe came to call his father to breakfast, he found him lying on the pile of dirt. He was bleeding at the mouth and forehead. Shovelfuls of dirt came flying out of the pit.

Jimmie thought someone had killed his father and was getting ready to bury him. He ran home in a frenzy of terror, and by telephone summoned a band of neighbors.

Half a dozen men crept up on the pit. Tularecito struggled like a wounded lion, and held his own until they struck him on the head with his own shovel. Then they tied him up and took him in to jail.

In Salinas a medical board examined the boy. When the doctors asked him questions, he smiled blandly at them and did not answer. Franklin Gomez told the board what he knew and asked the custody of him.

"We really can't do it, Mr. Gomez," the judge said finally. "You say he is a good boy. Just yesterday he tried to kill a man. You must see that we cannot let him go loose. Sooner or later he will succeed in killing someone."

After a short deliberation, he committed Tularecito to the asylum for the criminal insane at Napa.

V

Helen Van Deventer was a tall woman with a sharp, handsome face and tragic eyes. A strong awareness of tragedy ran through her life. At fifteen she had looked like a widow after her Persian kitten was poisoned. She mourned for it during six months, not ostentatiously, but with a subdued voice and a hushed manner. When her father died, at the end of the kitten's six months, the mourning continued uninterrupted. Seemingly she hungered for tragedy and life had lavishly heaped it upon her.

At twenty-five she married Hubert Van Deventer, a florid hunting man who spent six months out of every year trying to shoot some kind of creature or other. Three months after the wedding he shot himself when a blackberry vine tripped him up. Hubert was a fairly gallant man. As he lay dying under a tree, one of his companions asked whether he wanted to leave any message for his wife.

"Yes," said Hubert. "Tell her to have me mounted for that place in the library between the bull moose and the bighorn! Tell her I didn't buy this one from the guide!"

Helen Van Deventer closed off the drawing room with its trophies. Thereafter the room was holy to the spirit of Hubert. The curtains remained drawn. Anyone who felt it necessary to speak in the drawing room spoke softly. Helen did not weep, for it was not in her nature to weep, but her eyes grew larger, and she stared a great deal, with the vacant staring of one who travels over other times. Hubert had left her the house on Russian Hill in San Francisco, and a fairly large fortune.

Her daughter Hilda, born six months after Hubert was killed, was a pretty, doll-like baby, with her mother's great eyes. Hilda was never very well; she took all the children's diseases with startling promptness. Her temper, which at first wore itself out with howling, became destructive as soon as she could move about. She shattered any breakable thing which came into the pathway of her anger. Helen Van Deventer soothed and petted her and usually succeeded in increasing the temper.

When Hilda was six years old, Dr. Phillips, the family physician, told Mrs. Van Deventer the thing she had suspected for a long time.

"You must realize it," he said. "Hilda is not completely well in her mind. I suggest that she be taken to a psychiatrist."

The dark eyes of the mother widened with pain. "You are sure, doctor?"

"Fairly sure. I am not a specialist. You'll have to take her to someone who knows more than I do."

Helen stared away from him. "I have thought so too, doctor, but I can't take her to another man. You've always had the care of us. I know you. I shouldn't ever be sure of another man."

"What do you mean, 'sure'?" Dr. Phillips exploded. "Don't you know we might cure her if we went about it right?"

Helen's hands rose a trifle, and then dropped with hopelessness. "She won't ever get well, doctor. She was born at the wrong time. Her father's death—it was too much for me. I didn't have the strength to bear a perfect child, you see."

"Then what do you intend to do? Your idea is foolish, if I may be permitted."

"What is there to do, doctor? I can wait and hope. I know I can see it through, but I can't take her to another man. I'll just watch her and care for her. That seems to be my life." She smiled very sadly and her hands rose again.

"It seems to me you force hardships upon yourself," the doctor said testily.

"We take what is given us. I can endure. I am sure of that, and I am proud of it. No amount of tragedy can break down my endurance. But there is one thing I cannot bear, doctor. Hilda cannot be taken away from me. I will keep her with me, and you will come as always, but no one else must interfere."

Dr. Phillips left the house in disgust. The obvious and needless endurance of the woman always put him in a fury. "If I were Fate," he mused, "I'd be tempted to smash her placid resistance too."

It wasn't long after this that visions and dreams began to come to Hilda. Terrible creatures of the night, with claws and teeth, tried to kill her while she slept. Ugly little men pinched her and gritted their teeth in her ear, and Helen Van Deventer accepted the visions as new personalities come to test her.

"A tiger came and pulled the covers," Hilda cried in the morning.

"You mustn't let him frighten you, dear."

"But he tried to get his teeth through the blanket, mother."

"I'll sit with you tonight, darling. Then he can't come."

She began to sit by the little girl's bedside until dawn. Her eyes grew brighter and more feverish with the frenzied resistance of her spirit.

One thing bothered her more than the dreams. Hilda had begun to tell lies. "I went out into the garden this morning, mother. An old man was sitting in the street. He asked me to go to his house, so I went. He had a big gold elephant, and he let me ride on it." The little girl's eyes were far away as she made up the tale.

"Don't say such things, darling," her mother pleaded. "You know you didn't do any of those things."

"But I did, mother. And the old man gave me a watch. I'll show you. Here." She held out a wrist watch set with diamonds. Helen's hand shook with terror as she took the watch. For a second her face lost its look of resistance, and anger took its place.

"Where did you get it, Hilda?"

"The old man gave it to me, mother."

"No—tell me where you found it! You did find it, didn't you?"

"The old man gave it to me."

On the back of the watch a monogram was cut, initials unknown to Helen. She stared helplessly at the carved letters. "Mother will take this," she said harshly. That night she crept into the garden, found a trowel and buried the watch deep in the earth. That week she had a high iron fence built around the garden, and Hilda was never permitted to go out alone after that.

When she was thirteen, Hilda escaped and ran away. Helen hired private detectives to find her, but at the end of four days a policeman discovered Hilda sleeping in a deserted real estate tract office in Los Angeles. Helen rescued her daughter from the police station. "Why did you run away, darling?" she asked.

"Well, I wanted to play on a piano."

"But we have one at home. Why didn't you play on it?"

"Oh, I wanted to play on the other kind, the tall kind."

Helen took Hilda on her lap and hugged her tightly. "And what did you do then, dear?"

"I was out in the street and a man asked me to ride with him. He gave me five dollars. Then I found some gypsies, and I went to live with them. They made me queen. Then I was married to a young gypsy man, and we were going to have a little baby, but I got tired and sat down. Then a policeman took me."

"Darling, poor darling," Helen replied. "You know that isn't true. None of it is true."

"But it is true, mother."

Helen called Dr. Phillips. "She says she married a gypsy. You don't think—really you don't think she could have? I couldn't stand that."

The doctor looked at the little girl carefully. At the end of his examination he spoke almost viciously. "I've told you she should be put in the hands of a specialist." He approached the little girl. "Has the mean old woman been in your bedroom lately, Hilda?"

Hilda's hands twitched. "Last night she came with a monkey, a great big monkey. It tried to bite me."

"Well, just remember she can't ever hurt you because I'm taking care of you. That old woman's afraid of me. If she comes again, just tell her I'm looking after you and see how quick she runs away."

The little girl smiled wearily. "Will the monkey run away too?"

"Of course, and while I think of it, here's a little candy cane for your daughter." He drew a stick of stripey peppermint from his pocket. "You'd better give that to Babette, isn't that her name?" Hilda snatched the candy and ran out of the room.

"Now!" said the doctor to Helen, "my knowledge and my experience are sadly lacking, but I do know this much. Hilda will be very much worse now. She's reaching her maturity. The period of change, with its accompanying emotional overflow, invariably intensifies mental trouble. I can't tell what may happen. She may turn homicidal, and on the other hand, she may run off with the first man she sees. If you don't put her in expert hands, if you don't have her carefully watched, something you'll regret may happen. This last escapade is only a forerunner. You simply cannot go on as you are. It isn't fair to yourself."

Helen sat rigidly before him. In her face was that resistance which so enraged him. "What would you suggest?" she asked huskily.

"A hospital for the insane," he said, and it delighted him that his reply was brutal.

Her face tightened. Her resistance became a little more tense. "I won't do it," she cried. "She's mine, and I'm responsible for her. I'll stay with her myself, doctor. I won't let her out of my sight. But I will not send her away."

"You know the consequences," he said gruffly. Then the impossibility of reasoning with this woman overwhelmed him. "Helen, I've been your friend for years. Why should you take this load of misery and danger on your own shoulders?"

"I can endure anything, but I cannot send her away."

"You love the hair shirt," he growled. "Your pain is a pleasure. You won't give up any little shred of tragedy." He became furious. "Helen, every man must some time or other want to beat a woman. I think I'm a mild man, but right now I want to beat your face with my fists." He looked into her dark eyes and saw that he had only put a new tragedy upon her, had only given her a new situation to endure. "I'm going away now," he said. "Don't call me any more. Why—I'm beginning to hate you."

The people of the Pastures of Heaven learned with interest and resentment that a rich woman was coming to live in the valley. They watched truckloads of logs and lumber going up Christmas Canyon, and they laughed a little scornfully at the expense of hauling in logs to make a cabin. Bert Munroe walked up Christmas Canyon, and for half a day he watched the carpenters putting up a house.

"It's going to be nice," he reported at the General Store. "Every log is perfect, and what do you know, they've got gardeners working there already. They're bringing in big plants and trees all in bloom, and setting them in the ground. This Mrs. Van Deventer must be pretty rich."

"They sure lay it on," agreed Pat Humbert. "Them rich people sure do lay it on."

"And listen to this," Bert continued. "Isn't this like a woman? Guess what they got on some of the windows—bars! Not iron bars, but big thick oak ones. I guess the old lady's scared of coyotes."

"I wonder if she'll bring a lot of servants," T. B. Allen spoke hopefully, "but I guess she'd buy her stuff in town, though. All people like that buy their stuff in town."

When the house and the garden were completed, Helen Van Deventer and Hilda, a Chinese cook and a Filipino house-boy drove up Christmas Canyon. It was a beautiful log house. The carpenters had aged the logs with acids, and the gardeners had made it seem an old garden. Bays and oaks were left in the lawn and under them grew cinerarias, purple and white and blue. The walks were hedged with lobelias of incredible blue.

The cook and the house-boy scurried to their posts, but Helen took Hilda by the arm and walked in the garden for a while.

"Isn't it beautiful," Helen cried. Her face had lost some of its resistance. "Darling, don't you think we'll like it here?"

Hilda pulled up a cineraria and switched at an oak trunk with it. "I liked it better at home."

"But why, darling? We didn't have such pretty flowers, and there weren't any big trees. Here we can go walking in the hills every day."

"I liked it better at home."

"But why, darling?"

"Well, all my friends were there. I could look out through the fence and see the people go by."

"You'll like it better here, Hilda, when you get used to it."

"No I won't. I won't ever like it here, ever." Hilda began to cry, and then without transition she began screaming with rage. Suddenly she plucked a garden stick from the ground and struck her mother across the breast with it. Silently the house-boy appeared behind the girl, pinioned her arms, and carried her, kicking and screaming, into the house.

In the room that had been prepared for her, Hilda methodically broke the furniture. She slit the pillows and shook feathers about the room. Lastly she broke out the panes of her window, beat at the oaken bars and screamed with anger. Helen sat in her room, her lips drawn tight. Once she started up as though to go to Hilda's room, and then sank back into her chair again. For a moment the dumb endurance had nearly broken, but instantly it settled back more strongly than ever, and the shrieks from Hilda's room had no effect. The house-boy slipped into the room.

"Close the shutters, Missie?"

"No, Joe. We're far enough away from anyone. No one can hear it."

Bert Munroe saw the automobile drive by, bearing the new people up Christmas Canyon to the log cabin.

"It'll be pretty hard for a woman to get started alone," he said to his wife. "I think I ought to walk up and see if they need anything."

"You're just curious," his wife said banteringly.

"Well, of course if that's the way you feel about it, I won't go."

"I was just fooling, Bert," she protested. "I think it

would be a nice neighborly thing to do. Later on I'll get Mrs. Whiteside to go and call with me. That's the real way to do it. But you run along now and see how they're making out."

He swung along up the pleasant stream which sang in the bottom of Christmas Canyon. "It's not a place to farm," he said to himself, "but it's a nice place to live. I could be living in a place like this, just living—if the armistice hadn't come when it did." As usual he felt ashamed of wishing the war had continued for a while.

Hilda's shrieks came to his ears when he was still a quarter of a mile from the house. "Now what the devil," he said. "Sounds like they were killing someone." He hurried up the road to see.

Hilda's barred window looked out on the path which led to the front entrance of the house. Bert saw the girl clinging to the bars, her eyes mad with rage and fear.

"Hello!" he said. "What's the matter? What have they got you locked up for?"

Hilda's eyes narrowed. "They're starving me," she said. "They want me to die."

"That's foolish," said Bert. "Why would anyone want you to die."

"Oh! it's my money," she confided. "They can't get my money until I'm dead."

"Why, you're just a little girl."

"I am not," Hilda said sullenly. "I'm a big grown-up woman. I look little because they starve me and beat me."

Bert's face darkened. "Well, I'll just see about that," he said.

"Oh! don't tell them. Just help me out of here, and then I'll get my money, and then I'll marry you.

For the first time Bert began to suspect what the trouble was. "Sure, I'll help you," he said soothingly. "You just wait a little while, and I'll help you out."

He walked around to the front entrance and knocked at the door. In a moment it opened a crack; the stolid eyes of the house-boy looked out.

"Can I see the lady of the house?" Bert asked.

"No," said the boy, and he shut the door.

For a moment Bert blushed with shame at the rebuff, but then he knocked angrily. Again the door opened two inches, and the black eyes looked out.

"I tell you I've got to see the lady of the house. I've got to see her about the little girl that's locked up."

"Lady very sick. So sorry," said the boy. He closed the door again. This time Bert heard the bolt shoot home. He strode away down the path. "I'll sure tell my wife not to call on them," he said to himself. "A crazy girl and a lousy servant. They can go to hell!"

Helen called from her bedroom, "What was it, Joe?"

The boy stood in the doorway. "A man come. Say he got to see you. I tell him you sick."

"That's good. Who was he? Did he say why he wanted to see me?"

"Don't know who. Say he got to see you about Missie Hilda."

Instantly Helen was standing over him. Her face was angry. "What did he want? Who was he?"

"Don't know, Missie."

"And you sent him away. You take too many liberties. Now get out of here."

She dropped back on her chair and covered her eyes.

"Yes, Missie." Joe turned slowly away.

"Oh, Joe, come back!"

He stood beside her chair before she uncovered her eyes. "Forgive me, Joe. I didn't know what I said. You did right. You'll stay with me, won't you?"

"Yes, Missie."

Helen stood up and walked restlessly to the window. "I don't know what's the matter with me today. Is Miss Hilda all right?"

"Yes, Missie quiet now."

"Well, build a fire in the living-room fireplace, will you? And later bring her in."

In her design for the living room of the cabin Helen felt that she had created a kind of memorial to her husband. She had made it look as much as possible like a hunting lodge. It was a huge room, paneled and beamed with redwood. At intervals the mounted heads of various kinds of deer thrust out inquisitive noses. One side of the room was dominated by a great cobblestone fireplace over which hung a torn French battle flag Hubert had picked up somewhere. In a locked, glass-fronted case, all of Hubert's guns were lined up in racks. Helen felt that she would not completely lose her husband as long as she had a room like this to sit in.

In the Russian Hill drawing room she had practiced a dream that was pleasant to her. She wished she could continue it here in the new house. The dream was materialized almost by a ritual. Helen sat before the fire and folded her hands. Then she looked for a long moment at each of the mounted trophies, repeating for each one, "Hubert handled that." And finally the dream came. She almost saw him before her. In her mind she went over the shape of his hands, the narrowness of his hips and the length and straightness of his legs. After a while she remembered how he said things, where his accents fell, and the way his face seemed to glow and redden when he was excited. Helen recalled how he took his guests from one trophy to another. In front of each one Hubert rocked on his heels and folded his hands behind his back while he told of the killing of the animal in the tiniest detail.

"The moon wasn't right and there wasn't a sign anywhere. Fred (Fred was the guide) said we hadn't a chance to get anything. I remember we were out of bacon that morning. But you know I just had a feeling that we ought to stroll out for a look-see."

Helen could hear him telling the stupid, pointless stories which invariably ended up, "Well, the range was too long and there was a devilish wind blowing from the left, but I set my sights for it, and I thought, 'Well, here goes nothing,' and darned if I didn't knock him over. Of course it was just luck."

Hubert didn't really want his listeners to believe it was just luck. That was his graceful gesture as a sportsman. Helen remembered wondering why a sportsman wasn't permitted to acknowledge that he did anything well.

But that was the way the dream went. She built up his image until it possessed the room and filled it with the surging vitality of the great hunter. Then, when she had completed the dream, she smashed it. The doorbell had seemed to have a particularly dolorous note. Helen remembered the faces of the men, sad and embarrassed while they told her about the accident. The dream always stopped where they had carried the body up the front steps. A blinding wave of sadness filled her chest, and she sank back in her chair.

By this means she kept her husband alive, tenaciously refusing to let his image grow dim in her memory. She had only been married for three months, she told herself. Only three months! She resigned herself to a feeling of hopeless gloom. She knew that she encouraged this feeling, but she felt that it was Hubert's right, a kind of memorial that must be paid to him. She must resist sadness, but not by trying to escape from it.

Helen had looked forward to this first night in her new house. With logs blazing on the hearth, the light shining on the glass eyes of the animals' heads, she intended to welcome her dream into its new home.

Joe came back into the bedroom. "The fire going, Missie. I call Missie Hilda now?"

Helen glanced out of her window. The dusk was coming down from the hilltops. Already a few bats looped nervously about. The quail were calling to one another as they went to water, and far down the canyon the cows were lowing on their way in toward the milking sheds. A change was stealing over Helen. She was filled with a new sense of peace; she felt protected and clothed against the tragedies which had beset her for so long. She stretched her arms outward and backward, and sighed comfortably. Joe still waited in the doorway.

"What?" Helen said, "Miss Hilda? No, don't bring her yet. Dinner must be almost ready. If Hilda doesn't want to come out to dinner, I'll see her afterwards." She didn't want to see Hilda. This new, delicious peacefulness would be broken if she did. She wanted to sit in the strange luminosity of the dusk, to sit listening to the quail calling to one another as they came down from the brushy hillsides to drink before the night fell.

Helen threw a silken shawl about her shoulders and went out into the garden. Peace, it seemed, came sweeping down from the hillsides and enveloped her. In a flower bed she saw a little grey rabbit with a white tail, and seeing it made her quiver with pleasure. The rabbit turned its head and looked at her for a moment, and then went on nibbling at the new plants. Suddenly Helen felt foolishly happy. Something delicious and exciting was going to happen, something very delightful. In her sudden joy she talked to the rabbit. "Go on eating, you can have the old flowers. Tomorrow I'll plant cabbages for you. You'd like that, wouldn't you,

Peter? You know, Peter, is your name Peter? Silly, all rabbits are named Peter. Anyway, Peter, I haven't looked forward to anything for ages. Isn't that funny? Or is it sad? But now I'm looking forward to something. I'm just bursting with anticipation. And I don't know what the something can be. Isn't that silly, Peter?" She strolled on and waved her hand at the rabbit. "I should think the cinerarias would be better to eat," she said.

The singing of water drew her down the path toward the streamside. As she neared the bank, a flock of quail scudded into the brush with stuttering cries of alarm. Helen was ashamed that she had disturbed them. "Come back!" she called. "I won't shoot you. The rabbit didn't mind me. Why, I couldn't shoot you if I wanted to." Suddenly she recalled how Hubert had taken her out to teach her to shoot a shotgun. He had grown religiously solemn as he taught her how to hold the weapon and how to sight with both eyes open. "Now I'll throw up a can," he said. "I don't want you ever to shoot at a still target—ever. It is a poor sportsman who will shoot a resting bird." She had fired wildly at the flying can until her shoulder was stiff, and as they drove home he patted her. "It'll be a long time before you knock over a quail," he said. "But in a little while you ought to be able to pot rabbits." Then she thought of the leather quail strings he brought home with clusters of birds hung by their necks. "When they drop off the strings they're hung long enough to eat," he said solemnly. All of a sudden Helen realized that she didn't want to think of Hubert any more. The retrospection had almost killed her sense of peace.

It was almost dark. The night was sweet with the odor of sage. She heard the cook in the kitchen rattling the cow-bell she had bought as a dinner signal. Helen pulled her shawl close and shivered and went in.

In the dining room she found her daughter before her. All traces of the afternoon's rage were gone from Hilda's face; she looked happy, and very satisfied with herself.

"My darling. You're feeling better, aren't you?" Helen cried.

"Oh, yes."

Helen walked around the table and kissed her on the forehead. Then for a moment she hugged Hilda convulsively. "When you see how beautiful it is here, you'll love it. I know you will."

Hilda did not answer, but her eyes became wily.

"You will like it, won't you, darling?" Helen insisted as she went back to her place.

Hilda was mysterious. "Well maybe I'll like it. Maybe I won't have to like it."

"What do you mean, dear?"

"Maybe I won't be here very long."

"Won't be here very long?" Helen looked quickly across the table. Obviously Hilda was trying to keep some kind of secret, but it was too slippery.

"Maybe I might run away and be married."

Helen sank back in her chair and smiled. "Oh, I see. Surely you might. It would be better to wait a few years though. Who is it this time, dear? The prince again?"

"No, it's not the prince. It's a poor man, but I will love him. We made all of our plans today. He'll come for me, I guess."

Something stirred in Helen's memory. "Is it the man who came to the house this afternoon?"

Hilda started up from the table. "I won't tell you another thing," she cried. "You haven't any right to ask me. You just wait a little while—I'll show you I don't have to stay in this old house." She ran from the room and slammed her bedroom door after her.

Helen rang for the house-boy. "Joe, exactly what did the man who came today say?"

"Say he got to see you about little girl."

"Well what kind of a man was he?—how old?"

"Not old man, Missie, not young man. Maybe fifty years, I guess."

Helen sighed. It was just another of the stories, the little dramas Hilda thought out and told. And they were so real to her, poor child. Helen ate slowly, and afterwards, in the big living room, she sat before the fire—idly knocking coals from the glowing logs. She turned all the lights off. The fire glinted on the eyes of the stuffed heads on the wall, and Helen's old habit reasserted itself. She found herself imagining how Hubert's hands looked, how narrow his hips were, and how straight his legs. And then she made a discovery: When her mind dropped his hands they disappeared. She was not building the figure of her husband. He was gone, completely gone. For the first time in years, Helen put her hands to her face and cried, for the peace had come back, and the bursting expectancy. She dried her eyes and walked slowly about the room, smiling up at the heads with the casual eyes of a stranger who didn't know how each animal had died. The room looked different and felt different. She fumbled with the new window bolts and threw open the wide windows to the night. And the night wind sighed in and bathed her bare shoulders with its cool peace. She leaned out of the window and listened. So many little noises came from the garden and from the hill beyond the garden. "It's just infested with life," she thought. "It's just bursting with life." Gradually as she listened she became aware of a rasping sound from the other side of the house. "If there were beavers, it would be a beaver cutting down a tree. Maybe it's a porcupine eating out the foundations. I've heard of that. But there aren't any porcupines here either." There were vibrations of the rasping in the house itself. "It must be something gnawing on the logs," she said. There came a little crash. The noise stopped. Helen started uneasily. She walked quickly down a passageway and stopped before the door of Hilda's room. With her hand on the strong outside bolt she called, "Are you all right, darling?" There was no answer. Helen slipped the bolt very quietly and entered the room. One of the oaken bars was hacked out and Hilda was gone.

For a moment Helen stood rigidly at the open window, looking wistfully into the grey night. Then her face paled and her lips set in the old line of endurance. Her movements were mechanical as she retraced her steps to the living room. She climbed up on a chair, unlocked the gun case and took down a shotgun.

Dr. Phillips sat beside Helen Van Deventer in the coroner's office. He had to come as the child's doctor, of course, but also he thought he could keep Helen from being afraid. She didn't look afraid. In her severe, her almost savage mourning, she looked as enduring as a sea-washed stone.

"And you expected it?" the coroner was saying. "You thought it might happen?"

Dr. Phillips looked uneasily at Helen and cleared his throat. "She had been my patient since she was born. In a case like this, she might have committed suicide or murder, depending on circumstances. Then again she might have lived on harmlessly. She could have gone all her life without making any violent move. It was impossible to say, you see."

The coroner was signing papers. "It was a beastly way for her to do it. Of course the girl was insane, and there isn't any reason to look into her motives. Her motives might have been tiny things. But it was a horrible way to do it. She never knew that, though. Her head in the stream and the gun beside her. I'll instruct a suicide verdict. I'm sorry to have to talk this way before you, Mrs. Van Deventer. Finding her must have been a terrible shock to you."

The doctor helped Helen down the steps of the courthouse. "Don't look that way," he cried. "You look as though you were going to an execution. It's better so, I tell you. You must not suffer so."

She didn't look at him. "I know now. By this time I know what my life expects of me," she said softly. "Now I know what I have always suspected. And I have the strength to endure, Doctor. Don't you worry about me."

VI

Junius Maltby was a small young man of good and cultured family and decent education. When his father died bankrupt, Junius got himself inextricably entangled in a clerkship, against which he feebly struggled for ten years.

After work Junius retired to his furnished room, patted the cushions of his morris chair and spent the evening reading. Stevenson's essays he thought nearly the finest things in English; he read *Travels with a Donkey* many times.

One evening soon after his thirty-fifth birthday, Junius fainted on the steps of his boarding house. When he recovered consciousness, he noticed for the first time that his breathing was difficult and unsatisfactory. He wondered how long it had been that way. The doctor whom he consulted was kind and even hopeful.

"You're by no means too far gone to get well," he said. "But you really must take those lungs out of San Francisco. If you stay here in the fog, you won't live a year. Move to a warm, dry climate."

The accident to his health filled Junius with pleasure, for it cut the strings he had been unable to sever for himself. He had five hundred dollars, not that he ever saved any money; he had simply forgotten to spend it. "With that much," he said, "I'll either recover and make a clean, new start, or else I'll die and be through with the whole business."

A man in his office told him of the warm, protected valley, the Pastures of Heaven, and Junius went there immediately. The name pleased him. "It's either an omen that I'm not going to live," he thought, "or else it's a nice symbolic substitute for death." He felt that the name meant something personal to him, and he was very glad, because for ten years nothing in the world had been personal to him.

There were, in the Pastures of Heaven, several families who wanted to take boarders. Junius inspected each one, and finally went to live on the farm of the widow Quaker. She needed the money, and besides, he could sleep in a shed separated from the farmhouse. Mrs. Quaker had two small boys and kept a hired man to work the farm.

The warm climate worked tenderly with Junius' lungs. Within the year his color was good and he had gained in weight. He was quiet and happy on the farm, and what pleased him more, he had thrown out the ten years of the office and had grown superbly lazy. Junius' thin blond hair went uncombed; he wore his glasses far down on his square nose, for his eyes were getting stronger and only the habit of feeling spectacles caused him to wear them. Throughout the day he had always some small stick protruding from his mouth, a habit only the laziest and most ruminative of men acquire. This convalescence took place in 1910.

In 1911, Mrs. Quaker began to worry about what the neighbors were saying. When she considered the implication of having a single man in her house, she became upset and nervous. As soon as Junius' recovery seemed sure beyond doubt, the widow confessed her trepidations. He married her, immediately and gladly. Now he had a home and a golden future, for the new Mrs. Maltby owned two hundred acres of grassy hillside and five acres of orchard and vegetable bottom. Junius sent for his books, his morris chair with the adjustable back, and his good copy of Velasquez' *Cardinal*. The future was a pleasant and sunshiny afternoon to him.

Mrs. Maltby promptly discharged the hired man and tried to put her husband to work; but in this she encountered a resistance the more bewildering because it presented no hard front to strike at. During his convalescence, Junius had grown to love laziness. He liked the valley and the farm, but he liked them as they were; he didn't want to plant new things, nor to tear out old. When Mrs. Maltby put a hoe in his hand and set him to work in the vegetable garden, she found him, likely enough, hours later, dangling his feet in the meadow stream and reading his pocket copy of *Kidnapped*. He was sorry; he didn't know how it had happened. And that was the truth.

At first she nagged him a great deal about his laziness and his sloppiness of dress, but he soon developed a faculty for never listening to her. It would be impolite, he considered, to notice her when she was not being a lady. It would be like staring at a cripple. And Mrs. Maltby, after she had battered at his resistance of fog for a time, took to sniveling and neglecting her hair.

Between 1911 and 1917, the Maltbys grew very poor. Junius simply would not take care of the farm. They even sold a few acres of pasture land to get money for food and clothing, and even then there was never enough to eat. Poverty sat cross-legged on the farm, and the Maltbys were ragged. They had never any new clothes at all, but Junius had discovered the essays of David Grayson. He wore overalls and sat under the sycamores that lined the meadow stream. Sometimes he read *Adventures in Contentment* to his wife and two sons.

Early in 1917, Mrs. Maltby found that she was going to have a baby, and late in the same year the wartime influenza epidemic struck the family with a dry viciousness. Perhaps because they were undernourished, the two boys were stricken simultaneously. For three days the house seemed filled to overflowing with flushed, feverish children whose nervous fingers strove to cling to life by the threads of their bed-clothes. For three days they struggled weakly, and on the fourth, both of the boys died. Their mother didn't know it, for she was confined, and the neighbors who came to help in the house hadn't the courage nor the cruelty to tell her. The black fever came upon her while she was in labor and killed her before she ever saw her child.

The neighbor women who helped at the birth told the story throughout the valley that Junius Maltby read books by the stream while his wife and children died. But this was only partly true. On the day of their seizure, he dangled his feet in the stream, because he didn't know they were ill, but thereafter he wandered vaguely from one to the other of the dying children, and talked nonsense to them. He told the eldest boy how diamonds are made. At the bedside of the other, he explained the beauty, the antiquity and the symbolism of the swastika. One life went out while he read aloud the second chapter of *Treasure Island*, and he didn't even know it had happened until he finished the chapter and looked up. During those days he was bewildered. He brought out the only things he had and offered them, but they had no potency with death. He knew in advance they wouldn't have, and that made it all the more terrible to him.

When the bodies were all gone, Junius went back to the stream and read a few pages of *Travels with a Donkey*. He chuckled uncertainly over the obstinacy of Modestine. Who but Stevenson could have named a donkey "Modestine"?

One of the neighbor women called him in and cursed him so violently that he was embarrassed and didn't listen. She put her hands on her hips and glared at him with contempt. And then she brought his child, a son, and laid it in his arms. When she looked back at him from the gate, he was standing with the howling little brute in his arms. He couldn't see any place to put it down, so he held it for a long time.

The people of the valley told many stories about Junius. Sometimes they hated him with the loathing busy people have for lazy ones, and sometimes they envied his laziness; but often they pitied him because he blundered so. No one in the valley ever realized that he was happy.

They told how, on a doctor's advice, Junius bought a goat to milk for the baby. He didn't inquire into the sex of his purchase nor give his reason for wanting a goat. When it arrived he looked under it, and very seriously asked, "Is this a normal goat?"

"Sure," said the owner.

"But shouldn't there be a bag or something immediately between the hind legs?—for the milk, I mean."

The people of the valley roared about that. Later, when a new and better goat was provided, Junius fiddled with it for two days and could not draw a drop of milk. He wanted to return this goat as defective until the owner showed him how to milk it. Some people claimed that he held the baby under the goat and let it suck its own milk, but this was untrue. The people of the valley declared they didn't know how he ever reared the child.

One day Junius went into Monterey and hired an old German to help him on the farm. He gave his new servant five dollars on account, and never paid him again. Within two weeks the hired man was so entangled in laziness that he did no more work than his employer. The two of them sat around the place together discussing things which interested and puzzled them—how color comes to flowers—whether there is a symbology in nature—where Atlantis lay—how the Incas interred their dead.

In the spring they planted potatoes, always too late, and without a covering of ashes to keep the bugs out. They sowed beans and corn and peas, watched them for a time, and then forgot them. The weeds covered everything from sight. It was no unusual thing to see Junius burrow into a perfect thicket of mallow weeds and emerge carrying a pale cucumber. He had stopped wearing shoes because he liked the feeling of the warm earth on his feet, and because he had no shoes.

In the afternoon Junius talked to Jakob Stutz a great deal. "You know," he said, "when the children died, I thought I had reached a peculiar high peak of horror. Then, almost while I thought it, the horror turned to sorrow and the sorrow dwindled to sadness. I didn't know my wife nor the children very well, I guess. Perhaps they were too near to me. It's a strange thing, this *knowing*. It is nothing but an awareness of details. There are long-visioned minds and short-visioned. I've never been able to see things that are close to me. For instance, I am much more aware of the Parthenon than of my own house over there." Suddenly Junius' face seemed to quiver with feeling, and his eyes brightened with enthusiasm. "Jakob," he said, "have you ever seen a picture of the frieze of the Parthenon?"

"Yes, and it is good, too," said Jakob.

Junius laid a hand on his hired man's knee. "Those horses," he said. "Those lovely horses—bound for a celestial pasture. Those eager and yet dignified young men setting out for an incredible fiesta that's being celebrated just around the cornice. I wonder how a man can know what a horse feels like when it is very happy; and that sculptor must have known or he couldn't have carved them so."

That was the way it went. Junius could not stay on a subject. Often the men went hungry because they failed to find a hen's nest in the grass when it came suppertime.

The son of Junius was named Robert Louis. Junius called him that when he thought of it, but Jakob Stutz rebelled at what he considered a kind of literary preciousness. "Boys must be named like dogs," he maintained. "One sound is sufficient for the name. Even Robert is too long. He should be called 'Bob.' " Jakob nearly got his way.

"I'll compromise with you," said Junius. "We'll call him Robbie. Robbie is really shorter than Robert, don't you think?"

He often gave way before Jakob, for Jakob continually struggled a little against the webs that were being spun about him. Now and then, with a kind of virtuous fury, he cleaned the house.

Robbie grew up gravely. He followed the men about, listening to their discussions. Junius never treated him like a little boy, because he didn't know how little boys should be treated. If Robbie made an observation the two men listened courteously and included the remark in their conversation, or even used it as the germ of an investigation. They tracked down many things in the course of an afternoon. Every day there were several raids on Junius' Encyclopedia.

A huge sycamore put out a horizontal limb over the meadow stream, and on it the three sat, the men hanging their feet into the water and moving pebbles with their toes while Robbie tried extravagantly to imitate them. Reaching the water was one of his criteria of manhood. Jakob had by this time given up shoes; Robbie had never worn any in his life.

The discussions were erudite. Robbie couldn't use childish talk, for he had never heard any. They didn't make conversation; rather they let a seedling of thought sprout by itself, and then watched with wonder while it sent out branching limbs. They were surprised at the strange fruit their conversation bore, for they didn't direct their thinking, nor trellis nor trim it the way so many people do.

There on the limb the three sat. Their clothes were rags and their hair was only hacked off to keep it out of their eyes. The men wore long, untrimmed beards. They watched the water-skaters on the surface of the pool below them, a pool which had been deepened by idling toes. The giant tree above them whisked softly in the wind, and occasionally dropped a leaf like a brown handkerchief. Robbie was five years old.

"I think sycamore trees are good," he observed when a leaf fell in his lap. Jakob picked up the leaf and stripped the parchment from its ribs.

"Yes," he agreed, "they grow by water. Good things love water. Bad things always been dry."

"Sycamores are big and good," said Junius. "It seems to me that a good thing or a kind thing must be very large to survive. Little good things are always destroyed by evil little things. Rarely is a big thing poisonous or treacherous. For this reason, in human thinking, bigness is an attribute of good and littleness of evil. Do you see that, Robbie?"

"Yes," said Robbie. "I see that. Like elephants."

"Elephants are often evil, but when we think of them, they seem gentle and good."

"But water," Jakob broke in. "Do you see about water too?"

"No, not about water."

"But I see," said Junius. "You mean that water is the seed of life. Of the three elements water is the sperm, earth the womb and sunshine the mold of growth."

Thus they taught him nonsense.

The people of the Pastures of Heaven recoiled from Junius Maltby after the death of his wife and his two boys. Stories of his callousness during the epidemic grew to such proportions that eventually they fell down of their own weight and were nearly forgotten. But although his neighbors forgot that Junius had read while his children died, they could not forget the problem he was becoming. Here in the fertile valley he lived in fearful poverty. While other families built small fortunes, bought Fords and radios, put in electricity and went twice a week to the moving pictures in Monterey or Salinas, Junius degenerated and became a ragged savage. The men of the valley resented his good bottom land, all overgrown with weeds, his untrimmed fruit trees and his fallen fences. The women thought with loathing of his unclean house with its littered dooryard and dirty windows. Both men and women hated his idleness and his complete lack of pride. For a while they went to visit him, hoping by their near examples to drag him from his slothfulness. But he received them naturally and with the friendliness of equality. He wasn't a bit ashamed of his poverty nor of his rags. Gradually his neighbors came to think of Junius as an outcast. No one drove up the private road to his house any more. They outlawed him from decent society and resolved never to receive him should he visit them.

Junius knew nothing about the dislike of his neighbors. He was still gloriously happy. His life was as unreal, as romantic and as unimportant as his thinking. He was content to sit in the sun and to dangle his feet in the stream. If he had no good clothes, at least he had no place to go which required good clothes.

Although the people almost hated Junius, they had only pity for the little boy Robbie. The women told one another how horrible it was to let the child grow up in such squalor. But, because they were mostly good people, they felt a strong reluctance for interfering with Junius' affairs.

"Wait until he's school age," Mrs. Banks said to a group of ladies in her own parlor. "We couldn't do anything now if we wanted to. He belongs to that father of his. But just as soon as the child is six, the county'll have something to say, let me tell you."

Mrs. Allen nodded and closed her eyes earnestly. "We keep forgetting that he's Mamie Quaker's child as much as

Maltby's. I think we should have stepped in long ago. But when he goes to school we'll give the poor little fellow a few things he never had."

"The least we can do is to see that he has enough clothes to cover him," another of the women agreed.

It seemed that the valley lay crouched in waiting for the time when Robbie should go to school. When, at term opening, after his sixth birthday, he did not appear, John Whiteside, the clerk of the school board, wrote a letter to Junius Maltby.

"I hadn't thought of it," Junius said when he read it. "I guess you'll have to go to school."

"I don't want to go," said Robbie.

"I know. I don't much want you to go, either. But we have laws. The law has a self-protective appendage called penalty. We have to balance the pleasure of breaking the law against the punishment. The Carthaginians punished even misfortune. If a general lost a battle through bad luck, he was executed. At present we punish people for accidents of birth and circumstance in much the same manner."

In the ensuing discussion they forgot all about the letter. John Whiteside wrote a very curt note.

"Well, Robbie, I guess you'll have to go," said Junius, when he received it. "Of course they'll teach you a great many useful things."

"Why don't you teach me?" Robbie pleaded.

"Oh, I can't. You see I've forgotten the things they teach."

"I don't want to go at all. I don't want to learn things."

"I know you don't, but I can't see any other way out."

And so one morning Robbie trudged to school. He was clad in an ancient pair of overalls, out at the knees and seat, a blue shirt from which the collar was gone, and nothing else. His long hair hung over his grey eyes like the forelock of a range pony.

The children made a circle around him in the school yard and stared at him in silence. They had all heard of the poverty of the Maltbys and of Junius' laziness. The boys looked forward to this moment when they could torture Robbie. Here was the time come; he stood in their circle, and they only stared at him. No one said, "Where'd you get them clothes," or, "Look at his hair," the way they had intended to. The children were puzzled by their failure to torment Robbie.

As for Robbie, he regarded the circle with serious eyes. He was not in the least frightened. "Don't you play games?" he asked. "My father said you'd play games."

And then the circle broke up with howls. "He doesn't know any games."—"Let's teach him pewee."—"No, nigger-baby." "Listen! Listen! Prisoner's base first."—"He doesn't know any games."

And, although they didn't know why, they thought it rather a fine thing not to know games. Robbie's thin face was studious. "We'll try pewee first," he decided. He was clumsy at the new games, but his teachers did not hoot at him. Instead they quarreled for the privilege of showing him how to hold the pewee stick. There are several schools of technique in pewee. Robbie stood aside listening for a while, and at last chose his own instructor.

Robbie's effect on the school was immediate. The older boys let him entirely alone, but the younger ones imitated him in everything, even tearing holes in the knees of their overalls. When they sat in the sun with their backs to the school wall, eating their lunches, Robbie told them about his father and about the sycamore tree. They listened intently and wished their fathers were lazy and gentle, too.

Sometimes a few of the boys, disobeying the orders of their parents, sneaked up to the Maltby place on a Saturday. Junius gravitated naturally to the sycamore limb, and while they sat on both sides of him, he read *Treasure Island* to them, or described the Gallic wars or the battle of Trafalgar. In no time at all, Robbie, with the backing of his father, became the king of the school yard. This is demonstrated by the facts that he had no chum, that they gave him no nickname, and that he arbitrated all the disputes. So exalted was his station that no one even tried to fight with him.

Only gradually did Robbie come to realize that he was the leader of the younger boys of the school. Something self-possessed and mature about him made his companions turn to him for leadership. It wasn't long before his was the voice which decided the game to be played. In baseball he was the umpire for the reason that no other boy could make a ruling without causing a riot. And while he played the games badly himself, questions of rules and ethics were invariably referred to him.

After a lengthy discussion with Junius and Jakob, Robbie invented two vastly popular games, one called Slinkey Coyote, a local version of Hare and Hounds, and the other named Broken Leg, a kind of glorified tag. For these two games he made rules as he needed them.

Miss Morgan's interest was aroused by the little boy, for he was as much a surprise in the schoolroom as he was in the yard. He could read perfectly and used a man's vocabulary, but he could not write. He was familiar with numbers, no matter how large, yet he refused to learn even the simplest arithmetic. Robbie learned to write with the greatest of difficulty. His hand wavered crazy letters on his school pad. At length Miss Morgan tried to help him.

"Take one thing and do it over and over until you get it perfectly," she suggested. "Be very careful with each letter."

Robbie searched his memory for something he liked. At length he wrote, "There is nothing so monsterous but we can belief it of ourselfs." He loved that "monsterous." It gave timbre and profundity to the thing. If there were words, which through their very sound-power could drag unwilling genii from the earth, 'monsterous' was surely one of them. Over and over he wrote the sentence, putting the greatest of care and drawing on his 'monsterous.' At the end of an hour, Miss Morgan came to see how he was getting on.

"Why, Robert, where in the world did you hear that?"

"It's from Stevenson, ma'am. My father knows it by heart almost."

Of course Miss Morgan had heard all the bad stories of Junius, and in spite of them had approved of him. But now she began to have a strong desire to meet him.

Games in the school yard were beginning to fall off in interest. Robbie lamented the fact to Junius one morning before he started off to school. Junius scratched his beard and thought. "Spy is a good game," he said at last. "I remember I used to like Spy."

"Who shall we spy on, though?"

"Oh, anyone. It doesn't matter. We used to spy on Italians."

Robbie ran off excitedly to school, and that afternoon, following a lengthy recourse to the school dictionary, he organized the B.A.S.S.F.E.A.J. Translated, which it never was above a whisper, this was the Boys' Auxiliary Secret Service For Espionage Against the Japanese. If for no other reason, the very magnificence of the name of this organization would have made it a force to be reckoned with. One by one Robbie took the boys into the dim greenness under the school-yard willow tree, and there swore them to secrecy with an oath so ferocious that it would have done credit to a lodge. Later, he brought the group together. Robbie explained to the boys that we would undoubtedly go to war with Japan some day.

"It behoofs us to be ready," he said. "The more we can find out about the nefarious practices of this nefarious race, the more spy information we can give our country when war breaks out."

The candidates succumbed before this glorious diction. They were appalled by the seriousness of a situation which required words like these. Since spying was now the business of the school, little Takashi Kato, who was in the third grade, didn't spend a private moment from then on. If Takashi raised two fingers in school, Robbie glanced meaningly at one of the Boy Auxiliaries, and a second hand sprung frantically into the air. When Takashi walked home after school, at least five boys crept through the brush beside the road. Eventually, however, Mr. Kato, Takashi's father, fired a shot into the dark one night, after seeing a white face looking in his window. Robbie reluctantly called the Auxiliary together and ordered that espionage be stopped at sundown. "They couldn't do anything really important at night," he explained.

In the long run Takashi did not suffer from the espionage practiced on him, for, since the Auxiliaries had to watch him, they could make no important excursions without taking him along. He found himself invited everywhere, because no one would consent to be left behind to watch him.

The Boy Auxiliaries received their death blow when Takashi, who had in some way learned of their existence, applied for admittance.

"I don't see how we can let you in," Robbie explained kindly. "You see you're a Japanese, and we hate them."

Takashi was almost in tears. "I was born here, the same

as you," he cried. "I'm just as good American as you, ain't I?"

Robbie thought hard. He didn't want to be cruel to Takashi. Then his brow cleared. "Say, do you speak Japanese?" he demanded.

"Sure, pretty good."

"Well, then you can be our interpreter and figure out secret messages."

Takashi beamed with pleasure. "Sure I can," he cried enthusiastically. "And if you guys want, we'll spy on my old man."

But the thing was broken. There was no one left to fight but Mr. Kato, and Mr. Kato was too nervous with his shotgun.

Hallowe'en went past, and Thanksgiving. In that time Robbie's effect on the boys was indicated by a growth in their vocabularies, and by a positive hatred for shoes or of any kind of good clothing for that matter. Although he didn't realize it, Robbie had set a style, not new, perhaps, but more rigid than it had been. It was unmanly to wear good clothes, and even more than that, it was considered an insult to Robbie.

One Friday afternoon Robbie wrote fourteen notes, and secretly passed them to fourteen boys in the school yard. The notes were all the same. They said: "A lot of indians are going to burn the Pres. of the U. S. to the stake at my house tomorrow at ten o'clock. Sneak out and bark like a fox down by our lower field. I will come and lead you to the rescue of this poor soul."

For several months Miss Morgan had intended to call upon Junius Maltby. The stories told of him, and her contact with his son, had raised her interest to a high point. Every now and then, in the schoolroom, one of the boys imparted a piece of astounding information. For example, one child who was really famous for his stupidity, told her that Hengest and Horsa invaded Britain. When pressed he admitted that the information came from Junius Maltby, and that in some way it was a kind of a secret. The old story of the goat amused the teacher so much that she wrote it for a magazine, but no magazine bought it. Over and over she had set a date to walk out to the Maltby farm.

She awakened on a December Saturday morning and found frost in the air and a brilliant sun shining. After breakfast she put on her corduroy skirt and her hiking boots, and left the house. In the yard she tried to persuade the ranch dogs to accompany her, but they only flopped their tails and went back to sleep in the sun.

The Maltby place lay about two miles away in the little canyon called Gato Amarillo. A stream ran beside the road, and sword ferns grew rankly under the alders. It was almost cold in the canyon, for the sun had not yet climbed over the mountain. Once during her walk Miss Morgan thought she heard footsteps and voices ahead of her, but when she hurried around the bend, no one was in sight. However, the brush beside the road crackled mysteriously.

Although she had never been there before, Miss Morgan knew the Maltby land when she came to it. Fences reclined tiredly on the ground under an overload of bramble. The fruit trees stretched bare branches clear of a forest of weeds. Wild blackberry vines clambered up the apple trees; squirrels and rabbits bolted from under her feet, and soft-voiced doves flew away with whistling wings. In a tall wild pear tree a congress of bluejays squawked a cacophonous argument. Then, beside an elm tree which wore a shaggy coat of frost-bitten morning glory, Miss Morgan saw the mossy, curled shingles of the Maltby roof. The place, in its quietness, might have been deserted for a hundred years. "How run-down and slovenly," she thought. "How utterly lovely and slipshod!" She let herself into the yard through a wicket gate which hung to its post by one iron band. The farm buildings were grey with weathering, and, up the sides of the walls, outlawed climbers pushed their fingers. Miss Morgan turned the corner of the house and stopped in her tracks; her mouth fell open and a chill shriveled on her spine. In the center of the yard a stout post was set up, and to it an old and ragged man was bound with many lengths of rope. Another man, younger and smaller, but even more ragged, piled brush about the feet of the captive. Miss Morgan shivered and backed around the house corner again. "Such things don't happen," she insisted. "You're dreaming. Such things just can't happen." And then she heard the most amiable of conversations going on between the two men.

"It's nearly ten," said the torturer.

The captive replied, "Yes, and you be careful how you put fire to that brush. You be sure to see them coming before you light it."

Miss Morgan nearly screamed with relief. She walked a little unsteadily toward the stake. The free man turned and saw her. For a second he seemed surprised, but immediately recovering, he bowed. Coming from a man with torn overalls and a matted beard, the bow was ridiculous and charming.

"I'm the teacher," Miss Morgan explained breathlessly "I was just out for a walk, and I saw this house. For a moment I thought this auto-da-fé was serious."

Junius smiled. "But it *is* serious. It's more serious than you think. For a moment I thought you were the rescue. The relief is due at ten o'clock, you know."

A savage barking of foxes broke out below the house among the willows. "That will be the relief," Junius continued. "Pardon me, Miss Morgan, isn't it? I am Junius Maltby and this gentleman on ordinary days is Jakob Stutz. Today, though, he is President of the United States being burned by Indians. For a time we thought he'd be Guinevere, but even without the full figure, he makes a better President than a Guinevere, don't you think? Besides he refused to wear a skirt."

"Damn foolishness," said the President complacently.

Miss Morgan laughed. "May I watch the rescue, Mr. Maltby?"

"I'm not Mr. Maltby, I'm three hundred Indians."

The barking of foxes broke out again. "Over by the steps," said the three hundred Indians. "You won't be taken for a redskin and massacred over there." He gazed toward the stream. A willow branch was shaking wildly. Junius scratched a match on his trousers and set fire to the brush at the foot of the stake. As the flame leaped up, the willow trees seemed to burst into pieces and each piece became a shrieking joy. The mass charged forward, armed as haphazardly and as terribly as the French people were when they stormed the Bastille. Even as the fire licked toward the President, it was kicked violently aside. The rescuers unwound the ropes with fervent hands, and Jakob Stutz stood free and happy. Nor was the following ceremony less impressive than the rescue. As the boys stood at salute, the President marched down the line and to each overall bib pinned a leaden slug on which the word HERO was deeply scratched. The game was over.

"Next Saturday we hang the guilty villains who have attempted this dastardly plot," Robbie announced.

"Why not now? Let's hang 'em now!" the troop screamed.

"No, my men. There are lots of things to do. We have to make a gallows." He turned to his father. "I guess we'll have to hang both of you," he said. For a moment he looked covetously at Miss Morgan, and then reluctantly gave her up.

That afternoon was one of the most pleasant Miss Morgan had ever spent. Although she was given a seat of honor on the sycamore limb, the boys had ceased to regard her as the teacher.

"It's nicer if you take off your shoes," Robbie invited her, and it was nicer she found, when her boots were off and her feet dangled in the water.

That afternoon Junius talked of cannibal societies among the Aleutian Indians. He told how the mercenaries turned against Carthage. He described the Lacedaemonians combing their hair before they died at Thermopylae. He explained the origin of macaroni, and told of the discovery of copper as though he had been there. Finally when the dour Jakob opposed his idea of the eviction from the Garden of Eden, a mild quarrel broke out, and the boys started for home. Miss Morgan allowed them to distance her, for she wanted to think quietly about the strange gentleman.

The day when the school board visited was looked forward to with terror by both the teacher and her pupils. It was a day of tense ceremony. Lessons were recited nervously and the misspelling of a word seemed a capital crime. There was no day on which the children made more blunders, nor on which the teacher's nerves were thinner worn.

The school board of the Pastures of Heaven visited on the afternoon of December 15. Immediately after lunch they filed in, looking somber and funereal and a little ashamed. First came John Whiteside, the clerk, old and white-haired, with an easy attitude toward education which was sometimes criticized in the valley. Pat Humbert came after him. Pat was elected because he wanted to be. He was a lonely man who had no initiative in meeting people, and who took every possible means to be thrown into their contact. His clothes were as uncompromising, as unhappy as the bronze suit on the seated statue of Lincoln in Washington. T. B. Allen followed, dumpily rolling up the aisle. Since he was the only merchant in the valley, his seat on the board belonged to him by right. Behind him strode Raymond Banks, big and jolly and very red of hands and face. Last in the line was Bert Munroe, the newly elected member. Since it was his first visit to the school, Bert seemed a little sheepish as he followed the other members to their seats at the front of the room.

When the board was seated magisterially, their wives came in and found seats at the back of the room, behind the children. The pupils squirmed uneasily. They felt that they were surrounded, that escape, should they need to escape, was cut off. When they twisted in their seats, they saw that the women were smiling benevolently on them. They caught sight of a large paper bundle which Mrs. Munroe held on her lap.

School opened. Miss Morgan, with a strained smile on her face, welcomed the school board. "We will do nothing out of the ordinary, gentlemen," she said. "I think it will be more interesting to you in your official capacities, to see the school as it operates every day." Very little later, she wished she hadn't said that. Never within her recollection, had she seen such stupid children. Those who did manage to force words past their frozen palates, made the most hideous mistakes. Their spelling was abominable. Their reading sounded like the jibbering of the insane. The board tried to be dignified, but they could not help smiling a little from embarrassment for the children. A light perspiration formed on Miss Morgan's forehead. She had visions of being dismissed from her position by an outraged board. The wives in the rear smiled on, nervously, and time dripped by. When the arithmetic had been muddled and travestied, John Whiteside arose from his chair.

"Thank you, Miss Morgan," he said. "If you'll allow it, I'll just say a few words to the children, and then you can dismiss them. They ought to have some payment for having us here."

The teacher sighed with relief. "Then you do understand they weren't doing as well as usual? I'm glad you know that."

John Whiteside smiled. He had seen so many nervous young teachers on school board days. "If I thought they were doing their best, I'd close the school," he said. Then he spoke to the children for five minutes—told them they should study hard and love their teacher. It was the short and painless little speech he had used for years. The older pupils had heard it often. When it was done, he asked the teacher to dismiss the school. The pupils filed quietly out, but, once in the air, their relief was too much for them. With howls and shrieks they did their best to kill each other by disembowelment and decapitation.

John Whiteside shook hands with Miss Morgan. "We've never had a teacher who kept better order," he said kindly. "I think if you knew how much the children like you, you'd be embarrassed."

"But they're good children," she insisted loyally. "They're awfully good children."

"Of course," John Whiteside agreed. "By the way, how is the little Maltby boy getting along?"

"Why, he's a bright youngster, a curious child. I think he has almost a brilliant mind."

"We've been talking about him in board meeting, Miss Morgan. You know, of course, that his home life isn't all that it ought to be. I noticed him this afternoon especially. The poor child's hardly clothed."

"Well, it's a strange home." Miss Morgan felt that she had to defend Junius. "It's not the usual kind of home, but it isn't bad."

"Don't mistake me, Miss Morgan. We aren't going to interfere. We just thought we ought to give him a few things. His father's very poor, you know."

"I know," she said gently.

"Mrs. Munroe bought him a few clothes. If you'll call him in, we'll give them to him."

"Oh. No, I wouldn't—" she began.

"Why not? We only have a few little shirts and a pair of overalls and some shoes."

"But Mr. Whiteside, it might embarrass him. He's quite a proud little chap."

"Embarrass him to have decent clothes? Nonsense! I should think it would embarrass him more not to have them. But aside from that, it's too cold for him to go barefoot at this time of year. There's been frost on the ground every morning for a week."

"I wish you wouldn't," she said helplessly. "I really wish you wouldn't do it."

"Miss Morgan, don't you think you're making too much of this? Mrs. Munroe has been kind enough to buy the things for him. Please call him in so she can give them to him."

A moment later Robbie stood before them. His unkempt hair fell over his face, and his eyes still glittered with the fierceness of the play in the yard. The group gathered at the front of the room regarded him kindly, trying not to look too pointedly at his ragged clothes. Robbie gazed uneasily about.

"Mrs. Munroe has something to give you, Robert," Miss Morgan said.

Then Mrs. Munroe came forward and put the bundle in his arms. "What a nice little boy!"

Robbie placed the package carefully on the floor and put his hands behind him.

"Open it, Robert," T. B. Allen said sternly. "Where are your manners?"

Robbie gazed resentfully at him. "Yes, sir," he said, and untied the string. The shirts and the new overalls lay open before him, and he stared at them uncomprehendingly. Suddenly he seemed to realize what they were. His face flushed warmly. For a moment he looked about nervously like a trapped animal, and then he bolted through the door, leaving the little heap of clothing behind him. The school board heard two steps on the porch, and Robbie was gone.

Mrs. Munroe turned helplessly to the teacher. "What's wrong with him anyway?"

"I think he was embarrassed," said Miss Morgan.

"But why should he be? We were nice to him."

The teacher tried to explain, and became a little angry with them in trying. "I think, you see—why, I don't think he ever knew he was poor until a moment ago."

"It was my mistake," John Whiteside apologized. "I'm sorry, Miss Morgan."

"What can we do about him?" Bert Munroe asked.

"I don't know. I really don't know."

Mrs. Munroe turned to her husband. "Bert, I think if you went out and had a talk with Mr. Maltby it might help. I don't mean you to be anything but kind. Just tell him little boys shouldn't walk around in bare feet in the frost. Maybe just a word like that'll help. Mr. Maltby could tell little Robert he must take the clothes. What do you think, Mr. Whiteside?"

"I don't like it. You'll have to vote to overrule my objection. I've done enough harm."

"I think his health is more important than his feelings," Mrs. Munroe insisted.

School closed for Christmas week on the twentieth of December. Miss Morgan planned to spend her vacation in Los Angeles. While she waited at the crossroads for a bus to Salinas, she saw a man and a little boy walking down the Pastures of Heaven road toward her. They were dressed in cheap new clothes, and both of them walked as though their feet were sore. As they neared her, Miss Morgan looked closely at the little boy, and saw that it was Robbie. His face was sullen and unhappy.

"Why, Robert," she cried. "What's the matter? Where are you going?"

The man spoke. "We're going to San Francisco, Miss Morgan."

She looked up quickly. It was Junius shorn of his beard. She hadn't realized that he was so old. Even his eyes, which had been young, looked old. But of course he was pale because the beard had protected his skin from sunburn. On his face there was a look of deep puzzlement.

"Are you going up for the holidays?" Miss Morgan asked. "I love the stores in the city around Christmas. I could look in them for days."

"No," Junius replied slowly. "I guess we're going to be up there for good. I am an accountant, Miss Morgan. At least I was an accountant twenty years ago. I'm going to try to get a job." There was pain in his voice.

"But why do you do that?" she demanded.

"You see," he explained simply. "I didn't know I was doing an injury to the boy, here. I hadn't thought about it. I suppose I should have thought about it. You can see that he shouldn't be brought up in poverty. You can see that, can't you? I didn't know what people were saying about us."

"Why don't you stay on the ranch? It's a good ranch, isn't it?"

"But I couldn't make a living on it, Miss Morgan. I don't know anything about farming. Jakob is going to try to run the ranch, but you know, Jakob is very lazy. Later, when I can, I'll sell the ranch so Robbie can have a few things he never had."

Miss Morgan was angry, but at the same time she felt she was going to cry. "You don't believe everything silly people tell you, do you?"

He looked at her in surprise. "Of course not. But you can see for yourself that a growing boy shouldn't be brought up like a little animal, can't you?"

The bus came into sight on the highway and bore down on them. Junius pointed to Robbie. "He didn't want to come. He ran away into the hills. Jakob and I caught him last night. He's lived like a little animal too long, you see. Besides, Miss Morgan, he doesn't know how nice it will be in San Francisco."

The bus squealed to a stop. Junius and Robbie climbed into the back seat. Miss Morgan was about to get in beside them. Suddenly she turned and took her seat beside the driver. "Of course," she said to herself. "Of course, they want to be alone."

VII

Old Guiermo Lopez died when his daughters were fairly well grown, leaving them forty acres of rocky hillside and no money at all. They lived in a whitewashed, clapboard shack with an outhouse, a well and a shed beside it. Practically nothing would grow on the starved soil except tumble-weed and flowering sage, and, although the sisters toiled mightily over a little garden, they succeeded in producing very few vegetables. For a time, with grim martyrdom, they went hungry, but in the end the flesh conquered. They were too fat and too jolly to make martyrs of themselves over an unreligious matter like eating.

One day Rosa had an idea. "Are we not the best makers of tortillas in the valley?" she asked of her sister.

"We had that art from our mother," Maria responded piously.

"Then we are saved. We will make enchiladas, tortillas, tamales. We will sell them to the people of Las Pasturas del Cielo."

"Will those people buy, do you think?" Maria asked skeptically.

"Listen to this from me, Maria. In Monterey there are several places where tortillas, only one finger as good as ours, are sold. And those people who sell them are very rich. They have a new dress thrice a year. And do their tortillas compare with ours? I ask that of you, remembering our mother."

Maria's eyes brimmed with tears of emotion. "They do not," she declared passionately. "In the whole world there are none like those tortillas beaten by the sainted hands of our mother."

"Well, then, adelante!" said Rosa with finality. "If they are so good, the people will buy."

There followed a week of frenzied preparation in which the perspiring sisters scrubbed and decorated. When they had finished, their little house wore a new coat of whitewash inside and out. Geranium cuttings were planted by the door-step, and the trash of years had been collected and burned. The front room of the house was transformed into a restaurant containing two tables which were covered with yellow oilcloth. A pine board on the fence next to the county road proclaimed: TORTILLAS, ENCHILADAS, TAMALES AND SOME OTHER SPANISH COOKINGS, R. & M. LOPEZ.

Business did not come with a rush. Indeed very little came at all. The sisters sat at their own yellow tables and waited. They were childlike and jovial and not very clean. Sitting in the chairs they waited on fortune. But let a customer enter the shop, and they leaped instantly to attention. They laughed delightedly at everything their client said; they boasted of their tortillas. They rolled their sleeves to the elbows to show the whiteness of their skin in passionate denial of Indian blood. But very few customers came. The sisters began to find difficulties in their business. They could not make a quantity of their product, for it would spoil if kept for long. Tamales require fresh meat. So it was that they began to set traps for birds and rabbits; sparrows, blackbirds and larks were kept in cages until they were needed for tamales. And still the business languished.

One morning Rosa confronted her sister. "You must harness old Lindo, Maria. There are no more corn husks." She placed a piece of silver in Maria's hand. "Buy only a few in Monterey," she said. "When the business is better we will buy very many." Maria obediently kissed her and started out toward the shed.

"And Maria—if there is any money over, a sweet for you and for me—a big one."

When Maria drove back to the house that afternoon, she found her sister strangely quiet. The shrieks, the little squeals, the demands for every detail of the journey, which usually followed a reunion, were missing. Rosa sat in a chair at one of the tables, and on her face there was a scowl of concentration.

Maria approached timidly. "I bought the husks very cheaply," she said. "And here, Rosa, here is the sweet. The biggest kind, and only four cents!"

Rosa took the proffered candy bar and put one huge end of it in her mouth. She still scowled with thought. Maria settled herself nearby, smiling gently, quizzically, silently pleading for a share of her sister's burden. Rosa sat like a rock and sucked her candy bar. Suddenly she glared into Maria's eyes. "Today," she said solemnly, "today I gave myself to a customer."

Maria sobbed with excitement and interest.

"Do not make a mistake," Rosa continued. "I did not take money. The man had eaten three enchiladas—three!"

Maria broke into a thin, childish wail of nervousness.

"Be still," said Rosa. "What do you think I should do now? It is necessary to encourage our customers if we are to succeed. And he had three, Maria, three enchiladas! And he paid for them. Well? What do you think?"

Maria sniffled and clutched at a moral bravery in the face of her sister's argument. "I think, Rosa, I think our mother would be glad, and I think your own soul would be glad if you should ask forgiveness of the Mother Virgin and of Santa Rosa."

Rosa smiled broadly and took Maria in her arms. "That is what I did. Just as soon as he went away. He was hardly out of the house before I did that."

Maria tore herself away, and with streaming eyes went into her bedroom. Ten minutes she kneeled before the little Virgin on the wall. Then she arose and flung herself into Rosa's arms. "Rosa, my sister," she cried happily. "I think —I think I shall encourage the customers, too."

The Lopez sisters smothered each other in a huge embrace and mingled their tears of joy.

That day marked the turning point of the affairs of the Lopez sisters. It is true that business did not flourish, but from then on, they sold enough of their "Spanish Cookings" to keep food in the kitchen and bright print dresses on their broad, round backs. They remained persistently religious. When either of them had sinned she went directly to the little porcelain Virgin, now conveniently placed in the hall to be accessible from both bedrooms, and prayed for forgiveness. Sins were not allowed to pile up. They confessed each one as it was committed. Under the Virgin there was a polished place on the floor where they had knelt in their nightdresses.

Life became very pleasant to the Lopez sisters. There was not even a taint of rivalry, for although Rosa was older and braver, they looked almost exactly alike. Maria was a little fatter, but Rosa was a little taller, and there you had it.

Now the house was filled with laughter and with squeals of enthusiasm. They sang over the flat stones while they patted out the tortillas with their fat, strong hands. Let a customer say something funny, let Tom Breman say to them, as he ate his third tamale, "Rosa, you're living too high. This rich living is going to bust your gut wide open if you don't cut it out," and both of the sisters would be racked with giggles for half an hour afterwards. A whole day later, while they patted out the tortillas on the stone, they would remember this funny thing and laugh all over again. For these sisters knew how to preserve laughter, how to pet and coax it along until their spirits drank the last dregs of its potentiality. Don Tom was a fine man, they said. A funny man—and a rich man. Once he ate five plates of chile con carne. But also, something you did not often find in a rich man, he was an *hombre fuerte*, oh, very strong! Over the tortilla stones they nodded their heads wisely and reminiscently at this observation, like two connoisseurs remembering a good wine.

It must not be supposed that the sisters were prodigal of their encouragement. They accepted no money for anything except their cooking. However, if a man ate three or more of their dishes, the soft hearts of the sisters broke with gratitude, and that man became a candidate for encouragement.

On an unfortunate night, a man whose appetite was not equal to three enchiladas offered to Rosa the money of shame. There were several other customers in the house at the time. The offer was cast into a crackle of conversation. Instantly the noise ceased, leaving a horrified silence. Maria hid her face in her hands. Rosa grew pale and then flushed brilliant with furious blood. She panted with emotion and her eyes sparkled. Her fat, strong hands rose like eagles and settled on her hips. But when she spoke, it was with a curious emotional restraint. "It is an insult to me," she said huskily. "You do not know, perhaps, that General Vallejo is nearly our ancestor, so close as that we are related. In our veins the pure blood is. What would General Vallejo say if he heard? Do you think his hand could stay from his sword to hear you insult two ladies so nearly in his family? Do you think it? You say to us, 'You are shameful women!' We, who make the finest, the thinnest tortillas in all California." She panted with the effort to restrain herself.

"I didn't mean nothing," the offender whined. "Honest to God, Rosa, I didn't mean nothing."

Her anger left her then. One of her hands took flight

from her hip, this time like a lark, and motioned almost sadly toward the door. "Go," she said gently. "I do not think you meant bad, but the insult is still." And as the culprit slunk out of the doorway, "Now, would anyone else like a dish of chiles con frijoles? Which one here? Chiles con frijoles like none in the world."

Ordinarily they were happy, these sisters. Maria, whose nature was very delicate and sweet, planted more geraniums around the house, and lined the fence with hollyhocks. On a trip to Salinas, Rosa and Maria bought and presented to each other boudoir caps like inverted nests of blue and pink ribbons. It was the ultimate! Side by side they looked in a mirror and then turned their heads and smiled a little sadly at each other, thinking, "This is the great day. This is the time we shall remember always as the happy time. What a shame it cannot last."

In fear that it would not last, Maria kept large vases of flowers in front of her Virgin.

But their foreboding came seldom upon them. Maria bought a little phonograph with records—tangoes, waltzes. When the sisters worked over the stones, they set the machine to playing and patted out the tortillas in time to the music.

Inevitably, in the valley of the Pastures of Heaven, the whisper went about that the Lopez sisters were bad women. Ladies of the valley spoke coldly to them when they passed. It is impossible to say how these ladies knew. Certainly their husbands didn't tell them, but nevertheless they knew; they always know.

Before daylight on a Saturday morning, Maria carried out the old, string-mended harness and festooned it on the bones of Lindo. "Have courage, my friend," she said to the horse, as she buckled the crupper and, "The mouth, please, my Lindo," as she inserted the bit. Then she backed him between the shafts of an ancient buggy. Lindo purposely stumbled over the shafts, just as he had for thirty years. When Maria hooked the traces, he looked around at her with a heavy, philosophic sadness. Old Lindo had no interest in destinations any more. He was too old even to be excited about going home once he was out. Now he lifted his lips from his long, yellow teeth, and grinned despairingly. "The way is not long," Maria soothed him. "We will go slowly. You must not fear the journey, Lindo." But Lindo did fear the journey. He loathed the journey to Monterey and back.

The buggy sagged alarmingly when Maria clambered into it. She took the lines gingerly in her hands. "Go, my friend," she said, and fluttered the lines. Lindo shivered and looked around at her. "Do you hear? We must go! There are things to buy in Monterey." Lindo shook his head and drooped one knee in a kind of curtsey. "Listen to me, Lindo!" Maria cried imperiously. "I say we must go. I am firm! I am even angry." She fluttered the lines ferociously about his shoulders. Lindo drooped his head nearly to the earth, like a scenting hound, and moved slowly out of the yard. Nine miles he must go to Monterey, and nine miles back. Lindo knew it, and despaired at the knowledge. But now that her firmness and her anger were over, Maria settled back in the seat and hummed the chorus of the "Waltz Moon" tango.

The hills glittered with dew. Maria, breathing the fresh damp air, sang more loudly, and even Lindo found youth enough in his old nostrils to snort. A meadow lark flew ahead from post to post, singing furiously. For ahead Maria saw a man walking in the road. Before she caught up with him, she knew from the shambling, ape-like stride that it was Allen Hueneker, the ugliest, shyest man in the valley.

Allen Hueneker not only walked like an ape, he looked like an ape. Little boys who wanted to insult their friends did so by pointing to Allen and saying, "There goes your brother." It was a deadly satire. Allen was so shy and so horrified at his appearance that he tried to grow whiskers to cover up his face, but the coarse, sparse stubble grew in the wrong places and only intensified his simian appearance. His wife had married him because she was thirty-seven, and because Allen was the only man of her acquaintance who could not protect himself. Later it developed that she was a woman whose system required jealousy properly to function. Finding nothing in Allen's life of which she could be jealous, she manufactured things. To her neighbors she told stories of his prowess with women, of his untrustworthiness, of his obscure delinquencies. She told these stories until she believed them, but her neighbors laughed behind her back when she spoke of Allen's sins, for everyone in the Pastures of Heaven knew how shy and terrified the ugly little man was.

The ancient Lindo stumbled abreast of Allen Hueneker. Maria tugged on the lines as though she pulled up a thunderously galloping speed. "Steady, Lindo! Be calm!" she called. At the lightest pressure of the lines, Lindo turned to stone and sunk into his loose-jointed, hang-necked posture of complete repose.

"Good morning," said Maria politely.

Allen edged shyly over toward the side of the road. "Morning," he said, and turned to look with affected interest up a side hill.

"I go to Monterey," Maria continued. "Do you wish to ride?"

Allen squirmed and searched the sky for clouds or hawks. "I ain't going only to the bus stop," he said sullenly.

"And what then? It is a little ride, no?"

The man scratched among his whiskers, trying to make up his mind. And then, more to end the situation than for the sake of a ride, he climbed into the buggy beside the fat Maria. She rolled aside to make room for him, and then oozed back. "Lindo, go!" she called. "Lindo, do you hear me? Go before I grow angry again." The lines clattered about Lindo's neck. His nose dropped toward the ground, and he sauntered on.

For a little while they rode in silence, but soon Maria remembered how polite it was to encourage conversation. "You go on a trip, yes?" she asked.

Allen glared at an oak tree and said nothing.

"I have not been on a train," Maria confided after a moment, "but my sister, Rosa, has ridden on trains. Once she rode to San Francisco, and once she rode back. I have heard very rich men say it is good to travel. My own sister, Rosa, says so too."

"I ain't going only to Salinas," said Allen.

"Ah, of course I have been there many times. Rosa and I have such friends in Salinas. Our mother came from there. And our father often went there with wood."

Allen struggled against his embarrassment. "Couldn't get the old Ford going, or I'd've gone in it."

"You have, then, a Ford?" Maria was impressed.

"Just an old Ford."

"We have said, Rosa and I, that some day we, too, may have a Ford. Then we will travel to many places. I have heard very rich men say it is good to travel."

As though to punctuate the conversation, an old Ford appeared over the hill and came roaring down on them. Maria gripped the lines. "Lindo, be calm!" she called. Lindo paid not the slightest attention either to Maria or to the Ford.

Mr. and Mrs. Munroe were in the Ford. Bert craned his neck back as they passed. "God! Did you see that?" he demanded, laughing. "Did you see that old woman-killer with Maria Lopez?"

Mrs. Munroe smiled.

"Say," Bert cried. "It'd be a good joke to tell old lady Hueneker we saw her old man running off with Maria Lopez."

"Don't you do anything of the kind," his wife insisted.

"But it'd be a good joke. You know how she talks about him."

"No, don't you do it, Bert!"

Meanwhile Maria drove on, conversing guilelessly with her reluctant guest. "You do not come to our house for enchiladas. There are no enchiladas like ours. For look! we learned from our mother. When our mother was living, it was said as far as San Juan, even as far as Gilroy, that no one else could make tortillas so flat, so thin. You must know it is the beating, always the beating that makes goodness and thinness to a tortilla. No one ever beat so long as our mother, not even Rosa. I go now to Monterey for flour because it is cheaper there."

Allen Hueneker sank into his side of the seat and wished for the bus station.

It was late in the afternoon before Maria neared home again. "Soon we are there," she called happily to Lindo. "Have courage, my friend, the way is short now." Maria was bubbling with anticipation. In a riot of extravagance she had bought four candy bars, but that was not all. For Rosa she had a present, a pair of broad silken garters with huge red poppies appliquéd on their sides. In her imagination she could see Rosa putting them on and then lifting her skirt, but very modestly, of course. The two of them would look at the garters in a mirror standing on the floor. Rosa would point her toe a trifle, and then the sisters would cry with happiness.

In the yard Maria slowly unharnessed Lindo. It was good, she knew, to put off joy, for by doing so, one increased joy.

The house was very quiet. There were no vehicles in front to indicate the presence of customers. Maria hung up the old harness, and turned Lindo into the pasture. Then she took out the candy bars and the garters and walked slowly into the house. Rosa sat at one of the little tables, a silent, restrained Rosa, a grim and suffering Rosa. Her eyes seemed glazed and sightless. Her fat, firm hands were clenched on the table in front of her. She did not turn nor give any sign of recognition when Maria entered. Maria stopped and stared at her.

"Rosa," she said timidly. "I'm back home, Rosa."

Her sister turned slowly. "Yes," she said.

"Are you sick, Rosa?"

The glazed eyes had turned back to the table again. "No."

"I have a present, Rosa. Look, Rosa." She held up the magnificent garters.

Slowly, very slowly, Rosa's eyes crept up to the brilliant red poppies and then to Maria's face. Maria was poised to break into squealing enthusiasm. Rosa's eyes dropped, and two fat tears ran down the furrows beside her nose.

"Rosa, do you see the present? Don't you like them, Rosa? Won't you put them on, Rosa?"

"You are my good little sister."

"Rosa, tell me, what is the matter? You are sick. You must tell your Maria. Did someone come?"

"Yes," said Rosa hollowly, "the sheriff came."

Now Maria fairly chattered with excitement. "The sheriff, he came? Now we are on the road. Now we will be rich. How many enchiladas, Rosa? Tell me how many for the sheriff."

Rosa shook off her apathy. She went to Maria and put motherly arms about her. "My poor little sister," she said. "Now we cannot ever sell any more enchiladas. Now we must live again in the old way with no new dresses."

"Rosa, you are crazy. Why you talk this way to me?"

"It is true. It was the sheriff. 'I have a complaint,' he said to me. 'I have a complaint that you are running a bad house.' 'But that is a lie,' I said. 'A lie and an insult to our mother and to General Vallejo.' 'I have a complaint,' he told me. 'You must close your doors or else I must arrest you for running a bad house.' 'But it is a lie,' I tried to make him understand. 'I got a complaint this afternoon,' he said. 'When I have a complaint, there is nothing I can do, for see, Rosa,' he said to me as a friend, 'I am only the servant of the people who make complaints.' And now you see, Maria, my sister, we must go back to the old living." She left the stricken Maria and turned back to her table. For a moment Maria tried to understand it, and then she sobbed hysterically. "Be still, Maria! I have been thinking. You know it is true that we will starve if we cannot sell enchiladas. Do not blame me too much when I tell you this. I have made up my mind. See, Maria! I will go to San Francisco and be a bad woman." Her head dropped low over her fat hands. Maria's sobbing had stopped. She crept close to her sister.

"For money?" she whispered in horror.

"Yes," cried Rosa bitterly. "For money. For a great deal of money. And may the good Mother forgive me."

Maria left her then, and scuttled into the hallway where she stood in front of the porcelain Mary. "I have placed candles," she cried. "I have put flowers every day. Holy Mother, what is the matter with us? Why do you let this happen?" Then she dropped on her knees and prayed, fifty Hail Marys! She crossed herself and rose to her feet. Her face was strained but determined.

In the other room Rosa still sat bent over her table.

"Rosa," Maria cried shrilly. "I am your sister. I am what you are." She gulped a great breath. "Rosa, I will go to San Francisco with you. I, too, will be a bad woman—"

Then the reserve of Rosa broke. She stood up and opened her huge embrace. And for a long time the Lopez sisters cried hysterically in each other's arms.

VIII

Molly Morgan got off the train in Salinas and waited three quarters of an hour for the bus. The big automobile was empty except for the driver and Molly.

"I've never been to the Pastures of Heaven, you know," she said. "Is it far from the main road?"

"About three miles," said the driver.

"Will there be a car to take me into the valley?"

"No, not unless you're met."

"But how do people get in there?"

The driver ran over the flattened body of a jack rabbit with apparent satisfaction. "I only hit 'em when they're dead," he apologized. "In the dark, when they get caught in the lights, I try to miss 'em."

"Yes, but how am I going to get into the Pastures of Heaven?"

"I dunno. Walk, I guess. Most people walk if they ain't met."

When he set her down at the entrance to the dirt side-road, Molly Morgan grimly picked up her suitcase and marched toward the draw in the hills. An old Ford truck squeaked up beside her.

"Goin' into the valley, ma'am?"

"Oh—yes, yes I am."

"Well, get in, then. Needn't be scared. I'm Pat Humbert. I got a place in the Pastures."

Molly surveyed the grimy man and acknowledged his introduction. "I'm the new schoolteacher. I mean, I think I am. Do you know where Mr. Whiteside lives?"

"Sure, I go right by there. He's clerk of the board. I'm on the school board myself, you know. We wondered what you'd look like." Then he grew embarrassed at what he had said, and flushed under his coating of dirt. " 'Course I mean what you'd *be* like. Last teacher we had gave a good deal of trouble. She was all right, but she was sick—I mean, sick and nervous. Finally quit because she was sick."

Molly picked at the fingertips of her gloves. "My letter says I'm to call on Mr. Whiteside. Is he all right? I don't mean that. I mean—is he—what kind of a man is he?"

"Oh, you'll get along with him all right. He's a fine old man. Born in that house he lives in. Been to college, too. He's a good man. Been clerk of the board for over twenty years."

When he put her down in front of the big old house of John Whiteside, she was really frightened. "Now it's coming," she said to herself. "But there's nothing to be afraid of. He can't do anything to me." Molly was only nineteen. She felt that this moment of interview for her first job was a tremendous inch in her whole existence.

The walk up to the door did not reassure her, for the path lay between tight little flower beds hedged in with clipped box, seemingly planted with the admonition, "Now grow and multiply, but don't grow too high, nor multiply too greatly, and above all things, keep out of this path!" There was a hand on those flowers, a guiding and a correcting hand. The large white house was very dignified. Venetian blinds of yellow wood were tilted down to keep out the noon sun. Halfway up the path she came in sight of the entrance. There was a veranda as broad and warm and welcoming as an embrace. Through her mind flew the thought, "Surely you can tell the hospitality of a house by its entrance. Suppose it had a little door and no porch." But in spite of the welcoming of the wide steps and the big doorway, her timidities clung to her when she rang the bell. The big door opened, and a large, comfortable woman stood smiling at Molly.

"I hope you're not selling something," said Mrs. Whiteside. "I never want to buy anything, and I always do, and then I'm mad."

Molly laughed. She felt suddenly very happy. Until that moment she hadn't known how frightened she really was. "Oh, no," she cried. "I'm the new schoolteacher. My letter says I'm to interview Mr. Whiteside. Can I see him?"

"Well, it's noon, and he's just finishing his dinner. Did you have dinner?"

"Oh, of course. I mean, no."

Mrs. Whiteside chuckled and stood aside for her to enter. "Well, I'm glad you're sure." She led Molly into a large dining room, lined with mahogany, glass-fronted dish closets. The square table was littered with the dishes of a meal. "Why, John must have finished and gone. Sit down, young woman. I'll bring back the roast."

"Oh, no. Really, thank you, no, I'll just talk to Mr. Whiteside and then go along."

"Sit down. You'll need nourishment to face John."

"Is—is he very stern, with new teachers, I mean?"

"Well," said Mrs. Whiteside. "That depends. If they haven't had their dinner, he's a regular bear. He shouts at them. But when they've just got up from the table, he's only just fierce."

Molly laughed happily. "You have children," she said. "Oh, you've raised lots of children—and you like them."

Mrs. Whiteside scowled. "One child raised me. Raised me right through the roof. It was too hard on me. He's out raising cows now, poor devils. I don't think I raised him very high."

When Molly had finished eating, Mrs. Whiteside threw

open a side door and called, "John, here's someone to see you." She pushed Molly through the doorway into a room that was a kind of library, for big bookcases were loaded with thick, old comfortable books, all filigreed in gold. And it was a kind of a sitting room. There was a fireplace of brick with a mantel of little red tile bricks and the most extraordinary vases on the mantel. Hung on a nail over the mantel, slung really, like a rifle on a shoulder strap, was a huge meerschaum pipe in the Jaegar fashion. Big leather chairs with leather tassels hanging to them, stood about the fireplace, all of them patent rocking chairs with the kind of springs that chant when you rock them. And lastly, the room was a kind of an office, for there was an old-fashioned roll-top desk, and behind it sat John Whiteside. When he looked up, Molly saw that he had at once the kindest and the sternest eyes she had ever seen, and the whitest hair, too. Real blue-white, silky hair, a great duster of it.

"I am Mary Morgan," she began formally.

"Oh, yes, Miss Morgan, I've been expecting you. Won't you sit down?"

She sat in one of the big rockers, and the springs cried with sweet pain. "I love these chairs," she said. "We used to have one when I was a little girl." Then she felt silly. "I've come to interview you about this position. My letter said to do that."

"Don't be so tense, Miss Morgan. I've interviewed every teacher we've had for years. And," he said, smiling, "I still don't know how to go about it."

"Oh—I'm glad, Mr. Whiteside. I never asked for a job before. I was really afraid of it."

"Well, Miss Mary Morgan, as near as I can figure, the purpose of this interview is to give me a little knowledge of your past and of the kind of person you are. I'm supposed to know something about you when you've finished. And now that you know my purpose, I suppose you'll be self-conscious and anxious to give a good impression. Maybe if you just tell me a little about yourself, everything'll be all right. Just a few words about the kind of girl you are, and where you came from."

Molly nodded quickly. "Yes, I'll try to do that, Mr. Whiteside," and she dropped her mind back into the past.

There was the old, squalid, unpainted house with its wide back porch and the round washtubs leaning against the rail. High in the great willow tree her two brothers, Joe and Tom, crashed about crying, "Now I'm an eagle." "I'm a parrot." "Now I'm an old chicken." "Watch me!"

The screen door on the back porch opened, and their mother leaned tiredly out. Her hair would not lie smoothly no matter how much she combed it. Thick strings of it hung down beside her face. Her eyes were always a little red, and her hands and wrists painfully cracked. "Tom, Joe," she called. "You'll get hurt up there. Don't worry me so, boys! Don't you love your mother at all?" The voices in the tree were hushed. The shrieking spirits of the eagle and the old chicken were drenched in self-reproach. Molly sat in the dust, wrapping a rag around a stick and doing her best to imagine it a tall lady in a dress. "Molly, come in and stay with your mother. I'm so tired today."

Molly stood up the stick in the deep dust. "You, miss," she whispered fiercely. "You'll get whipped on your bare bottom when I come back." Then she obediently went into the house.

Her mother sat in a straight chair in the kitchen. "Draw up, Molly. Just sit with me for a little while. Love me, Molly! Love your mother a little bit. You are mother's good little girl, aren't you?" Molly squirmed on her chair. "Don't you love your mother, Molly?"

The little girl was very miserable. She knew her mother would cry in a moment, and then she would be compelled to stroke the stringy hair. Both she and her brothers knew they should love their mother. She did everything for them, everything. They were ashamed that they hated to be near her, but they couldn't help it. When she called to them and they were not in sight, they pretended not to hear, and crept away, talking in whispers.

"Well, to begin with, we were very poor," Molly said to John Whiteside. "I guess we were really poverty-stricken. I had two brothers a little older than I. My father was a traveling salesman, but even so, my mother had to work. She worked terribly hard for us."

About once in every six months a great event occurred. In the morning the mother crept silently out of the bedroom. Her hair was brushed as smoothly as it could be; her eyes sparkled, and she looked happy and almost pretty. She whispered, "Quiet, children! Your father's home."

Molly and her brothers sneaked out of the house, but even in the yard they talked in excited whispers. The news traveled quickly about the neighborhood. Soon the yard was filled with whispering children. "They say their father's home." "Is your father really home?" "Where's he been this time?" By noon there were a dozen children in the yard, standing in expectant little groups, cautioning one another to be quiet.

About noon the screen door on the porch sprang open and whacked against the wall. Their father leaped out. "Hi," he yelled. "Hi, kids!" Molly and her brothers flung themselves upon him and hugged his legs, while he plucked them off and hurled them into the air like kittens.

Mrs. Morgan fluttered about, clucking with excitement. "Children, children. Don't muss your father's clothes."

The neighbor children threw handsprings and wrestled and shrieked with joy. It was better than any holiday.

"Wait till you see," their father cried. "Wait till you see what I brought you. It's a secret now." And when the hysteria had quieted a little he carried his suitcase out on the porch and opened it. There were presents such as no one had ever seen, mechanical

toys unknown before—tin bugs that crawled, dancing wooden niggers and astounding steam shovels that worked in sand. There were superb glass marbles with bears and dogs right in their centers. He had something for everyone, several things for everyone. It was all the great holidays packed into one.

Usually it was midafternoon before the children became calm enough not to shriek occasionally. But eventually George Morgan sat on the steps, and they all gathered about while he told his adventures. This time he had been to Mexico while there was a revolution. Again he had gone to Honolulu, had seen the volcano and had himself ridden on a surfboard. Always there were cities and people, strange people; always adventures and a hundred funny incidents, funnier than anything they had ever heard. It couldn't all be told at one time. After school they had to gather to hear more and more. Throughout the world George Morgan tramped, collecting glorious adventures.

"As far as my home life went," Miss Morgan said, "I guess I almost didn't have any father. He was able to get home very seldom from his business trips."

John Whiteside nodded gravely.

Molly's hands rustled in her lap and her eyes were dim.

One time he brought a dumpy, woolly puppy in a box, and it wet on the floor immediately.

"What kind of a dog is it?" Tom asked in his most sophisticated manner.

Their father laughed loudly. He was so young! He looked twenty years younger than their mother. "It's a dollar and a half dog," he explained. "You get an awful lot of kinds of dog for a dollar and a half. It's like this. . . . Suppose you go into a candy store and say, 'I want a nickel's worth of peppermints and gumdrops and licorice and raspberry chews.' Well, I went in and said, 'Give me a dollar and a half's worth of mixed dog.' That's the kind it is. It's Molly's dog, and she has to name it."

"I'm going to name it George," said Molly.

Her father bowed strangely to her, and said, "Thank you, Molly." They all noticed that he wasn't laughing at her, either.

Molly got up very early the next morning and took George about the yard to show him the secrets. She opened the board where two pennies and a gold policeman's button were buried. She hooked his little front paws over the back fence so he could look down the street at the schoolhouse. Lastly she climbed into the willow tree, carrying George under one arm. Tom came out of the house and sauntered under the tree. "Look out you don't drop him," Tom called, and just at that moment the puppy squirmed out of her arms and fell. He landed on the hard ground with a disgusting little thump. One leg bent out at a crazy angle, and the puppy screamed long, horrible screams, with sobs between breaths. Molly scrambled out of the tree, dull and stunned by the accident. Tom was standing over the puppy, his face white and twisted with pain, and George, the puppy, screamed on and on.

"We can't let him," Tom cried. "We can't let him." He ran to the woodpile and brought back a hatchet. Molly was too stupefied to look away, but Tom closed his eyes and struck. The screams stopped suddenly. Tom threw the hatchet from him and leaped over the back fence. Molly saw him running away as though he were being chased.

At that moment Joe and her father came out of the back door. Molly remembered how haggard and thin and grey her father's face was when he looked at the puppy. It was something in her father's face that started Molly to crying. "I dropped him out of the tree, and he hurt himself, and Tom hit him, and then Tom ran away." Her voice sounded sulky. Her father hugged Molly's head against his hip.

"Poor Tom!" he said. "Molly, you must remember never to say anything to Tom about it, and never to look at him as though you remembered." He threw a gunny sack over the puppy. "We must have a funeral," he said. "Did I ever tell you about the Chinese funeral I went to, about the colored paper they throw in

the air, and the little fat roast pigs on the grave?" Joe edged in closer, and even Molly's eyes took on a gleam of interest. "Well, it was this way. . . ."

Molly looked up at John Whiteside and saw that he seemed to be studying a piece of paper on his desk. "When I was twelve years old, my father was killed in an accident," she said.

The great visits usually lasted about two weeks. Always there came an afternoon when George Morgan walked out into the town and did not come back until late at night. The mother made the children go to bed early, but they could hear him come home, stumbling a little against the furniture, and they could hear his voice through the wall. These were the only times when his voice was sad and discouraged. Lying with held breaths, in their beds, the children knew what that meant. In the morning he would be gone, and their hearts would be gone with him.

They had endless discussions about what he was doing. Their father was a glad argonaut, a silver knight. Virtue and Courage and Beauty—he wore a coat of them. "Sometime," the boys said, "sometime when we're big, we'll go with him and see all those things."

"I'll go, too," Molly insisted.

"Oh, you're a girl. You couldn't go, you know."

"But he'd let me go, you know he would. Sometime he'll take me with him. You see if he doesn't."

When he was gone their mother grew plaintive again, and her eyes reddened. Querulously she demanded their love, as though it were a package they could put in her hand.

One time their father went away, and he never came back. He had never sent any money, nor had he ever written to them, but this time he just disappeared for good. For two years they waited, and then their mother said he must be dead. The children shuddered at the thought, but they refused to believe it, because no one so beautiful and fine as their father could be dead. Some place in the world he was having adventures. There was some good reason why he couldn't come back to them. Some day when the reason was gone, he would come: some morning he would be there with finer presents and better stories than ever before. But their mother said he must have had an accident. He must be dead. Their mother was distracted. She read those advertisements which offered to help her make money at home. The children made paper flowers and shamefacedly tried to sell them. The boys tried to develop magazine routes, and the whole family nearly starved. Finally, when they couldn't stand it any longer, the boys ran away and joined the Navy. After that Molly saw them as seldom as she had seen her father, and they were so changed, so hard and boisterous, that she didn't even care, for her brothers were strangers to her.

"I went through high school, and then I went to San Jose and entered Teachers' College. I worked for my board and room at the home of Mrs. Allen Morit. Before I finished school my mother died, so I guess I'm a kind of an orphan, you see."

"I'm sorry," John Whiteside murmured gently.

Molly flushed. "That wasn't a bid for sympathy, Mr. Whiteside. You said you wanted to know about me. Everyone has to be an orphan some time."

"Yes," he agreed. "I'm an orphan too, I guess."

Molly worked for her board and room. She did the work of a full-time servant, only she received no pay. Money for clothes had to be accumulated by working in a store during summer vacation. Mrs. Morit trained her girls. "I can take a green girl, not worth a cent," she often said, "and when that girl's worked for me six months, she can get fifty dollars a month. Lots of women know it, and they just snap up my girls. This is the first schoolgirl I've tried, but even she shows a lot of improvement. She reads too much though. I always say a servant should be asleep by ten o'clock, or else she can't do her work right."

Mrs. Morit's method was one of constant criticism and nagging, carried on in a just, firm tone. "Now, Molly, I don't want to find fault, but if you don't wipe the silver drier than that, it'll have streaks."—"The butter knife goes this way, Molly. Then you can put the tumbler here."

"I always give a reason for everything," she told her friends.

In the evening, after the dishes were washed, Molly sat on her bed and studied, and when the light was off, she lay on her bed and thought of her father. It was ridiculous to do it, she knew. It was a waste of time. Her father came up to the door, wearing a cutaway coat, and striped trousers and a top hat. He carried a huge bouquet of red roses in his hand. "I couldn't come before, Molly. Get on your coat quickly. First we're going down to get that evening dress in the windows of Prussia's, but we'll have to hurry. I have tickets for the train to New York tonight. Hurry up, Molly! Don't stand there gawping." It was silly. Her father was dead. No, she didn't really believe he was dead. Somewhere in the world he lived beautifully, and sometime he would come back.

Molly told one of her friends at school, "I don't really believe it, you see, but I don't disbelieve it. If I ever knew he was dead, why it would be awful. I don't know what I'd do then. I don't want to think about knowing *he's dead."*

When her mother died, she felt little besides shame. Her mother had wanted so much to be loved, and she hadn't known how to draw love. Her importunities had bothered the children and driven them away.

"Well, that's about all," Molly finished. "I got my di ploma, and then I was sent down here."

"It was about the easiest interview I ever had," John Whiteside said.

"Do you think I'll get the position, then?"

The old man gave a quick, twinkly glance at the big meerschaum hanging over the mantel.

"That's his friend," Molly thought. "He has secrets with that pipe."

"Yes, I think you'll get the job. I think you have it already. Now, Miss Morgan, where are you going to live? You must find board and room some place."

Before she knew she was going to say it, she had blurted, "I want to live here."

John Whiteside opened his eyes in astonishment. "But we never take boarders, Miss Morgan."

"Oh, I'm sorry I said that. I just liked it so much here, you see."

He called, "Willa," and when his wife stood in the half-open door, "This young lady wants to board with us. She's the new teacher."

Mrs. Whiteside frowned. "Couldn't think of it. We never take boarders. She's too pretty to be around that fool of a Bill. What would happen to those cows of his? It'd be a lot of trouble. You can sleep in the third bedroom upstairs," she said to Molly. "It doesn't catch much sun anyway."

Life changed its face. All of a sudden Molly found she was a queen. From the first day the children of the school adored her, for she understood them, and what was more, she let them understand her. It took her some time to realize that she had become an important person. If two men got to arguing at the store about a point of history or literature or mathematics, and the argument deadlocked, it ended up, "Take it to the teacher! If she doesn't know, she'll find it." Molly was very proud to be able to decide such questions. At parties she had to help with the decorations and to plan refreshments.

"I think we'll put pine boughs around everywhere. They're pretty, and they smell so good. They smell like a party." She was supposed to know everything and to help with everything, and she loved it.

At the Whiteside home she slaved in the kitchen under the mutterings of Willa. At the end of six months, Mrs.

Whiteside grumbled to her husband, "Now if Bill only had any sense. But then," she continued, "if *she* has any sense—" and there she left it.

At night Molly wrote letters to the few friends she had made in Teachers' College, letters full of little stories about her neighbors, and full of joy. She must attend every party because of the social prestige of her position. On Saturdays she ran about the hills and brought back ferns and wild flowers to plant about the house.

Bill Whiteside took one look at Molly and scuttled back to his cows. It was a long time before he found the courage to talk to her very much. He was a big, simple young man who had neither his father's balance nor his mother's humor. Eventually, however, he trailed after Molly and looked after her from distances.

One evening, with a kind of feeling of thanksgiving for her happiness, Molly told Bill about her father. They were sitting in canvas chairs on the wide veranda, waiting for the moon. She told him about the visits, and then about the disappearance. "Do you see what I have, Bill?" she cried. "My lovely father is some place. He's mine. You think he's living, don't you, Bill?"

"Might be," said Bill. "From what you say, he was a kind of an irresponsible cuss, though. Excuse me, Molly. Still, if he's alive, it's funny he never wrote."

Molly felt cold. It was just the kind of reasoning she had successfully avoided for so long. "Of course," she said stiffly, "I know that. I have to do some work now, Bill."

High up on a hill that edged the valley of the Pastures of Heaven, there was an old cabin which commanded a view of the whole country and of all the roads in the vicinity. It was said that the bandit Vasquez had built the cabin and lived in it for a year while the posses went crashing through the country looking for him. It was a landmark. All the people of the valley had been to see it at one time or another. Nearly everyone asked Molly whether she had been there yet. "No," she said, "but I will go up some day. I'll go some Saturday. I know where the trail to it is." One morning she dressed in her new hiking boots and corduroy skirt. Bill sidled up and offered to accompany her. "No," she said. "You have work to do. I can't take you away from it."

"Work be hanged!" said Bill.

"Well, I'd rather go alone. I don't want to hurt your feelings, but I just want to go alone, Bill." She was sorry not to let him accompany her, but his remark about her father had frightened her. "I want to have an adventure," she said to herself. "If Bill comes along, it won't be an adventure at all. It'll just be a trip." It took her an hour and a half to climb up the steep trail under the oaks. The leaves on the ground were as slippery as glass, and the sun was hot. The good smell of ferns and dank moss and yerba buena filled the air. When Molly came at last to the ridge crest, she was damp and winded. The cabin stood in a small clearing in the brush, a little square wooden room with no windows. Its doorless entrance was a black shadow. The place was quiet, the kind of humming quiet that flies and bees and crickets make. The whole hillside sang softly in the sun. Molly approached on tiptoe. Her heart was beating violently.

"Now I'm having an adventure," she whispered. "Now I'm right in the middle of an adventure at Vasquez' cabin." She peered in at the doorway and saw a lizard scuttle out of sight. A cobweb fell across her forehead and seemed to try to restrain her. There was nothing at all in the cabin, nothing but the dirt floor and the rotting wooden walls, and the dry, deserted smell of the earth that has long been covered from the sun. Molly was filled with excitement. "At night he sat in there. Sometimes when he heard noises like men creeping up on him, he went out of the door like the ghost of a shadow, and just melted into the darkness." She looked down on the valley of the Pastures of Heaven. The orchards lay in dark green squares; the grain was yellow, and the hills behind, a light brown washed with lavender. Among the farms the roads twisted and curled, avoiding a field, looping around a huge tree, half circling a hill flank. Over the whole valley was stretched a veil of heat shimmer. "Unreal," Molly whispered, "fantastic. It's a story, a real story, and I'm having an adventure." A breeze rose out of the valley like the sigh of a sleeper, and then subsided.

"In the daytime that young Vasquez looked down on the valley just as I'm looking. He stood right here, and looked at the roads down there. He wore a purple vest braided with gold, and the trousers on his slim legs widened at the bottom like the mouths of trumpets. His spur rowels were wrapped with silk ribbons to keep them from clinking. Sometimes he saw the posses riding by on the road below. Lucky for him the men bent over their horses' necks, and didn't look up at the hilltops. Vasquez laughed, but he was afraid, too. Sometimes he sang. His songs were soft and sad because he knew he couldn't live very long."

Molly sat down on the slope and rested her chin in her cupped hands. Young Vasquez was standing beside her, and Vasquez had her father's gay face, his shining eyes as he came on the porch shouting, "Hi, kids!" This was the kind of adventure her father had. Molly shook herself and stood up. "Now I want to go back to the first and think it all over again."

In the late afternoon Mrs. Whiteside sent Bill out to look for Molly. "She might have turned an ankle, you know." But Molly emerged from the trail just as Bill approached it from the road.

"We were beginning to wonder if you'd got lost," he said. "Did you go up to the cabin?"

"Yes."

"Funny old box, isn't it? Just an old woodshed. There are a dozen just like it down here. You'd be surprised, though, how many people go up there to look at it. The funny part is, nobody's sure Vasquez was ever there."

"Oh, I think he must have been there."

"What makes you think that?"

"I don't know."

Bill became serious. "Everybody thinks Vasquez was a kind of a hero, when really he was just a thief. He started in stealing sheep and horses and ended up robbing stages. He had to kill a few people to do it. It seems to me, Molly, we ought to teach people to hate robbers, not worship them."

"Of course, Bill," she said wearily. "You're perfectly right. Would you mind not talking for a little while, Bill? I guess I'm a little tired, and nervous, too."

The year wheeled around. Pussywillows had their kittens, and wild flowers covered the hills. Molly found herself wanted and needed in the valley. She even attended school board meetings. There had been a time when those secret and august conferences were held behind closed doors, a mystery and a terror to everyone. Now that Molly was asked to step into John Whiteside's sitting room, she found that the board discussed crops, told stories, and circulated mild gossip.

Bert Munroe had been elected early in the fall, and by the springtime he was the most energetic member. He it was who planned dances at the schoolhouse, who insisted upon having plays and picnics. He even offered prizes for the best report cards in the school. The board was coming to rely pretty much on Bert Munroe.

One evening Molly came down late from her room. As always, when the board was meeting, Mrs. Whiteside sat in the dining room. "I don't think I'll go in to the meeting," Molly said. "Let them have one time to themselves. Sometimes I feel that they would tell other kinds of stories if I weren't there."

"You go on in, Molly! They can't hold a board meeting without you. They're so used to you, they'd be lost. Besides, I'm not at all sure I want them to tell those other stories."

Obediently Molly knocked on the door and went into the sitting room. Bert Munroe paused politely in the story he was narrating. "I was just telling about my new farm hand, Miss Morgan. I'll start over again, 'cause it's kind of funny. You see, I needed a hay hand, and I picked this fellow up under the Salinas River bridge. He was pretty drunk, but he wanted a job. Now I've got him, I find he isn't worth a cent as a hand, but I can't get rid of him. That son of a gun has been every place. You ought to hear him tell about the places he's been. My kids wouldn't let me get rid of him if I wanted to. Why he can take the littlest thing he's seen and make a fine story out of it. My kids just sit around with their ears spread, listening to him. Well, about twice a month he walks into Salinas and goes on a bust. He's one of those dirty, periodic drunks. The Salinas cops always call me up when they find him in a gutter, and I have to drive in to get him. And you know, when he comes out of it, he's always got some kind of present in his pocket for my kid Manny. There's nothing you can do with a man like that. He disarms you. I don't get a dollar's worth of work a month out of him."

Molly felt a sick dread rising in her. The men were laughing at the story. "You're too soft, Bert. You can't afford to keep an entertainer on the place. I'd sure get rid of him quick."

Molly stood up. She was dreadfully afraid someone would ask the man's name. "I'm not feeling very well tonight," she said. "If you gentlemen will excuse me, I think I'll go to bed." The men stood up while she left the room. In her bed she buried her head in the pillow. "It's crazy," she said to herself. "There isn't a chance in the world. I'm forgetting all about it right now." But she found to her dismay that she was crying.

The next few weeks were agonizing to Molly. She was reluctant to leave the house. Walking to and from school she watched the road ahead of her. "If I see any kind of a stranger I'll run away. But that's foolish. I'm being a fool." Only in her own room did she feel safe. Her terror was making her lose color, was taking the glint out of her eyes.

"Molly, you ought to go to bed," Mrs. Whiteside insisted. "Don't be a little idiot. Do I have to smack you the way I do Bill to make you go to bed?" But Molly would not go to bed. She thought too many things when she was in bed.

The next time the board met, Bert Munroe did not appear. Molly felt reassured and almost happy at his absence.

"You're feeling better, aren't you, Miss Morgan."

"Oh, yes. It was only a little thing, a kind of a cold. If I'd gone to bed I might have been really sick."

The meeting was an hour gone before Bert Munroe came in. "Sorry to be late," he apologized. "The same old thing happened. My so-called hay hand was asleep in the street in Salinas. What a mess! He's out in the car sleeping it off now. I'll have to hose the car out tomorrow."

Molly's throat closed with terror. For a second she thought she was going to faint. "Excuse me, I must go," she cried, and ran out of the room. She walked into the dark hallway and steadied herself against the wall. Then slowly and automatically she marched out of the front door and down the steps. The night was filled with whispers. Out in the road she could see the black mass that was Bert Munroe's car. She was surprised at the way her footsteps plodded down the path of their own volition. "Now I'm killing myself," she said. "Now I'm throwing everything away. I wonder why." The gate was under her hand, and her hand flexed to open it. Then a tiny breeze sprang up and brought to her nose the sharp foulness of vomit. She heard a blubbering, drunken snore. Instantly something whirled in her head. Molly spun around and ran frantically back to the house. In her room she locked the door and sat stiffly down, panting with the effort of her run. It seemed hours before she heard the men go out of the house, calling their good-nights. Then Bert's motor started, and the sound of it died away down the road. Now that she was ready to go she felt paralyzed.

John Whiteside was writing at his desk when Molly entered the sitting room. He looked up questioningly at her. "You aren't well, Miss Morgan. You need a doctor."

She planted herself woodenly beside the desk. "Could you get a substitute teacher for me?" she asked.

"Of course I could. You pile right into bed and I'll call a doctor."

"It isn't that, Mr. Whiteside. I want to go away tonight."

"What are you talking about? You aren't well."

"I told you my father was dead. I don't know whether he's dead or not. I'm afraid—I want to go away tonight."

He stared intently at her. "Tell me what you mean," he said softly.

"If I should see that drunken man of Mr. Munroe's—" she paused, suddenly terrified at what she was about to say.

John Whiteside nodded very slowly.

"No," she cried. "I don't think that. I'm sure I don't."

"I'd like to do something, Molly."

"I don't want to go, I love it here—But I'm afraid. It's so important to me."

John Whiteside stood up and came close to her and put his arm about her shoulders. "I don't think I understand, quite," he said. "I don't think I want to understand. That isn't necessary." He seemed to be talking to himself. "It wouldn't be quite courteous—to understand."

"Once I'm away I'll be able not to believe it," Molly whimpered.

He gave her shoulders one quick squeeze with his encircling arm. "You run upstairs and pack your things, Molly," he said. "I'll get out the car and drive you right in to Salinas now."

IX

Of all the farms in the Pastures of Heaven the one most admired was that of Raymond Banks. Raymond kept five thousand white chickens and one thousand white ducks. The farm lay on the northern flat, the prettiest place in the whole country. Raymond had laid out his land in squares of alfalfa and of kale. His long, low chicken houses were whitewashed so often that they looked always immaculate and new. There was never any of the filth so often associated with poultry farms, about Raymond's place.

For the ducks there was a large round pond into which fresh water constantly flowed from a two inch pipe. The overflow from the pond ran down rows of thick sturdy kale or spread itself out in the alfalfa patches. It was a fine thing on a sunny morning to see the great flock of clean, white chickens eating and scratching in the dark green alfalfa, and it was even finer to see the thousand white ducks sailing magnificently about on the pond. Ducks swam ponderously, as though they were as huge as the Leviathan. The ranch sang all day with the busy noise of chickens.

From the top of a nearby hill you could look down on the squares of alfalfa on which the thousands of moving white specks eddied and twisted like bits of dust on a green pool. Then perhaps a red-tail hawk would soar over, carefully watching Raymond's house. The white specks instantly stopped their meaningless movements and scuttled to the protecting roosters, and up from the fields came the despairing shrieks of thousands of hawk-frightened chickens. The back door of the farmhouse slammed, and Raymond sauntered out carrying a shotgun. The hawk swung up a hundred feet in the air and soared away. The little white bunches spread out again and the eddying continued.

The patches of green were fenced from each other so that one square could rest and recuperate while the chickens were working in another. From the hill you could see Raymond's whitewashed house set on the edge of a grove of oak trees. There were many flowers around the house: calendulas and big African marigolds and cosmos as high as trees; and, behind the house, there was the only rose garden worthy the name in the valley of the Pastures of Heaven. The local people looked upon this place as the model farm of the valley.

Raymond Banks was a strong man. His thick, short arms, wide shoulders and hips and heavy legs, even the stomach which bulged his overalls, made him seem magnificently strong, strong for pushing and pulling and lifting. Every exposed part of him was burned beef-red by the sun, his heavy arms to the elbows, his neck down into his collar, his face, and particularly his ears and nose were painfully burned and chapped. Thin blond hair could not protect his scalp from reddening under the sun. Raymond's eyes were remarkable, for, while his hair and eyebrows were pale yellow, the yellow that usually goes with light blue eyes, Raymond's eyes were black as soot. His mouth was full-lipped and jovial and completely at odds with his long and villainously beaked nose. Raymond's nose and ears were terribly punished by the sun. There was hardly a time during the year when they were not raw and peeled.

Raymond Banks was forty-five and very jolly. He never spoke softly, but always in a heavy half-shout full of mock fierceness. He said things, even the commonest of things, as though they were funny. People laughed whenever he spoke. At Christmas parties in the schoolhouse, Raymond was invariably chosen as the Santa Claus because of his hearty voice, his red face and his love for children. He abused children with such a heavy ferocity that he kept them laughing all the time. In or out of his red Santa Claus suit, the children of the valley regarded Raymond as a kind of Santa Claus. He had a way of flinging them about, of wrestling and mauling them, that was caressing and delightful. Now and then, he turned serious and told them things which had the import of huge lessons.

Sometimes on Saturday mornings a group of little boys walked to the Banks farm to watch Raymond working. He let them peep into the little glass windows of the incubators. Sometimes the chicks were just coming out of the shells, shaking their wet wings and wabbling about on clumsy legs. The boys were allowed to raise the covers of the brooders and to pick up whole armfuls of yellow, furry chicks which made a noise like a hundred little ungreased machines. Then they walked to the pond and threw pieces of bread to the grandly navigating ducks. Most of all, though, the boys liked the killing time. And strangely enough, this was the time when Raymond dropped his large bantering and became very serious.

Raymond picked a little rooster out of the trap and hung it by its legs on a wooden frame. He fastened the wildly beating wings with a wire clamp. The rooster squawked loudly. Raymond had the killing knife with its spear-shaped blade on the box beside him. How the boys admired that knife, the vicious shape of it and its shininess; the point was as sharp as a needle.

"Now then, old rooster, you're done for," said Raymond. The boys crowded closer. With sure, quick hands, Raymond grasped the chicken's head and forced the beak open. The knife slipped like a flash of light along the roof of the beak and into the brain and out again. The wings shuddered and beat against their clamp. For a moment the neck stretched yearningly from side to side, and a little rill of blood flowed from the tip of the beak.

"Now watch!" Raymond cried. His forked hand combed the breast and brought all the feathers with it. Another combing motion and the back was bare. The wings were not struggling so hard now. Raymond whipped the feathers off, all but the wing-tip feathers. Then the legs were stripped, a single movement for each one. "You see? You've got to do it quick," he explained as he worked. "There's just about two minutes that the feathers are loose. If you leave them in, they get set." He took the chicken down from the frame, snicked another knife twice, pulled, and there were the entrails in a pan. He wiped his red hands on a cloth.

"Look!" the boys shrieked. "Look! What's that?"

"That's the heart."

"But look! It's still moving. It's still alive."

"Oh, no, it isn't," Raymond assured them. "That rooster was dead just the second the knife touched his brain. That heart just beats on for a while, but the rooster is dead all right."

"Why don't you chop them like my father does, Mr. Banks?"

"Well, because this is cleaner and quicker, and the butchers want them with their heads on. They sell the heads in with the weight, you see. Now, come on, old rooster!" He reached into the trap for another struggling squawker. When the killing was over, Raymond took all the chicken crops out of the pan and distributed them among the boys. He taught them how to clean and blow up the crops to make chicken balloons. Raymond was always very serious when he was explaining his ranch. He refused to let the boys help with the killing, although they asked him many times.

"You might get excited and miss the brain," he said.

"That would hurt the chicken, if you didn't stick him just right."

Mrs. Banks laughed a great deal—clear, sweet laughter which indicated mild amusement or even inattention. She had a way of laughing appreciatively at everything anyone said, and, to merit this applause, people tried to say funny things when she was about. After her work in the house was finished, she dug in the flower garden. She had been a town girl; that was why she liked flowers, the neighbors said. Guests, driving up to the house, were welcomed by the high, clear laughter of Cleo Banks, and they chuckled when they heard it. She was so jolly. She made people feel good. No one could ever remember that she said anything, but months after hearing it, they could recall the exact tones of her laughter.

Raymond Banks rarely laughed at all. Instead he pretended a sullenness so overdrawn that it was accepted as humor. These two people were the most popular hosts in the valley. Now and then they invited everyone in the Pastures of Heaven to a barbecue in the oak grove beside their house. They broiled little chickens over coals of oak bark and set out hundreds of bottles of home brewed beer. These parties were looked forward to and remembered with great pleasure by the people of the valley.

When Raymond Banks was in high school, his chum had been a boy who later became the warden at San Quentin prison. The friendship had continued, too. At Christmas time they still exchanged little presents. They wrote to each other when any important thing happened. Raymond was proud of his acquaintance with the warden. Two or three times a year he received an invitation to be a witness at an execution, and he always accepted it. His trips to the prison were the only vacations he took.

Raymond liked to arrive at the warden's house the night

before the execution. He and his friend sat together and talked over their school days. They reminded each other of things both remembered perfectly. Always the same episodes were recalled and talked about. Then, the next morning, Raymond liked the excitement, the submerged hysteria of the other witnesses in the warden's office. The slow march of the condemned aroused his dramatic sense and moved him to a thrilling emotion. The hanging itself was not the important part, it was the sharp, keen air of the whole proceeding that impressed him. It was like a super-church, solemn and ceremonious and somber. The whole thing made him feel a fullness of experience, a holy emotion that nothing else in his life approached. Raymond didn't think of the condemned any more than he thought of the chicken when he pressed the blade into its brain. No strain of cruelty nor any gloating over suffering took him to the gallows. He had developed an appetite for profound emotion, and his meager imagination was unable to feed it. In the prison he could share the throbbing nerves of the other men. Had he been alone in the death chamber with no one present except the prisoner and the executioner, he would have been unaffected.

After the death was pronounced, Raymond liked the second gathering in the warden's office. The nerve-wracked men tried to use hilarity to restore their outraged imaginations. They were more jolly, more noisily happy than they ordinarily were. They sneered at the occasional witness, usually a young reporter, who fainted or came out of the chamber crying. Raymond enjoyed the whole thing. It made him feel alive; he seemed to be living more acutely than at other times.

After it was all over, he had a good dinner with the warden before he started home again. To some little extent the same emotion occurred to Raymond when the little boys came to watch him kill chickens. He was able to catch a slight spark of their excitement.

The Munroe family had not been long in the Pastures of Heaven before they heard about the fine ranch of Raymond Banks and about his visits to the prison. The people of the valley were interested, fascinated and not a little horrified by the excursions to see men hanged. Before he ever saw Raymond, Bert Munroe pictured him as a traditional executioner, a lank, dark man, with a dull, deathly eye; a cold, nerveless man. The very thought of Raymond filled Bert with a kind of interested foreboding.

When he finally met Raymond Banks and saw the jolly black eyes and the healthy, burned face, Bert was disillusioned, and at the same time a little disgusted. The very health and heartiness of Raymond seemed incongruous and strangely obscene. The paradox of his good nature and his love for children was unseemly.

On the first of May, the Bankses gave one of their parties under the oak trees on the flat. It was the loveliest season of the year; lupins and shooting stars, gallitos and wild violets smoldered with color in the new, short grass on the hillsides. The oaks had put on new leaves as shiny and clean as washed holly. The sun was warm enough to drench the air with sage, and all the birds made frantic, noisy holiday. From the chicken yards came the contented gabbling of scratching hens and the cynical, self-satisfied quacking of the ducks.

At least fifty people were standing about the long tables under the trees. Hundreds of bottles of beer were packed in washtubs of salt and ice, a mixture so cold that the beer froze in the necks of the bottles. Mrs. Banks went about among the guests, laughing in greeting and in response to greeting. She rarely said a word. At the barbecue pits, Raymond was grilling little chickens while a group of admiring men stood about, offering jocular advice.

"If any of you can do it better, just step up," Raymond shouted at them. "I'm going to put on the steaks now for anyone that's crazy enough not to want chicken."

Bert Munroe stood nearby watching the red hands of Raymond. He was drinking a bottle of the strong beer. Bert was fascinated by the powerful red hands constantly turning over the chickens on the grill.

When the big platters of broiled chicken were carried to the tables, Raymond went back to the pits to cook some more for those fine men who might require a second or even a third little chicken. Raymond was alone now, for his audience had all flocked to the tables. Bert Munroe looked up from his plate of beef steak and saw that Raymond was alone by the pits. He put down his fork and strolled over.

"What's the matter, Mr. Munroe? Wasn't your chicken good?" Raymond asked with genial anxiety.

"I had steak, and it was fine. I eat pretty fast, I guess. I never eat chicken, you know."

"That so? I never could understand how anyone wouldn't like chicken, but I know plenty of people don't. Let me put on another little piece of meat for you."

"Oh! I guess I've had enough. I always think people eat too much. You ought to get up from the table feeling a little bit hungry. Then you keep well, like the animals."

"I guess that's right," said Raymond. He turned the little carcasses over the fire. "I notice I feel better when I don't eat so much."

"Sure you do. So do I. So would everybody. Everybody eats too much." The two men smiled warmly at each other because they had agreed on this point, although neither of them believed it very strongly.

"You sure got a nice piece of land in here," Raymond observed, to double their growing friendship with a second agreement.

"Well, I don't know. They say there's loco weed on it, but I haven't seen any yet."

Raymond laughed. "They used to say the place was haunted before you came and fixed it up so nice. Haven't seen any ghosts, have you?"

"Not a ghost. I'm more scared of loco weed than I am of ghosts. I sure do hate loco weed."

"Don't know as I blame you. Course with chickens it doesn't bother me much, but it raises hell with you people that run stock."

Bert picked up a stick from the ground and knocked it gently on the winking coals. "I hear you're acquainted with the warden up to San Quentin."

"Know him well. I went to school with Ed when I was a kid. You acquainted with him, Mr. Munroe?"

"Oh, no—no. He's in the papers quite a bit. A man in his position gets in the papers quite a bit."

Raymond's voice was serious and proud. "Yeah. He gets a lot of publicity all right. But he's a nice fella, Mr. Munroe, as nice a fella as you'd want to meet. And in spite of having all those convicts on his hands, he's just as jolly and friendly. You wouldn't think, to talk to him, that he had a big responsibility like that."

"Is that so? You wouldn't think that. I mean, you'd think he'd be kind of worried with all those convicts on his hands. Do you see him often?"

"Well—yes. I do. I told you I went to school with him. I was kind of chums with him. Well, he hasn't forgot me. Every once in a while he asks me up to the prison when there's a hanging."

Bert shuddered in spite of the fact that he had been digging for this. "Is that so?"

"Yes. I think it's quite an honor. Not many people get in except newspaper men and official witnesses, sheriffs and police. I have a good visit with Ed every time too, of course."

A strange thing happened to Bert. He seemed to be standing apart from his body. His voice acted without his volition. He heard himself say, "I don't suppose the warden would like it if you brought a friend along." He listened to his words with astonishment. He had not wanted to say that at all.

Raymond was stirring the coals vigorously. He was embarrassed. "Why, I don't know, Mr. Munroe. I never thought about it. Did you want to go up with me?"

Again Bert's voice acted alone. "Yes," it said.

"Well, I'll tell you what I'll do then. I'll write to Ed (I write to him pretty often, you see, so he won't think anything of it). I'll just kind of slip it in the letter about you wanting to go up. Then maybe he'll send two invitations next time. Of course I can't promise, though. Won't you have another little piece of steak?"

Bert was nauseated. "No. I've had enough," he said. "I'm not feeling so good. I guess I'll go lie down under a tree for a little while."

"Maybe you shook up some of the yeast in that beer, Mr. Munroe. You've got to be pretty careful when you pour it."

Bert sat on the crackling dry leaves at the foot of an oak tree. The tables, lined with noisy guests, were on his right. The hoarse laughing of the men and the shrill cries of communicating women came to him faintly through a wall of thought. Between the tree trunks he could see Raymond Banks still moving about the meat pits, grilling chickens for those few incredible appetites that remained unappeased. The nausea which had forced him away was subtly changing. The choked feeling of illness was becoming a strange panting congestion of desire. The desire puzzled Bert and worried him. He didn't want to go to San Quentin. It would make him unhappy to see a man hanged. But he was glad he had asked to go. His very gladness worried him. As Bert watched, Raymond rolled his sleeves higher up on his thick red arms before he cleaned the grates. Bert jumped up and started toward the pits. Suddenly the nausea arose in him again. He swerved around and hurried to the table where his wife sat shrilling pleasantries around the gnawed carcass of a chicken.

"My husband never eats chicken," she was crying.

"I'm going to walk home," Bert said. "I feel rotten."

His wife laid down the carcass of the chicken and wiped her fingers and mouth on a paper napkin. "What's the matter with you, Bert?"

"I don't know. I just feel kind of rotten."

"Do you want me to go home with you in the car?"

"No, you stay. Jimmie'll drive you home."

"Well," said Mrs. Munroe, "you better say good-bye to Mr. and Mrs. Banks."

Bert turned doggedly away. "You tell them good-bye for me," he said. "I'm feeling too rotten." And he strode quickly away.

A week later Bert Munroe drove to the Banks farm and stopped his Ford in front of the gate. Raymond came from behind a bush where he had been trying a shot at a hawk. He sauntered out and shook hands with his caller.

"I've heard so much about your place, I thought I'd just come down for a look," Bert said.

Raymond was delighted. "Just let me put this gun away, and I'll show you around." For an hour they walked over the farm, Raymond explaining and Bert admiring the cleanliness and efficiency of the chicken ranch. "Come on in and have a glass of beer," Raymond said, when they had covered the place. "There's nothing like cold beer on a day like this."

When they were seated Bert began uneasily, "Did you write that letter to the warden, Mr. Banks?"

"Yes—I did. Ought to have an answer pretty soon now."

"I guess you wonder why I asked you. Well, I think a man ought to see everything he can. That's experience. The more experience a man has, the better. A man ought to see everything."

"I guess that's right, all right," Raymond agreed.

Bert drained his glass and wiped his mouth. "Of course I've read in the papers about hangings, but it isn't like seeing one really. They say there're thirteen steps up to the gallows for bad luck. That right?"

Raymond's face wore an expression of concentration. "Why, I don't know, Mr. Munroe. I never counted them."

"How do they—fight and struggle much after they're dropped?"

"I guess so. You see they're strapped and a black cloth is over their heads. You can't see much of anything. It's more like fluttering, I'd say, than struggling."

Bert's face was red and intent. His eyes glistened with interest. "The papers say it takes fifteen minutes to half an hour for them to die. Is that right?"

"I—I suppose it is. Of course they're really what you might call dead the minute they drop. It's like you cut a chicken's head off, and the chicken flutters around, but it's really dead."

"Yes—I guess that's right. Just reflex, they call it. I suppose it's pretty hard on some people seeing it for the first time."

Raymond smiled in faint amusement. "Sure. Nearly always somebody faints. Then the kid reporters from the papers cry sometimes, cry like babies, and some people are sick, you know, really sick—lose their dinner right there. Mostly first timers are that way. Let's have another bottle of beer, Mr. Munroe. It's good and cold, isn't it?"

"Yes, it's fine beer all right," Bert agreed absently. "I'll have to get your recipe. A man ought to have a little beer ready for the hot weather. I've got to go now, Mr. Banks. Thank you for showing me around the place. You could give some pointers to these Petaluma people about chickens, I guess."

Raymond flushed with pleasure. "I try to keep up with new things. I'll let you know when I hear from Ed, Mr. Munroe."

During the next two weeks Bert Munroe was nervous and extremely irritable. This was so unusual that his wife protested. "You're not well, Bert. Why don't you drive in and let a doctor look you over."

"Oh! I'm all right," he insisted. He spent most of his time at work on the farm, but his eyes roved to the county road every time an automobile drove by. It was on a Saturday that Raymond Banks drove up in his light truck and parked before the Munroe gate. Bert dropped a shovel and went out to meet him. When one farmer meets another they seldom go into a house. Instead, they walk slowly over the land, pulling bits of grass from the fields, or leaves from the trees and testing them with their fingers while they talk. Summer was beginning. The leaves on the fruit trees had not yet lost their tender, light greens, but the blossoms were all gone and the fruit set. Already the cherries were showing a little color. Bert and Raymond walked slowly over the cultivated ground under the orchard trees.

"Birds are thick this year," said Bert. "They'll get most of the cherries, I guess." He knew perfectly well why Raymond had come.

"Well, I heard from Ed, Mr. Munroe. He says it will be all right for you to go up with me. He says they don't let many come, because they try to keep the morbidly curious people away. But he says any friend of mine is all right. We'll go up next Thursday. There's an execution Friday." (Bert walked along in silence, his eyes on the ground). "Ed's a nice fellow. You'll like him," Raymond went on. "We'll stay with him Thursday night."

Bert picked up an overlooked pruning from the ground and bent it to a tense bow in his hands. "I've been thinking about it," he said. "Would it make any difference to you if I pulled out the last minute?"

Raymond stared at him. "Why, I thought you wanted to go. What's the matter?"

"You'll think I'm pretty soft, I guess, if I tell you. The fact is—I've been thinking about it and—I'm scared to go. I'm scared I couldn't get it out of my head afterwards."

"It's not as bad as it sounds," Raymond protested.

"Maybe it isn't. I don't know about that. But I'm scared it would be bad for me. Everybody don't see a thing the same way."

"No, that's true."

"I'll try to give you an idea how I feel, Mr. Banks. You know I don't eat chicken. I never tell anybody why I don't eat it. Just say I don't like it. I've put you to a lot of trouble. I'll tell you—to kind of explain." The stick snapped in his hands, and he threw the two ends away and thrust his hands in his pockets.

"When I was a kid, about twelve years old, I used to deliver a few groceries before school. Well, out by the brewery an old crippled man lived. He had one leg cut off at the thigh, and, instead of a wooden leg, he had one of those old-fashioned crutches—kind of a crescent on top of a round stick. You remember them. He got around on it pretty well, but kind of slow. One morning, when I went by with my basket of groceries, this old man was out in his yard killing a rooster. It was the biggest Rhode Island Red I ever saw. Or maybe it was because I was so little that the chicken looked so big. The old man had the crutch braced under his armpit, and he was holding the rooster by the legs." Bert stopped and picked another pruning from the ground. This one, too, bent under his hands. His face was growing pale as he talked.

"Well," he continued, "this old man had a hatchet in his other hand. Just as he made a cut at the rooster's neck, his crutch slipped a little bit, the chicken twisted in his hand, and he cut off one of the wings. Well, then that old man just about went crazy. He cut and he cut, always in the wrong place, into the breast and into the stomach. Then the crutch slipped some more and threw him clear off balance just as the hatchet was coming down. He cut off one of the chicken's legs and sliced right through his own finger." Bert wiped his forehead with his sleeve. Raymond was heaping a little mountain of dirt with the side of his shoe.

"Well, when that happened, the old man just dropped the rooster on the ground and hobbled into the house holding on to his finger. And that rooster went crawling off with all its guts hanging out on the ground—went crawling off and kind of croaking." The stick snapped again, and this time he threw the pieces violently from him. "Well, Mr. Banks, I've never killed a chicken since then, and I've never eaten one. I've tried to eat them, but every time, I see that damned Rhode Island Red crawling away." For the first time he looked directly at Raymond Banks. "Do you see how that would happen?"

Raymond dodged his eyes and looked away. "Yes. Yes, sir, that must have been pretty awful."

Bert crowded on. "Well, I got to thinking about this hanging. It might be like the chicken. I dreamed about that chicken over and over again, when I was a kid. Every time my stomach would get upset and give me a nightmare, I'd dream about that chicken. Now suppose I went to this hanging with you. I might dream about it, too. Not long ago they hung a woman in Arizona, and the rope pulled her head right off. Suppose that happened. It would be a hundred times worse than the chicken. Why I'd never get over a thing like that."

"But that practically never happens," Raymond protested. "I tell you it's not nearly as bad as it sounds."

Bert seemed not to hear him. His face was working with horror at his thoughts. "Then you say some people get sick and some of them faint. I know why that is. It's because those people are imagining they're up on the gallows with the rope around their necks. They really feel like the man it's happening to. I've done that myself. I imagined I was going to be hung in twenty-four hours. It's like the most god-awful nightmare in the world. And I've been thinking —what's the use of going up there and horrifying myself? I'd be sick. I know I would. I'd just go through everything the poor devil on the gallows did. Just thinking about it last night, I felt the rope around my neck. Then I went to sleep, and the sheet got over my face, and I dreamed it was that damned black cap."

"I tell you, you don't think things like that," Raymond cried angrily. "If you think things like that you haven't got any right to go up with me. I tell you it isn't as terrible as that, when you see it. It's nothing. You said you wanted to go up, and I got permission for you. What do you want to go talking like this for? There's no need to talk like you just did. If you don't want to go, why the hell don't you just say so and then shut up?"

The look of horror went out of Bert's eyes. Almost eagerly he seized upon anger. "No need to get mad, Mr. Banks. I was just telling you why I didn't want to go. If you had any imagination, I wouldn't have to tell you. If you had any imagination, you'd see for yourself, and you wouldn't go up to see some poor devil get killed."

Raymond turned away contemptuously. "You're just yellow," he said and strode away to his truck. He drove furiously over the road to his ranch, but when he had arrived and covered the truck, he walked slowly toward his house. His wife was cutting roses.

"What's the matter with you, Ray? You look sick," she cried.

Raymond scowled. "I've got a headache, that's all. It'll go away. You know Bert Munroe that wanted to go up with me next week?"

"Yes."

"Well, now he don't want to go."

"What's the matter with him?"

"He's lost his nerve, that's what. He's scared to see it."

His wife laughed uneasily. "Well, I don't know as I'd *like* to see it myself."

"You're a woman, but he's supposed to be a man."

The next morning Raymond sat down listlessly to breakfast and ate very little. His wife looked worried. "You've still got that headache, Ray. Why don't you do something for it?"

Raymond ignored her question. "I've got to write to Ed, and I don't know what to say to him."

"What do you mean, you don't know."

"Well, I'm afraid I'm getting a cold. I don't know whether I'll be in shape to go up there Thursday. It's a long trip, and cold crossing the bay."

Mrs. Banks sat in thought. "Why don't you ask him to come down here sometime. He's never been here; you've been there lots of times."

Raymond brightened up. "By George! That's an idea.

I've been going up to see him for years. I'll just drop him a note to come and see us."

"We could give him a barbecue," Mrs. Banks suggested.

Raymond's face clouded over. "Oh, I don't think so. A close friend like Ed would rather not have a crowd. But beer—say, you should see how Ed loves his beer. I'll drop him a note now." He got out a pen and a little pad of writing paper and an ink bottle. As his pen hesitated over the paper, his face dropped back into a scowl. "Damn that Munroe anyway! I went to a lot of trouble for him. How'd I know he was going to turn yellow on me."

X

Pat Humbert's parents were middle-aged when he was born; they had grown old and stiff and spiteful before he was twenty. All of Pat's life had been spent in an atmosphere of age, of the aches and illness, of the complaints and self-sufficiency of age. While he was growing up, his parents held his opinions in contempt because he was young. "When you've lived as long as we have, you'll see things different," they told him. Later, they found his youth hateful because it was painless. Their age, so they implied, was a superior state, a state approaching god-head in dignity and infallibility. Even rheumatism was desirable as a price for the great wisdom of age. Pat was led to believe that no young thing had any virtue. Youth was a clumsy, fumbling preparation for excellent old age. Youth should think of nothing but the duty it owed to age, of the courtesy and veneration due to age. On the other hand, age owed no courtesy whatever to youth.

When Pat was sixteen, the whole work of the farm fell upon him. His father retired to a rocking chair beside the air-tight stove in the sitting room, from which he issued orders, edicts and criticisms.

The Humberts dwelt in an old, rambling farmhouse of five rooms: a locked parlor, cold and awful as doom, a hot, stuffy sitting room smelling always of pungent salves and patent medicines, two bedrooms and a large kitchen. The old people sat in cushioned rocking chairs and complained bitterly if Pat did not come in from the farm work to replenish the fire in the stove several times a day. Toward the end of their lives, they really hated Pat for being young.

They lived a long time. Pat was thirty when they died

within a month of each other. They were unhappy and bitter and discontented with their lives, and yet each one clung tenaciously to the poor spark and only died after a long struggle.

There were two months of horror for Pat. For three weeks he nursed his mother while she lay rigid on the bed, her breath clattering in and out of her lungs. She watched him with stony, accusing eyes as he tried to make her comfortable. When she was dead, her eyes still accused him.

Pat unlocked the terrible parlor; the neighbors sat in rows before the coffin, a kind of audience, while the service went on. From the bedroom came the sound of old Mr. Humbert's peevish weeping.

The second period of nursing began immediately after the first funeral, and continued for three weeks more. Then the neighbors sat in rows before another coffin. Before the funerals, the parlor had always been locked except during the monthly cleaning. The blinds were drawn down to protect the green carpets from the sun. In the center of the room stood a gilt-legged marble topped table which bore, on a tapestry of Millet's "Angelus," a huge Bible with a deeply tooled cover. On either side of the Bible sat squat vases holding tight bouquets of everlasting flowers. There were four straight chairs in the parlor, one against each of the four walls—two for the coffin and two for the watchers. Three large pictures in gilt frames hung on the walls: colored, enlarged photographs of each of the old Humberts looking stern and dead, but so taken that their eyes followed an intruder about the room. The third picture showed the corpse of Elaine in its boat on the thin sad river. The shroud hung over the gunwale and dipped into the water. On a corner table stood a tall glass bell in which three stuffed orioles sat on a cherry branch. So cold and sepulchral was this parlor that it had never been entered except by corpses and their attendants. It was indeed a little private mortuary chamber. Pat had seen three aunts and an uncle buried from that parlor.

Pat stood quietly by the graveside while his neighbors shaped up a tent of earth. Already his mother's grave had sunk a little, leaving a jagged crack all around its mound. The men were patting the new mound now, drawing a straight ridgepole and smoothing the slope of the sides. They were good workmen with the soil; they liked to make a good job with it whether it be furrow or grave mound. After it was perfect, they still walked about patting it lightly here and there. The women had gone back to the buggies and were waiting for their husbands to come. Each man walked up to Pat and shook his hand and murmured some solemn friendly thing to him. The wagons and surreys and buggies were all moving away now, disappearing one by one in the distance. Still Pat stood in the cemetery staring at the two graves. He didn't know what to do now there was no one to demand anything of him.

Fall was in the air, the sharp smell of it and the little jerky winds of it breathing up and then dying in mid-blow. Wild doves sat in a line on the cemetery fence all facing one way, all motionless. A piece of old brown newspaper scudded along the ground and clung about Pat's ankles. He stooped and picked it off, looked at it for a moment and then threw it away. The sound of grating buggy wheels came from the road. T. B. Allen tied his horse to the fence and walked up to Pat. "We thought you'd be going someplace tonight," he said in an embarrassed voice. "If you feel like it, we'd like you to come to supper at our house—and stay the night, too."

Pat started out of the coma that had fallen on him. "I should be going away from here," he said. He fumbled for another thought. "I'm not doing any good here."

"It's better to get away from it," Allen said.

"It's hard to leave, Mr. Allen. It's a thing you'll sometimes want to remember, and other times you'll want to forget it, I guess. But it's hard to leave because then you know it's all over—forever."

"Well, why don't you come to supper over at our house?"

All of Pat's guards were down; he confessed, "I never had supper away from home in my life. They"—he nodded toward the graves—"They didn't like to be out after dark. Night air wasn't good for them."

"Then maybe it would be good for you to eat at our house. You shouldn't go back to the empty place, at least not tonight. A man ought to save himself a little." He took Pat's arm and swung him toward the gate. "You follow me in your wagon." And as they went out of the gate a little elegy escaped from him. "It's a fit thing to die in the fall," he said. "It wouldn't be good to die in the spring and never to know about the rainfall nor how the crops shaped. But in the fall everything's over."

"They wouldn't care, Mr. Allen. They didn't ever ask about the crops, and they hated the rain because of their rheumatism. They just wanted to live. I don't know why."

For supper there were cold cuts of beef, and potatoes fried raw with a few onions, and bread pudding with raisins. Mrs. Allen tried to help Pat in his trouble by speaking often of his parents, of how good and kind they were, of his father's honesty and his mother's famous cookery. Pat knew she was lying about them to help him, and he didn't need it. He was in no agony of grief. The thick lethargy still hung over him so that it was a great effort to move or to speak.

He was remembering something that had happened at the funeral. When the pall-bearers lifted the casket from its two chairs, one of the men tripped against the marble-topped table. The accident tipped over one of the vases of everlastings and pushed the Bible askew on its tapestry. Pat knew that in decency he should restore the old order. The chairs should be pushed against their walls and the Bible set straight. Finally he should lock up the parlor again. The memory of his mother demanded these things of him.

The Allens urged him to stay the night, but after a while, he bade them a listless good night and dragged himself out to harness his horse. The sky was black and cold between the sharp stars, and the hills hummed faintly under a lowering temperature. Through his lethargy, Pat heard the clopping of the horse's hooves on the road, the crying of night birds and the whisk of wind through the drying leaves. But more real to him were his parents' voices sounding in his head. "There'll be frost," his father said. "I hate the frost worse than rats." And his mother chimed in, "Speaking of rats—I have a feeling there's rats in the cellar. I wonder if Pat has set the traps this year past. I told him to, but he forgets everything I tell him."

Pat answered the voices. "I put poison in the cellar. Traps aren't as good as poison."

"A cat is best," his mother's whining voice said. "I don't know why we never have a cat or two. Pat never has a cat."

"I get cats, mother, but they eat gophers and go wild and run away. I can't keep cats."

The house was black and unutterably dreary when he arrived. Pat lighted the reflector lamp and built a fire in the stove to warm the kitchen. As the flame roared through the wood, he sank into a chair and found that he was very comfortable. It would be nice, he thought, to bring his bed into the kitchen and to sleep beside the stove. The straightening of the house could be done tomorrow, or any day for that matter.

When he threw open the door into the sitting room, a

wave of cold, lifeless air met him. His nostrils were assailed by the smell of funeral flowers and age and medicine. He walked quickly to his bedroom and carried his cot into the warm and lighted kitchen.

After a while Pat blew out the light and went to bed. The fire cricked softly in the stove. For a time the night was still, and then gradually the house began to swarm with malignant life. Pat discovered that his body was tense and cold. He was listening for sounds from the sitting room, for the creak of the rocking chairs and for the loud breathing of the old people. The house cracked, and although he had been listening for sounds, Pat started violently. His head and legs became damp with perspiration. Silently and miserably he crept from his bed and locked the door into the sitting room. Then he went back to his cot and lay shivering under the covers. The night had become very still, and he was lonely.

The next morning Pat awakened with a cold sense of duty to be performed. He tried to remember what it was. Of course, it was the Bible lying off-center on its table. That should be put straight. The vase of everlastings should be set upright, and after that the whole house should be cleaned. Pat knew he should do these things in spite of the reluctance he felt for opening the door into the sitting room. His mind shrank from the things he would see when he opened the door—the two rocking chairs, one on either side of the stove; the pillows in the chair seats would be holding the impressions of his parents' bodies. He knew the odors of age and of unguents and of stale flowers that were waiting for him on the other side of the door. But the thing was a duty. It must be done.

He built a fire and made his breakfast. It was while he drank the hot coffee that a line of reasoning foreign to his old manner of life came to him. The unusual thoughts that thronged upon him astounded him at once for their audacity and for their simplicity.

"Why should I go in there?" he demanded. "There's no one to care, no one even to know. I don't have to go in there if I don't want to." He felt like a boy who breaks school to walk in a deep and satisfying forest. But to combat his freedom, his mother's complaining voice came to his ears. "Pat ought to clean the house. Pat never takes care of things."

The joy of revolt surged up in him. "You're dead!" he told the voice. "You're just something that's happening in my mind. Nobody can expect me to do things any more. Nobody will ever know if I don't do things I ought to. I'm not going in there, and I'm never going in there." And while the spirit was still strong in him, he strode to the door, plucked out the key and threw it into the tall weeds behind the house. He closed the shutters on all the windows except those in the kitchen, and nailed them shut with long spikes.

The joy of his new freedom did not last long. In the daytime the farm work kept him busy, but before the day was out, he grew lonely for the old duties which ate up the hours and made the time short. He knew he was afraid to go into the house, afraid of those impressions in the cushions and of the disarranged Bible. He had locked up two thin old ghosts, but he had not taken away their power to trouble him.

That night, after he had cooked his supper, he sat beside the stove. An appalling loneliness like a desolate fog fell upon him. He listened to the stealthy sounds in the old house, the whispers and little knockings. So tensely did he listen that after a while he could hear the chairs rocking in the other room, and once he made out the rasping sound of a lid being unscrewed from a jar of salve. Pat could not stand it any longer. He went to the barn, harnessed his horse and drove to the Pastures of Heaven General Store.

Three men sat around the fat-bellied stove, contemplating its corrugations with rapt abstraction. They made room for Pat to draw up a chair. None of the men looked at him, because a man in mourning deserves the same social immunities a cripple does. Pat settled himself in his chair and gazed at the stove. "Remind me to get some flour before I go," he said.

All of the men knew what he meant. They knew he didn't need flour, but each one of them, under similar circumstances, would have made some such excuse. T. B. Allen opened the stove door and looked in and then spat on the coals. "A house like that is pretty lonely at first," he observed. Pat felt grateful to him although his words constituted a social blunder.

"I'll need some tobacco and some shotgun shells, too, Mr. Allen," he said by way of payment.

Pat changed his habits of living after that. Determinedly he sought groups of men. During the daytime he worked on his farm, but at night he was invariably to be found where two or three people were gathered. When a dance or a party was given at the schoolhouse, Pat arrived early and stayed until the last man was gone. He sat at the house of John Whiteside; he arrived first at fires. On election days he stayed at the polls until they closed. Wherever a group of people gathered, Pat was sure to show up. From constant stalking of company he came to have almost an instinct for discovering excitements which would draw crowds.

Pat was a homely man, gangling, big-nosed and heavy-jawed. He looked very much like Lincoln as a young man. His figure was as unfitted for clothes as Lincoln's was. His nostrils and ears were large and full of hair. They looked as though furry little animals were hiding in them. Pat had no conversation; he knew he added little to the gatherings he frequented, and he tried to make up for his lack by working, by doing favors, by arranging things. He liked to be appointed to committees for arranging school dances, for then he could call on the other committeemen to discuss plans; he could spend evenings decorating the school or running about the valley borrowing chairs from one family and dishes from another. If on any evening he could find no gathering to join, he drove his Ford truck to Salinas and sat through two moving-picture shows. After those first two nights of fearful loneliness, he never spent another evening in his closed-up house. The memory of the Bible, of the waiting chairs, or the years-old smells were terrifying to him.

For ten years Pat Humbert drove about the valley in search of company. He had himself elected to the school board; he joined the Masons and the Odd Fellows in Salinas and was never known to miss a meeting.

In spite of his craving for company, Pat never became a part of any group he joined. Rather he hung on the fringes, never speaking unless he was addressed. The people of the valley considered his presence inevitable. They used him unmercifully and hardly knew that he wished nothing better.

When the gatherings were over, when Pat was finally forced home, he drove his Ford into the barn and then rushed to bed. He tried with little success to forget the terrible rooms on the other side of the door. The picture of them edged into his mind sometimes. The dust would be thick now, and the cobwebs would be strung in all the corners and on all the furniture. When the vision invaded and destroyed his defenses before he could go to sleep, Pat shivered in his bed and tried every little soporific formula he knew.

Since he so hated his house, Pat took no care of it. The old building lay moldering with neglect. A white Banksia rose, which for years had been a stubby little bush, came suddenly to life and climbed up the front of the house. It covered the porch, hung festoons over the closed windows and dropped long streamers from the eaves. Within ten years the house looked like a huge mound of roses. People passing by on the county road paused to marvel at its size and beauty. Pat hardly knew about the rose. He refused to think about the house when he could refuse.

The Humbert farm was a good one. Pat kept it well and made money from it, and, since his expenses were small, he had quite a few thousand dollars in the bank. He loved the farm for itself, but he also loved it because it kept him from fear in the daytime. When he was working, the terror of being solitary, the freezing loneliness, could not attack him. He raised good fruit, but his berries were his chief interest. The lines of supported vines paralleled the county road. Every year he was able to market his berries earlier than anyone in the valley.

Pat was forty years old when the Munroes came into the valley. He welcomed them as his neighbors. Here was another house to which he might go to pass an evening. And since Bert Munroe was a friendly man, he liked to have Pat drop in to visit. Pat was a good farmer. Bert often asked his advice. Pat did not take very careful notice of Mae Munroe except to see, and to forget, that she was a pretty girl. He did not often think of people as individuals, but rather as antidotes for the poison of his loneliness, as escapes from the imprisoned ghosts.

One afternoon when the summer was dawning, Pat worked among his berry vines. He kneeled between the rows of vines and dug among the berry roots with a hoe. The berries were fast forming now, and the leaves were pale green and lovely. Pat worked slowly down the row. He was contented with the work, and he did not dread the coming night for he was to have supper at the Munroe house. As he worked he heard voices from the road. Although he was concealed among the vines, he knew from the tones that Mrs. Munroe and her daughter Mae were strolling by his house. Suddenly he heard Mae exclaim with pleasure.

"Mama, look at that!" Pat ceased his work to listen. "Did you ever see such a beautiful rose in your life, Mama?"

"It's pretty, all right," Mrs. Munroe said.

"I've just thought what it reminds me of," Mae continued. "Do you remember the postcard of that lovely house in Vermont? Uncle Keller sent it. This house, with the rose over it, looks just like that house in the picture. I'd like to see the inside of it."

"Well, there isn't much chance of that. Mrs. Allen says no one in the valley has been in that house since Pat's father and mother died, and that's ten years ago. She didn't say whether it was pretty."

"With a rose like that on the outside, the inside must be pretty. I wonder if Mr. Humbert will let me see it sometime." The two women walked on out of hearing.

When they were gone, Pat stood up and looked at the great rose. He had never seen how beautiful it was—a haystack of green leaves and nearly covered with white roses. "It is pretty," he said. "And it's like a nice house in Vermont. It's like a Vermont house, and—well, it *is* pretty, a pretty bush." Then, as though he had seen through the bush and through the wall, a vision of the parlor came to him. He went quickly back to his work among the berries, struggling to put the house out of his mind. But Mae's words came back to him over and over again, "It must be pretty inside." Pat wondered what a Vermont house looked like inside. John Whiteside's solid and grand house he knew, and, with the rest of the valley, he had admired the plush comfort of Bert Munroe's house, but a pretty house he had never seen, that is, a house he could really call pretty. In his mind he went over all the houses he knew and not one of them was what Mae must have meant. He remembered a picture in a magazine, a room with a polished floor and white woodwork and a staircase; it might have been Mt. Vernon. That picture had impressed him. Perhaps that was what Mae meant.

He wished he could see the postcard of the Vermont house, but if he asked to see it, they would know he had been listening. As he thought of it, Pat became obsessed with a desire to see a pretty house that looked like this. He put his hoe away and walked in front of his house. Truly the rose was marvelous. It dropped a canopy over the porch, hung awnings of white stars over the closed windows. Pat wondered why he had never noticed it before.

That night he did something he couldn't have contemplated before. At the Munroe door, he broke an engagement to spend an evening in company. "There's some business in Salinas I've got to attend to," he explained. "I stand to lose some money if I don't go right in."

In Salinas he went straight to the public library. "Have you got any pictures of Vermont houses—pretty ones?" he asked the librarian.

"You'll probably find some in the magazines. Come! I'll show you where to look."

They had to warn him when the library was about to close. He had found pictures of interiors, but of interiors he had never imagined. The rooms were built on a plan; each decoration, each piece of furniture, even the floors and walls were related, were a part of the plan. Some deep and instinctive feeling in him for arrangement, for color and line, had responded to the pictures. He hadn't known rooms could be like that—all in one piece. Every room he had ever seen was the result of a gradual and accidental accumulation. Aunt Sophie sent a vase, father bought a chair. They put a stove in the fireplace because it threw more heat; the Sperry Flour Company issued a big calendar and mother had its picture framed; a mail order house advertised a new kind of lamp. That was the way rooms were assembled. But in the pictures someone had an idea, and everything in the room was a part of the idea. Just before the library closed he came upon two pictures side by side. One showed a room like those he knew, and right beside it was another picture of the same room with all the clutter gone, and with the idea in it. It didn't look like the same place at all. For the first time in his life, Pat was anxious to go home. He wanted to lie in his bed and to think, for a strange new idea was squirming into being in the back of his mind.

Pat could not sleep that night. His head was too full of plans. Once he got up and lighted the lamp to look in his bank book. A little before daylight he dressed and cooked his breakfast, and while he ate, his eyes wandered again and again to the locked door. There was a light of malicious joy in his eyes. "It'll be dark in there," he said. "I better rip open the shutters before I go in there."

When the daylight came at last, he took a crowbar and walked around the house, tearing open the nailed shutters as he went. The parlor windows he did not touch, for he didn't want to disturb the rose bush. Finally he went back into the kitchen and stood before the locked door. For a moment the old vision stopped him. "But it will be just for a minute," he argued. "I'll start in tearing it to pieces right away." The crowbar poised and crashed on the lock. The door sprang open crying miserably on its dry hinges, and the horrible room lay before him. The air was foggy with cobwebs; a musty, ancient odor flowed through the door. There were the two rocking chairs on either side of the rusty stove. Even through the dust he could see the little hollows in their cushions. But these were not the terrible things. Pat knew where lay the center of his fears. He walked rapidly through the room, brushing the cobwebs from his eyes as he went. The parlor was still dark, for its shutters were closed. Pat didn't have to grope for the table; he knew exactly where it was. Hadn't it haunted him for ten years? He picked up table and Bible together, ran out through the kitchen and hurled them into the yard.

Now he could go more slowly. The fear was gone. The windows were stuck so hard that he had to use the bar to pry them open. First the rocking chairs went out, rolling and jumping when they hit the ground, then the pictures, the ornaments from the mantel, the stuffed orioles. And when the movable furniture, the clothing, the rugs and vases were scattered about under the windows, Pat ripped up the carpets and crammed them out, too. Finally he brought buckets of water and splashed the walls and ceilings thoroughly. The work was an intense pleasure to him. He tried to break the legs from the chairs when he threw them out. While the water was soaking into the old dark wallpaper, he collected all of the furniture from under the windows, piled it up and set fire to it. Old musty fabrics and varnished wood smoldered sullenly and threw out a foul stench of dust and dampness. Only when a bucket of kerosene was thrown over the pile did the flame leap up. The tables and chairs cracked as they released their ghosts into the fire. Pat surveyed the pile joyfully.

"You *would* sit in there all these years, wouldn't you?" he cried. "You thought I'd never get up the guts to burn you. Well, I just wish you could be around to see what I'm going to do, you rotten stinking trash." The green carpets burned through and left red, flaky coals. Old vases and jars cracked to pieces in the heat. Pat could hear the sizzle of mentholatum and painkiller gushing from containers and boiling into the fire. He felt that he was presiding at the death of his enemy. Only when the pile had burned down to coals did he leave it. The walls were soaked thoroughly by now, so that the wallpaper peeled off in long, broad ribbons.

That afternoon Pat drove in to Salinas and bought all the magazines on house decoration he could find. In the evening, after dinner, he searched the pages through. At last, in one of the magazines, he found the perfect room. There had been a question about some of the others; there was none about this one. And he could make it quite easily. With the partition between the sitting room and the parlor torn out, he would have a room thirty feet long and fifteen wide. The windows must be made wide, the fireplace enlarged and the floor sandpapered, stained and polished. Pat knew he could do all these things. His hands ached to be at work. "To-morrow I'll start," he said. Then another thought stopped him. "She thinks it's pretty now. I can't very well let her know I'm doing it now. Why, she'd know I heard her say that about the Vermont house. I can't let people know I'm doing it. They'd ask why I'm doing it." He wondered why he was doing it. "It's none of their darn business why," he explained to himself. "I don't have to go around telling people why. I've got my reasons. By God! I'll do it at night." Pat laughed softly to himself. The idea of secretly changing his house delighted him. He could work here alone, and no one would know. Then, when it was all finished, he could invite a few people in and pretend it was always that way. Nobody would remember how it was ten years ago.

This was the way he ordered his life: During the day he worked on the farm, and at night rushed into the house with a feeling of joy. The picture of the completed room was tacked up in the kitchen. Pat looked at it twenty times a day. While he was building window seats, putting up the French-grey paper, coating the woodwork with cream-colored enamel, he could see the completed room before him. When he needed supplies, he drove to Salinas late in the evening and brought back his materials after dark. He worked until midnight and went to bed breathlessly happy.

The people of the valley missed him from their gatherings. At the store they questioned him, but he had his excuse ready. "I'm taking one of those mail courses," he explained. "I'm studying at night." The men smiled. Loneliness was too much for a man, they knew. Bachelors on farms always got a little queer sooner or later.

"What are you studying, Pat?"

"Oh! What? Oh! I'm taking some lessons in—building."

"You ought to get married, Pat. You're getting along in years."

Pat blushed furiously. "Don't be a damn fool," he said.

As he worked on the room, Pat was developing a little play, and it went like this: The room was finished and the furniture in place. The fire burned redly; the lamps threw misty reflections on the polished floor and on the shiny furniture. "I'll go to her house, and I'll say, off-hand, 'I hear you like Vermont houses.' No! I can't say that. I'll say, 'Do you like Vermont houses? Well, I've got a room that's kind of like a Vermont room.' " The preliminaries were never quite satisfactory. He couldn't come on the perfect way for enticing her into his house. He ended by skipping that part. He could think it out later.

Now she was entering the kitchen. The kitchen wouldn't be changed, for that would make the other room a bigger surprise. She would stand in front of the door, and he would reach around her and throw it open. There was the room, rather dark, but full of dark light, really. The fire flowed up like a broad stream, and the lamps reflected on the floor. You could make out the glazed chintz hangings and the fat tiger of the overmantel hooked rug. The pewter glowed with a restrained richness. It was all so warm and snug. Pat's chest contracted with delight.

Anyway, she was standing in the door and—what would she say? Well, if she felt the way he did, maybe she wouldn't say anything. She might feel almost like crying. That was peculiar, the good full feeling as though you were about to cry. Maybe she'd stand there for a minute or two, just looking. Then Pat would say—"Won't you come in and sit for a while?" And of course that would break the spell. She would begin talking about the room in funny choked sentences. But Pat would be off-hand about it all. "Yes, I always kind of liked it." He said this out loud as he worked. "Yes, I always thought it was kind of nice. It came to me the other day that you might like to see it."

The play ended this way: Mae sat in the wingback chair in front of the fire. Her plump pretty hands lay in her lap. As she sat there, a far-away look came into her eyes. . . . And Pat never went any farther than that, for at that point a self-consciousness overcame him. If he went farther, it would be like peeking in a window at two people who wanted to be alone. The electric moment, the palpitating moment of the whole thing was when he threw open the door; when she stood on the threshhold, stunned by the beauty of the room.

At the end of three months the room was finished. Pat put the magazine picture in his wallet and went to San Francisco. In the office of a furniture company, he spread his picture on the desk. "I want furniture like that," he said.

"You don't mean originals, of course."

"What do you mean, originals?"

"Why, old pieces. You couldn't get them for under thirty thousand dollars."

Pat's face fell. His room seemed to collapse. "Oh!—I didn't know."

"We can get you good copies of everything here," the manager assured him.

"Why of course. That's good. That's fine. How much would the copies cost?"

A purchasing agent was called in. The three of them went over the articles in the picture and the manager made a list; pie-crust table, drop-leaf gate-leg table, chairs: one windsor, one rush seat ladderback, one wingback, one fireplace bench; rag rugs, glazed chintz hangings, lamps with frosted globes and crystal pendants; one open-faced cupboard, pictorial bone-china, pewter candlesticks and sconces.

"Well, it will be around three thousand dollars, Mr. Humbert."

Pat frowned with thought. After all, why should he save money? "How soon can you send it down?" he demanded.

While he waited for a notice that the furniture had arrived in Salinas, Pat rubbed the floor until it shone like a dull lake. He walked backward out of the room erasing his faint foot marks with a polisher. And then, at last, the crates arrived at the freight depot. It took four trips to Salinas in his truck to get them, trips made secretly in the night. There was an air of intrigue about the business.

Pat uncrated the pieces in the barn. He carried in chairs and tables, and, with a great many looks at the picture, arranged them in their exact places. That night the fire flowed up, and the frosted lamps reflected on the floor. The fat tiger on the hooked rug over the fireplace seemed to quiver in the dancing flame-light.

Pat went into the kitchen and closed the door. Then, very slowly he opened it again and stood looking in. The room glowed with warmth, with welcoming warmth. The pewter was even richer than he had thought it would be. The plates in the open-faced cupboard caught sparks on their rims. For a moment Pat stood in the doorway trying to get the right tone in his voice. "I always kind of liked it," he said in his most offhand manner. "It just came to me the other day that you might like to see it." He paused, for a horrible thought had come to him. "Why, she can't come here alone. A girl can't come to a single man's house at night. People would talk about her, and besides, she wouldn't do it." He was bitterly disappointed. "Her mother will have to come with her. But—maybe her mother won't get in the way. She can stand back here, kind of, out of the way."

Now that he was ready, a powerful reluctance stopped him. Evening after evening passed while he put off asking her to come. He went through his play until he knew exactly where she would stand, how she would look, what she would say. He had alternative things she might say. A week went by, and still he put off the visit that would bring her to see his room.

One afternoon he built up his courage with layers of will. "I can't put it off forever. I better go tonight." After dinner, he put on his best suit and set out to walk to the Munroe house. It was only a quarter of a mile away. He wouldn't ask her for tonight. He wanted to have the fire burning and the lamps lighted when she arrived. The night was cold and very dark. When Pat stumbled in the dust of the road, he thought with dismay how his polished shoes would look.

There were a great many lights in the Munroe house. In front of the gate, a number of cars were parked. "It's a party," Pat said to himself, "I'll ask her some other night. I couldn't do it in front of a lot of people." For a moment he even considered turning back. "It would look funny though, if I asked her the first time I saw her in months. She might suspect something."

When he entered the house, Bert Munroe grasped him by the hand. "It's Pat Humbert," he shouted. "Where have you been keeping yourself, Pat?"

"I've been studying at night."

"Well it's lucky you came over. I was going to go over to see you tomorrow. You heard the news, of course!"

"What news?"

"Why, Mae and Bill Whiteside are going to get married next Saturday. I was going to ask you to help at the wedding. It'll just be a home affair with refreshments afterwards. You used to help at the schoolhouse all the time before you got this studying streak." He took Pat's arm and tried to lead him down the hall. The sound of a number of voices came from the room at the end of the hall.

Pat resisted firmly. He exerted all his training in the offhand manner. "That's fine, Mr. Munroe. Next Saturday, you say? I'd be glad to help. No, I can't stay now. I got to run to the store right away." He shook hands again and walked slowly out the door.

In his misery he wanted to hide for a while, to burrow into some dark place where no one could see him. His way was automatically homeward. The rambling house was dark and unutterably dreary when he arrived. Pat went into the barn and with deliberate steps climbed the short ladder and lay down in the hay. His mind was shrunken and dry with disappointment. Above all things he did not want to go into the house. He was afraid he might lock up the door again. And then, in all the years to come, two puzzled spirits would live in the beautiful room, and in his kitchen, Pat would understand how they gazed wistfully into the ghost of a fire.

XI

When Richard Whiteside came to the far West in '50, he inspected the gold workings and gave them up as objects for his effort. "The earth gives only one crop of gold," he said. "When that crop is divided among a thousand tenants, it feeds no one for very long. This is bad husbandry."

Richard drove about over the fields and hills of California; in his mind there was the definite intention of founding a house for children not yet born and for their children. Few people in California in that day felt a responsibility toward their descendants.

On the evening of a fine clear day, he drove his two bay horses to the top of the little hills which surround the Pastures of Heaven. He pulled up his team and gazed down on the green valley. And Richard knew that he had found his home. In his wandering about the country he had come upon many beautiful places, but none of them had given him this feeling of consummation. He remembered the colonists from Athens and from Lacedaemon looking for new lands described by vague oracles; he thought of the Aztecs plodding forward after their guiding eagle. Richard said to himself, "Now if there could be a sign, it would be perfect. I know this is the place, but if only there could be an omen to remember and to tell the children." He looked into the sky, but it was clean of both birds and clouds. Then the breeze that blows over the hills in the evening sprang up. The oaks made furtive little gestures toward the valley, and on the hillside a tiny whirlwind picked up a few leaves and flung them forward. Richard chuckled. "Answer! Many a fine city was founded because of a hint from the gods no more broad than that."

After a little while he climbed out of his light wagon and unhitched his horses. Once hobbled, they moved off with little mincing steps toward the grass at the side of the road. Richard ate a supper of cold ham and bread, and afterwards he unrolled his blankets and laid them on the grass of the hillside. As the grey dusk thickened in the valley, he lay on his bed and gazed down on the Pastures of Heaven which was to be his home. On the far side, near a grove of fine oaks was the place; behind the chosen spot there was a hill and a little brushy crease, a stream surely. The light became uncertain and magical. Richard saw a beautiful white house with a trim garden in front of it and nearby, the white tower of a tank house. There were little yellow lights in the windows, little specks of welcoming lights. The broad front door opened, and a whole covey of children walked out on the veranda—at least six children. They peered out into the growing darkness, looked particularly up at the hill where Richard lay on his blankets. After a moment they went back into the house, and the door shut behind them. With the closing of the door, the house, the garden and the white tank house disappeared. Richard sighed with contentment and lay on his back. The sky was prickling with stars.

For a week Richard drove furiously about the valley. He bought two hundred and fifty acres in the Pastures of Heaven; he drove to Monterey to have the title searched and the deed recorded, and, when the land was surely his, he visited an architect.

It took six months to build his house, to carpet and furnish it, to bore a well and build the towering tank house over it. There were workmen about the Whiteside place the whole first year of Richard's ownership. The land was untouched with seed.

A neighbor who was worried by this kind of procedure

drove over and confronted the new owner. "Going to have your family come out, Mr. Whiteside?"

"I haven't any family," said Richard. "My parents are dead. I have no wife."

"Then what the hell are you building a big house like that for?"

Richard's face grew stern. "I'm going to live here. I've come to stay. My children and their children and theirs will live in this house. There will be a great many Whitesides born here, and a great many will die here. Properly cared for, the house will last five hundred years."

"I see what you mean, all right," said the neighbor. "It sounds fine, but that's not how we work out here. We build a little shack, and if the land pays, we build a little more on it. It isn't good to put too much into a place. You might want to move."

"I don't want to move," Richard cried. "That's just what I'm building against. I shall build a structure so strong that neither I nor my descendants will be able to move. As a precaution, I shall be buried here when I die. Men find it hard to leave the graves of their fathers." His face softened. "Why, man, don't you see what I'm doing? I'm founding a dynasty. I'm building a family and a family seat that will survive, not forever, but for several centuries at least. It pleases me, when I build this house, to know that my descendants will walk on its floors, that children whose great grandfathers aren't conceived will be born in it. I'll build the germ of a tradition into my house." Richard's eyes were sparkling as he talked. The pounding of carpenter's hammers punctuated his speech.

The neighbor thought he was dealing with a madman, but he felt a kind of reverence for the madness. He desired to salute it in some manner. Had he not been an American, he would have touched his hat with two fingers. This man's two grown sons were cutting timber three hundred miles away, and his daughter had married and gone to Nevada. His family was broken up before it was really started.

Richard built his house of redwood, which does not decay. He modeled it after the style of the fine country houses of New England, but, as a tribute to the climate of the Pastures of Heaven, he surrounded the whole building with a wide veranda. The roof was only temporarily shingled, but, as soon as his order could be received in Boston and a ship could get back again, the shingles were ripped off and eastern slate substituted. This roof was an important and symbolic thing to Richard. To the people of the valley the slate roof was the show piece of the country. More than anything else it made Richard Whiteside the first citizen of the valley. This man was steady, and his home was here. He didn't intend to run off to a new gold field. Why—his roof was slate. Besides, he was an educated man. He had been to Harvard. He had money, and he had the faith to build a big, luxurious house in the valley. He would rule the land. He was the founder and patriarch of a family, and his roof was of slate. The people appreciated and valued the Pastures of Heaven more because of the slate roof. Had Richard been a politician with a desire for local preferment, he could have made no more astute move than thus roofing his house with slate. It glimmered darkly in the rain; the sun made a steel mirror of it.

Finally the house was finished, two hired men were set to planting the orchards and to preparing the land for seed. A little band of sheep nibbled the grass on the hillside behind the house. Richard knew that his preparation was complete. He was ready for a wife. When a letter came from a distant relative, saying he had arrived in San Francisco with his wife and daughter and would be glad to see Richard, Richard knew he need not search farther. Before he went to San Francisco, he knew he would marry that daughter. It was the fit thing. There would be no accidents of blood if he married this girl.

Although they went through the form of courtship, the matter was settled as soon as they met. Alicia was glad to leave the domination of her mother and to begin a domestic empire of her own. The house had been made for her. She had not been in it twenty-four hours before she had spread scalloped and perforated papers on the pantry shelves, of the exact kind Richard remembered in his mother's pantry. She ordered the house in the old, comfortable manner, the unchangeable, the cyclic manner—washing Monday, ironing Tuesday and so forth—carpets up and beaten twice a year; jams, tomatoes and pickles preserved and shelved in the basement every fall. The farm prospered, the sheep and cows increased, and in the garden, bachelor buttons, sweet william, carnations, hollyhocks settled down to a yearly blooming. And Alicia was going to have a baby.

Richard had known all this would happen. The dynasty was established. The chimneys wore black smudges around their crowns. The fireplace in the sitting room smoked just enough to fill the house with a delicious incense of wood smoke. The great meerschaum pipe his father-in-law had given him was turning from its new, chalky white to a rich, creamy yellow.

When the child was coming, Richard treated Alicia almost like an invalid. In the evening when they sat before the fire, he tucked a robe about her feet. His great fear was that something would go wrong with the bearing of the child. They talked of the picture she should look at to influence the appearance of the firstling, and, to surprise her, Richard sent to San Francisco for a little bronze copy of the Michelangelo *David*. Alicia blushed at its nakedness, but before very long she became passionately fond of the little figure. When she went to bed it stood on her bedside table. During the day she took it from room to room with her as she worked, and in the evening it stood on the mantel in the sitting room. Often when she gazed at its clean, hard limbs a tiny smile of knowledge and of seeking came and went on her face. She was thoroughly convinced that her child would look like the *David*.

Richard sat beside her and stroked her hand soothingly. She liked to have him stroke the palm of her hand, firmly enough so it did not tickle. He talked to her quietly. "The curse is removed," he said. "You know, Alicia, my people, and yours a little farther removed, lived in one house for a hundred and thirty years. From that central hearth our blood was mingled with the good true blood of New England. One time my father told me that seventy-three children were born in the house. Our family multiplied until my grandfather's time. My father was an only child, and I was an only child. It was the sadness of my father's life. He was only sixty when he died, Alicia, and I was his only child. When I was twenty-five and hadn't really begun to live, the old house burned down. I don't know what started the fire." He laid her hand down on the arm of his chair as gently as though it were a weak little animal. An ember had rolled out of the fireplace and off the brick hearth. He pushed it back among the other coals and then took up Alicia's hand again. She smiled faintly at the *David* on the mantel.

"There was a practice in ancient times," Richard continued. His voice became soft and far away as though he spoke from those ancient times. Later in life Alicia could tell by the set of his head, by the tone of his voice and by his expression when he was about to speak of ancient times. For the Ancient Times of Herodotus, of Xenophon, of Thucydides were personal things to him. In the illiterate West the stories of Herodotus were as new as though he had invented them. He read the Persian War, the Peloponnesian Wars and the Ten Thousand every year. Now he stroked Alicia's hand a little more firmly.

"In ancient times when, through continued misfortunes, the people of a city came to believe themselves under a curse or even under disfavor of some god, they put all of their movable possessions in ships and sailed away to found a new city. They left their old city vacant and open to anyone who wanted it."

"Will you hand me the statue, Richard?" Alicia asked. "Sometimes I like to hold it in my hand." He jumped up and set the *David* in her lap.

"Listen, Alicia! There were only two children in the two generations before the house burned down. I put my possessions in a ship and sailed westward to found a new home. You must surely see that the home I lost took a hundred and thirty years to build. I couldn't replace it. A new house on the old land would have been painful to me. When I saw this valley, I knew it was the place for the new family seat. And now the generations are forming. I am very happy, Alicia."

She reached over to squeeze his hand in gratitude that she could make him happy. "Why," he said suddenly, "there was even an omen, when I first came into the valley. I inquired of the gods whether this was the place, and they answered. Is that good, Alicia? Shall I tell you about the omens and my first night on the hill?"

"Tell me tomorrow night," she said. "It will be better if I retire now." He stood up and helped her to unfold the rug from around her knees. Alicia leaned rather heavily on his arm as he helped her up the stairs. "There's something mystic in the house, Alicia, something marvelous. It's the new soul, the first native of the new race."

"He will look like the little statue," said Alicia.

When Richard had tucked in the covers so she could not catch cold, he went back to the sitting room. He could hear children in the house. They ran with pattering feet up and down the stairs, they dabbled in the ashes of the fireplace. He heard their voices softly calling to one another on the veranda. Before he went to bed, he put the three great books on the top shelf of the bookcase.

The birth was a very severe one. When it was over, and Alicia lay pale and exhausted in her bed, Richard brought the little son and put him beside her. "Yes," she said, complacently, "he looks like the statue. I knew he would, of course. And David will be his name, of course."

The Monterey doctor came downstairs and sat with Richard beside the fire. He puckered his brow gloomily and rolled a Masonic ring around and around on his third finger. Richard opened a bottle of brandy and poured two little glasses.

"I'm going to name this toast to my son, Doctor."

The doctor put his glass to his nose and sniffed like a horse. "Damn fine liquor. You better name it to your wife."

"Of course." They drank. "And this next one to my son."

"Name this one to your wife, too."

"Why?" Richard asked in surprise.

The doctor was almost dipping his nostrils in the glass. "Kind of a thank offering. You were damn near a widower."

Richard dumped his brandy down his throat. "I didn't know. I thought—I didn't know. I thought first ones were always hard to bear."

"Give me another drink," the doctor demanded. "You aren't going to have any more children."

Richard stopped in the act of pouring. "What do you mean by that? Of course I'm going to have more children."

"Not by this wife, you aren't. She's finished. Have another child and you won't have any wife."

Richard sat very still. The soft clattering of children he had heard in the house for the past month was suddenly stilled. He seemed to hear their secret feet stealing out the front door and down the steps.

The doctor laughed sourly. "Why don't you get drunk if that's the way you feel about it?"

"Oh! no, no. I don't think I could get drunk."

"Well, give me another drink before I go, anyway. It's going to be a cold drive home."

Richard did not tell his wife she could not have children until six months had passed. He wanted her to regain her strength before he exposed her to the shock of the revelation. When he finally did go to her, he felt the guilt of his secret. She was holding her child in her lap, and occasionally bending down to take one of his upstretched fingers in her mouth. The child stared up with vague eyes and smiled wetly while he waggled his straight fingers for her to suck. The sun flooded in the window. From a distance they could hear one of the hired men cursing a harrow team with singsong monotony. Alicia lifted her head and frowned slightly. "It's time he was christened, don't you think, Richard?"

"Yes," he agreed. "I'll make arrangements in Monterey."

She struggled with a weighty consideration. "Do you think it too late to change his name?"

"No, it's not too late. Why do you want to change it? What do you want to call him?"

"I want to have him called John. That's a New Testament name—" She looked up for his approval—"and besides, it's my father's name. My father will be pleased. Besides, I haven't felt quite right about naming him for that statue, even if it is a statue of the boy David. It isn't as though the statue had clothes on—"

Richard did not try to follow this logic. Instead he plunged into his confession. In a second it was over. He had not realized it would take so little time. Alicia was smiling a peculiar enigmatic smile that puzzled him. No matter how well he became acquainted with her, this smile, a little quizzical, a trifle sad, and filled with secret wisdom shut him out of her thoughts. She retired behind the smile. It said, "How silly you are. I know things which would make your knowledge seem ridiculous if I chose to tell you." The child stretched up its yearning fingers toward her face, and she flexed its fingers back and forth. "Wait a little," she said. "Doctors don't know everything. Just wait a little, Richard. We will have other children." She shifted the boy and slipped her hand under his diaper.

Richard went out and sat on his front steps. The house behind him was teeming with life again, whereas a few minutes ago it had been quiet and dead. There were thousands of things to do. The box hedge which held the garden in its place had not been clipped for six months. Long ago he had laid out a square in the side yard for a grass plot, and it lay waiting for the seed. There was no place for drying linen yet. The banister of the front steps was beside him. Richard put out his hand and stroked it as though it were the arched neck of a horse.

The Whitesides became the first family of the Pastures of Heaven almost as soon as they were settled. They were educated, they had a fine farm, and, while not rich, they were not pressed for money. Most important of all, they lived in comfort, in a fine house. The house was the symbol of the family—roomy, luxurious for that day, warm, hospitable and white. Its size gave an impression of substance, but it was the white paint, often renewed and washed, that placed it over the other houses of the valley as surely as a Rhine castle is placed over its village. The families admired the white house, and also they felt more secure because it was there. It embodied authority and culture and judgment and manners. The neighbors could tell by looking at his house that Richard Whiteside was a gentleman who would do no mean nor cruel nor unwise thing. They were proud of the house in the same way tenants of land in a duchy are proud of the manor house. While some of the neighbors were richer than Whiteside, they seemed to know they could not build a house like that even though they imitated it exactly. It was primarily because of his house that Richard became the valley's arbiter of manners, and, after that, a kind of extra-legal judge over small disputes. The reliance of his neighbors in turn bred in Richard a paternal feeling toward the valley. As he grew older he came to regard all the affairs of the valley as his affairs, and the people were proud to have it so.

Five years passed before her intuition told Alicia that she was ready to have another child. "I'll get the doctor," Richard said, when she told him. "The doctor will know whether it's safe or not."

"No, Richard. Doctors do not know. I tell you women know more about themselves than doctors do."

Richard obeyed her, because he was afraid of what the doctor would tell him. "It's the grain of deity in women," he explained to himself. "Nature has planted this sure knowledge in women in order that the race may increase."

Everything went well for six months, and then a devastating illness set in. When he was finally summoned, the doctor was too furious to speak to Richard. The confinement was a time of horror. Richard sat in his sitting room, gripping the arms of his chair and listening to the weak screaming in the bedroom above. His face was grey. After many hours the screaming stopped. Richard was so fuddled with apprehension that he did not even look up when the doctor came into the room.

"Get out the bottle," the doctor said, tiredly. "Let's name a toast to you for a God damn fool."

Richard did not look up nor answer. For a moment the doctor continued to scowl at him, and then he spoke more gently. "Your wife isn't dead, Heaven only knows why. She's gone through enough to kill a squad of soldiers. These weak women! They have the vitality of monsters. The baby is dead!" Suddenly he wanted to punish Richard for disregarding his first orders. "There isn't enough left of the baby to bury." He turned and left the house abruptly because he hated to be as sorry for anyone as he was for Richard Whiteside.

Alicia was an invalid. Little John could not remember when his mother had not been an invalid. All of his life that he could remember he had seen his father carry her up and down stairs in his arms. Alicia did not speak very often, but more and more the quizzical and wise smile was in her eyes. And in spite of her weakness, she ordered the house remarkably well. The rugged country girls, who served in the house as a coveted preparation for their own marriages, came for orders before every meal. Alicia, from her bed or from her rocking chair, planned everything.

Every night Richard carried her up to bed. When she was lying against her white pillows, he drew up a chair and sat by her bed for a little while, stroking the palm of her hand until she grew sleepy. Every night she asked, "Are you content, Richard?"

"I am content," he said. And then he told her about the farm and about the people of the valley. It was a kind of daily report of happenings. As he talked, the smile came upon her face and stayed there until her eyes drooped, and he blew out the light. It was a ritual.

On John's tenth birthday he was given a party. Children from all over the valley came and wandered on tip-toe through the big house, staring at the grandeur they had heard about. Alicia was sitting on the veranda. "You mustn't be so quiet, children," she said. "Run about and have a good time." But they could not run and shout in the Whiteside house. They might as well have shouted in church. When they had gone through all the rooms, they could stand the strain no longer. The whole party retired to the barn, from which their wild shrieks drifted back to the veranda where Alicia sat smiling.

That night, when she was in bed, she asked, "Are you content, Richard?"

His face still glowed with the pleasure he had taken in the party. "I am content," he said.

"You must not worry about the children, Richard," she continued. "Wait a little. Everything will be all right." This was her great, all-covering knowledge. "Wait a little. No sorrow can survive the smothering of a little time." And Richard knew that it was a greater knowledge than his.

"It isn't long to wait," Alicia went on.

"What isn't?"

"Why think, John. He's ten now. In ten years he will be married, and then, don't you see?—Teach him what you know. The family is safe, Richard."

"Of course, I know. The house is safe. I'm going to begin reading Herodotus to him, Alicia. He's old enough."

"I think Myrtle should clean all the spare bedrooms tomorrow. They haven't been aired for three months."

John Whiteside always remembered how his father read to him the three great authors, Herodotus, Thucydides, Xenophon. The meerschaum pipe was reddish brown by now, delicately and evenly colored. "All history is here," Richard said. "Everything mankind is capable of is recorded in these three books. The love and chicanery, the stupid dishonesty, the short-sightedness and bravery, nobility and sadness of the race. You may judge the future by these books, John, for nothing can happen which has not happened and been recorded in these books. Compared to these, the Bible is a very incomplete record of an obscure people."

And John remembered how his father felt about the house—how it was a symbol of the family, a temple built around the hearth.

John was in his last year in Harvard when his father suddenly died of pneumonia. His mother wrote to him telling him he must finish his course before he returned. "You would not be able to do anything that has not been done," she wrote. "It was your father's wish that you finish."

When he finally did go home, he found his mother a very aged woman. She was completely bedridden by now. John sat by her side and heard about his father's last days.

"He told me to tell you one thing," Alicia said. " 'Make John realize that he must keep us going. I want to survive in the generations,' and very soon after that he became delirious." John was looking out the window at the round hill behind the house. "Your father was delirious for two days. In all that time he talked of children—nothing but children. He heard them running up and down stairs and felt them pulling at the quilts of his bed. He wanted to take them up and hold them, John. Then just before he died the dreams cleared away. He was happy. He said, 'I have seen the future. There will be so many children. I am content, Alicia.' "

John was leaning his head in his palms now. And then his mother, who had never resisted anything, but had submitted every problem to time, pulled herself up in the bed and spoke harshly to him. "Get married!" she cried. "I want to see it. Get married—I want a strong woman who can have children. I couldn't have any after you. I would have died if I could have had one more. Find a wife quickly. I want to see her." She sank back on her pillows, but her eyes were unhappy and the smile of knowledge was not on her face.

John did not get married for six years. During that time his mother dried up until she was a tiny skeleton covered with bluish, almost transparent skin, and still she held on to life. Her eyes followed her son reproachfully; he felt ashamed when she looked at him. At length a classmate of John's came to the West to look about and brought his sister with him. They visited at the Whiteside farm for a month, and at the end of that time John proposed to Willa and was accepted. When he told his mother, she demanded to be alone with the girl. Half an hour later, Willa emerged from the sickroom blushing violently.

"What's the matter, dear?" John asked.

"Why, it's nothing. It's all right. Your mother asked me a great many questions, and then she looked at me for a long time."

"She's so old," John explained. "Her mind is so old." He went into his mother's room. The feverish frowning look was gone from her face and instead there was the old quizzical smile of knowledge.

"It's all right, John," she said. "I'd like to wait to see the children, but I can't. I've clung to life as long as I can. I'm tired of it." It was almost possible to see the tenacious will release its grip on her body. In the night she became unconscious and three days later she died as quietly and gently as though she had dozed.

John Whiteside did not think of the house exactly as his father had. He loved it more. It was the outer shell of his body. Just as his mind could leave his body and go traveling off, so could he leave the house, but just as surely he must come back to it. He renewed the white paint every two years, planted the garden himself and trimmed the box hedge. He did not occupy the powerful place in the valley his father had. John was less stern, less convinced of everything. Faced with an argument to decide, he was too prone to find endless ramifications on both sides. The big meerschaum pipe was very dark now, almost a black in which there were red lights.

Willa Whiteside loved the valley from the beginning. Alicia had been aloof and quiet, rather a frightening person. The people of the valley seldom saw her, and when they did, she treated them gently and kindly, was generous and careful of their feelings. She made them feel like peasants calling at the castle.

Willa liked to make calls on the women of the valley. She liked to sit in their kitchens drinking harsh tea and talking of the innumerable important things that bear on housekeeping. She grew to be an extensive trader of recipes. When she went to make a call, she carried a little notebook in which to write confided formulae. Her neighbors called her Willa and often came in the morning to drink tea in her kitchen. Perhaps it was partly her influence that caused John to become gregarious. He lost the power his father had held through aloofness. John liked his neighbors. On warm summer afternoons he sat in his canvas chair on the veranda and entertained such men as could get away from work. There were political caucuses on the veranda, little meetings over glasses of lemonade. The social and political structure of the whole valley was built on this porch, and always it was built amusingly. John looked at the life about him with a kind of amused irony, and due to his outlook, there ceased to exist in the valley any of the ferocious politics and violent religious opinions which usually poison rural districts. When, during the discussions among the men, some local or national climax or calamity was spoken of, John liked to bring out the three great books and to read aloud of some parallel situation in the ancient world. He had as great a love for the ancients as his father had.

There were the Sunday dinners with a neighbor couple and perhaps an itinerant minister as guests. The women helped in the kitchen until the mid-day dinner was ready. At the table the minister felt the pitiless fire of his mission slipping away in the air of gentle tolerance, until, when the dessert was brought in and the cider drunk, a fiery Baptist had been known to laugh heartily at a bit of quiet ridicule aimed at total immersion.

John enjoyed these things deeply, but his sitting room was the center of his existence. The leather chairs, whose hollows and bumps were casts of comfortable anatomy, were pieces of him. On the wall were the pictures he had grown up with, steel engravings of deer and Swiss Alpine climbers and of mountain goats. The pictures were so closely bound up with his life that he didn't see them any more, but the loss of any article would have been as painful as an amputation. In the evening his greatest pleasure came. A little fire was burning in the red brick fireplace. John sat in his chair caressing the big meerschaum. Now and then to oil it he stroked the polished bowl along the side of his nose. He was reading the Georgics or perhaps Varro on farming. Willa, under her own lamp, pursed her lips tightly while she embroidered doilies in floral designs as Christmas presents for eastern relatives who sent doilies to her.

John closed his book and went over to his desk. The roll top always stuck and required pampering. It gave suddenly and went clattering up. Willa unpursed her mouth. The look of intense agony she wore when she was doing a thing carefully left her face.

"What in the world are you doing?"

"Oh! Just seeing about some things."

For an hour he worked behind the desk, then—"Listen to this, Willa."

She relaxed again. "I thought so—poetry."

He read his verses and waited apologetically. Willa, with tact, kept silence. The silence lengthened until it was no longer tactful. "I guess it isn't very good." He laughed ruefully.

"No, it isn't."

He crumpled the paper and threw it into the fire. "For a few minutes I thought it was going to be good."

"What had you been reading, John?"

"Well, I was just looking through my Virgil and I thought I'd try my hand at a verse, because I didn't want to—oh, well, it's almost impossible to read a fine thing without wanting to do a fine thing. No matter." He rolled down the desk cover and picked a new book from the bookcase.

The sitting room was his home. Here he was complete, perfect and happy. Under the Rochester lamps every last scattered particle of him was gathered together into a definite, boundaried entity.

Most lives extend in a curve. There is a rise of ambition, a rounded peak of maturity, a gentle downward slope of disillusion and last a flattened grade of waiting for death. John Whiteside lived in a straight line. He was ambitionless; his farm not only made him a good living, but paid enough so he could hire men to work it for him. He wanted nothing beyond what he had or could easily procure. He was one of the few men who could savor a moment while he held it. And he knew it was a good life he was leading, a uniquely good life.

Only one need entered his existence. He had no children. The hunger for children was almost as strong in him as it had been in his father. Willa did not have children although she wanted them as badly as he did. The subject embarrassed them, and they never spoke of it.

In the eighth year of their marriage, through some accident, chemical or divine, Willa conceived, went through a painless, normal period of pregnancy and delivered a healthy child.

The accident never occurred again, but both Willa and John were thankful, almost devoutly thankful. The strong desire for self-perpetuation which had been more or less dormant in John rose up to the surface. For a few years he ripped the land with the plow, scratched it with the harrow and flogged it with the roller. Where he had been only a friend to the farm, the awakening duty to the generations changed him to a master. He plunged the seeds into the earth and waited covetously for the green crops to appear.

Willa did not change as her husband did. She took the boy William as a matter of course, called him Bill and refused to worship him. John saw his father in the boy although no one else did.

"Do you think he is bright?" John asked his wife. "You're with him more than I am. Do you think he has any intelligence?"

"Just so-so. Just normal."

"He seems to develop so slowly," John said impatiently. "I want the time to come when he'll begin to understand things."

On Bill's tenth birthday John opened his thick Herodotus and began to read to him. Bill sat on the floor, blankly regarding his father. Every night John read a few pages from the book. After about a week of it, he looked up from his book one evening and saw that Willa was laughing at him.

"What's the matter?" he demanded.

"Look under your chair."

He leaned down and saw that Bill had constructed a house of matches. The child was so absorbed in the work that he was not aware the reading had stopped. "Hasn't he been listening at all?"

"Not a word. He hasn't heard a word since the first night when he lost interest in the second paragraph."

John closed the book and put it in the bookcase. He did not want to show how badly he was wounded. "Probably he's not old enough. I'll wait a year and then try him again."

"He won't ever like it, John. He isn't built like you nor like your father."

"What is he interested in, then?" John asked in dismay.

"Just the things the other boys in the valley like, guns and horses and cows and dogs. He has escaped you, John, and I don't think you can ever catch him."

"Tell me the truth, Willa. Is he—stupid?"

"No," she said consideringly. "No, he's not stupid. In some ways he's harder and brighter than you are. He isn't your kind, John, and you might just as well know it now as later."

John Whiteside felt his interest in the land lapsing. The land was safe. Bill would farm it some day. The house was safe, too. Bill was not stupid. From the first he seemed to have a good deal of mechanical interest and ability. He made little wagons, and, as Christmas presents, demanded toy steam engines. John noticed another difference about the boy, a side that was strange to the Whiteside family. He was not only very secretive, but sharp in a business sense. He sold his possessions to other boys, and, when they were tired of them, bought them back at a lower price. Little gifts of money multiplied in his hands in mysterious ways. It was a long time before John would admit to himself that he could not communicate with his son. When he gave Bill a heifer, and Bill immediately traded it for a litter of pigs which he raised and sold, John laughed at himself.

"He is certainly brighter than I am," he told Willa. "Once my father gave me a heifer, and I kept her until she died of old age. Bill is a throwback of some kind, to a pirate, maybe. His children will probably be Whitesides. It's a powerful blood. I wish he weren't so secret about everything he does, though."

John's leather chair and his black meerschaum and his books reclaimed him again from the farm. He was elected clerk of the school board. Again the farmers gathered in his house to talk. John's hair was turning white, and his influence in the valley was growing stronger as his age came upon him.

The house of Whiteside was John's personality solidified. When the people of the valley thought of him, it was never of the man alone in a field, or in a wagon, or at the store. A mental picture of him was incomplete unless it included his house. He was sitting in his leather chair, smiling at his thick books, or reclining in one of the porch chairs on his wide, gracious veranda, or, with little shears and a basket, snipping flowers in the garden, or at the head of his own table carving a roast with artistry and care.

In the West, where, if two generations of one family have lived in a house, it is an old house and a pioneer family, a kind of veneration mixed with contempt is felt for old houses. There are very few old houses in the West. Those restless Americans who have settled up the land have never been able to stay in one place for very long. They build flimsy houses and soon move on to some new promise. Old houses are almost invariably cold and ugly.

When Bert Munroe moved his family to the Battle farm in the Pastures of Heaven, he was not long in understanding the position John Whiteside held. As soon as he could, he joined the men who gathered on the Whiteside veranda. His farm adjoined the Whiteside land. Soon after his arrival, Bert was elected to the school board, and then he was brought into official contact with John. One night at a Board meeting John quoted some lines from Thucydides. Bert waited until the other members had gone home.

"I wanted to ask you about that book you were talking about tonight, Mr. Whiteside."

"You mean the Peloponnesian Wars?" He brought the book and laid it in Bert's hands.

"I thought I'd like to read it, if you wouldn't mind lending it to me."

For a second John hesitated. "Of course—take it with you. It was my father's book. When you finish it, I have some others you might like to read."

From this incident a certain intimacy sprang up between the two families. They exchanged dinners and made little calls on each other. Bert felt at liberty to borrow tools from John.

On an evening when the Munroes had been in the valley for a year and a half, Bill walked stiffly into the Whiteside sitting room and confronted his parents. In his nervousness he was harsh. "I'm going to get married," he said. His manner made it seem like bad news.

"What's this?" John cried. "Why haven't you told us anything about it? Who is it?"

"Mae Munroe."

Suddenly John realized that this was good news, not a confession of a crime. "Why—why that's good! I'm glad. She's a fine girl—isn't she, Willa?" His wife avoided his eyes. She had been calling on the Munroes that morning.

Bill was planted stolidly in the center of the room. "When are you going to do it?" Willa asked. John thought her tone almost unfriendly.

"Pretty soon now. Just as soon as we get the house finished in Monterey."

John got up out of his chair, took the black meerschaum from the mantel and lighted it. Then he returned to his chair. "You've been very quiet about it," he observed steadily. "Why didn't you tell us?" Bill said nothing. "You say you're going to live in Monterey. Do you mean you aren't going to bring your wife here to live? Aren't you going to live in this house and farm this land?" Bill shook his head. "Are you ashamed of something, Bill?"

"No, sir," Bill said. "I'm not ashamed of anything. I never did like to talk about my affairs."

"Don't you think it a little of our affair, Bill?" John asked bitterly. "You are our family. Your children will be our grandchildren."

"Mae was raised in town," Bill broke in. "All of her friends live in Monterey, you know—friends she went to high school with. She doesn't like it out here where there's nothing doing."

"I see."

"So when she said she wanted to live in town I bought a partnership in the Ford agency. I always wanted to get into business."

John nodded slowly. His first anger was giving way now. "Don't you think she might consent to live in this house, Bill? We have so much room. We can do over any part she wants changed."

"But she doesn't like it in the country. All of her friends are in Monterey."

Willa's mouth was set grimly. "Look at your father, Bill!"

she ordered. John jerked his head upright and smiled gravely.

"Well, I guess that will be all right. Have you plenty of money?"

"Oh, sure! Plenty. And look here, father. We're getting a pretty big house, pretty big for two, that is. We talked about it, and we thought maybe you and mother would like to come to live with us."

John continued to smile with courteous gravity. "And then what would become of the house and the farm?"

"Well, we talked about that, too. You could sell the place and get enough for it to live all your lives in town. I could sell this place for you in a week."

John sighed and sank back against the cushions of his chair.

Willa said, "Bill, if I thought you would squeal, I'd beat you with a stick of wood."

John lighted his pipe and tamped the tobacco down in it. "You can't go away for long," he said gently. "Some day you'll get a homesickness you can't resist. This place is in your blood. When you have children you'll know that they can't grow up any place but here. You can go away for a little while, but you can't stay away. While you're in town, Bill, we'll just wait here and keep the house painted and the garden trimmed. You'll come back. Your children will play in the tank house. We'll wait for that. My father died dreaming of children," he smiled sheepishly. "I'd almost forgotten that."

"I could beat him with a stick," Willa muttered.

Bill left the room in embarrassment. "He'll come back," John repeated, after he had gone.

"Of course," his wife agreed grimly.

His head jerked up and he glanced at her suspiciously. "You really think that, don't you, Willa? You're not just saying it for me? That would make me feel old."

"Of course I think it. Do you think I'm wasting my breath?"

Bill was married in the late summer, and immediately afterward moved to his new stucco house in Monterey. In the fall John Whiteside grew restless again just as he had before Bill was born. He painted the house although it did not need it very badly. He mercilessly trimmed the shrubs in the garden.

"The land isn't producing enough," he told Bert Munroe. "I've let it go for a long time. I could be raising a lot more on it than I am."

"Yes," said Bert. "None of us make our land produce enough. I've always wondered why you didn't have a band of sheep. Seems to me your hills would carry quite a flock."

"We used to have a flock in my father's time. That seems a long time ago. But, as I tell you, I've let the place go. The brush has got thick."

"Burn it off," said Bert. "If you burn that brush this fall you'll get fine pasture next spring."

"That's a good idea. The brush comes down pretty close to the house, though. I'll have to get a good deal of help."

"Well, I'll help you, and I'll bring Jimmie. You have two men, and counting yourself, that'll be five. If we start in the morning when there's no wind, and wait for a little rain first, there won't be any danger."

The fall set in early. By October the willows along the creeks of the Pastures of Heaven were yellow as flames. Almost out of sight in the air, great squadrons of ducks flew southward, and in the barnyard the tame mallards flapped their wings and stretched their necks and honked yearningly. The blackbirds wheeled over the fields, uniting under a leader. There was a little early frost in the air. John Whiteside fretted against the winter. All day he worked in the orchard, helping to prune the trees.

One night he awakened to hear a light rain whispering on the slates and plashing softly in the garden.

"Are you awake, Willa?" he asked quietly.

"Of course."

"It's the first rain. I wanted you to hear it."

"I was awake when it started," she said complacently. "You missed the best part of it, the gusty part. You were snoring."

"Well, it won't last long. It's just a little first rain to wash off the dust."

In the morning, the sun shone through an atmosphere glistening with water. There was a crystalline quality in the sunlight. Breakfast was just over when Bert Munroe and his son Jimmie tramped up the back steps and into the kitchen.

" 'Morning, Mrs. Whiteside! 'Morning, John! I thought it was a good time to burn off that brush today. It was a nice little rain we had last night."

"That's a good idea. Sit down and have a cup of coffee."

"We just got up from breakfast, John. Couldn't swallow another thing."

"You, Jimmie? Cup of coffee?"

"Couldn't swallow another thing," said Jimmie.

"Well, then, let's get started before the grass dries out."

John went into the large basement which opened its sloping door beside the kitchen steps. In a moment he brought out a can of kerosene. When the two hired men had come in from the orchard, John provided all the men with wet gunny sacks.

"No wind," said Bert. "This is a good time for it. Start it right here, John! We'll stay between the fire and the house until we get a big strip burned off. It don't pay to take chances."

John plunged a kerosene torch into the thick brush and

drew a line of fire along its edge. The brush crackled and snapped fiercely. The flame ran along the ground among the resinous stems. Slowly the men worked along behind the fire, up the sharp little hill.

"That's about enough here," Bert called. "There's plenty of distance from the house now. I think two of us better fire it from the upper side now." He started walking up around the brush patch, followed by Jimmie. At that moment a little autumn whirlwind danced down the hill, twisting and careening as it came. It made a coquettish dash into the fire, picked up sparks and embers and flung them against the white house. Then, as though tired of the game, the little column of air collapsed. Bert and Jimmy were running back. The five men searched the ground and stamped out every spark. "It's lucky we saw that," said John. "Silly little thing like that might burn the house down."

Bert and Jimmy circled the patch and fired it from the upper side. John and his two men worked up the hill, keeping between the flames and the house. The air was dense and blue with smoke. In a quarter of an hour the brush patch was nearly burned off.

Suddenly they heard a scream from the direction of the house. The house itself was barely visible through the smoke from the burning brush. All five of the men turned about and broke into a run. As the smoke grew thinner, they could see a thick, grey eddy gushing from one of the upper windows.

Willa was running distractedly toward them over the burned ground. John stopped when he came to her.

"I heard a noise in the basement," she cried. "I opened the door in the kitchen that leads to the basement, and the thing just swooped past me. It's all over the house now."

Bert and Jimmie charged up to them. "Are the hoses by the tank house?" Bert shouted.

John tore his gaze from the burning house. "I don't know," he said uncertainly.

Bert took him by the arm. "Come on! What are you waiting for? We can save some of it. We can get some of the furniture out anyway."

John disengaged his arm and started to saunter down the hill toward the house. "I don't think I want to save any of it," he said.

"You're crazy," Bert cried. He ran on and plunged about the tank house, looking for the hoses.

Now the smoke and flame were pouring from the window. From inside the house came a noise of furious commotion; the old building was fighting for its life.

One of the hired men walked up beside John. "If only that window was closed, we'd have a chance," he said in a tone of apology. "It's so dry, that house. And it's got a draft like a chimbley."

John walked to the wood-pile and sat in the sawbuck. Willa looked at his face for a moment and then stood quietly beside him. The outside walls were smoking now, and the house roared with the noise of a great wind.

Then a very strange and a very cruel thing happened. The side wall fell outward like a stage set, and there, twelve feet above the ground, was the sitting room untouched as yet by the fire. As they watched the long tongues lashed into the room. The leather chairs shivered and shrank like live things from the heat. The glass on the pictures shattered and the steel engravings shriveled to black rags. They could see the big black meerschaum pipe hanging over the mantel. Then the flame covered the square of the room and blotted it out. The heavy slate roof crashed down, crushing walls and floors under its weight, and the house became a huge bonfire without shape.

Bert had come back and was standing helplessly beside

John. "It must of been that whirlwind," he explained. "A spark must of gone down the cellar and got into the coal oil. Yes, sir, it must of been that coal oil."

John looked up at him and smiled with a kind of horrified amusement. "Yes, sir, it must have been that coal oil," he echoed.

The fire burned smoothly now that its victory was gained; a field of growing flame rose high in the air. It no longer resembled a house at all. John Whiteside stood up from the saw-buck and straightened his shoulders and sighed. His eyes rested for a moment on a place in the flame fifteen feet from the ground where the sitting room had been. "Well, that's over," he said. "And I think I know how a soul feels when it sees its body buried in the ground and lost. Let's go to your house, Bert. I want to telephone Bill. He will probably have a room for us."

"Why don't you stay with us? We have plenty of room."

"No, we'll go to Bill." John looked around once more at the burning pile. Willa put out her hand to take his arm, but withdrew it before she had touched him. He saw the gesture and smiled at her. "I wish I could have saved my pipe," he said.

"Yes, sir," Bert broke in effusively. "That was the best colored meerschaum I ever saw. They have pipes in museums that aren't colored any better than that. That pipe must have been smoked a long time."

"It was," John agreed. "A very long time. And you know, it had a good taste, too."

XII

At two o'clock in the afternoon the sightseeing bus left its station in Monterey for a tour of the peninsula. As it moved along over the roads of the publicized Seventeen Mile Drive, the travelers peered out at the spectacular houses of very rich people. The sightseers felt a little shy as they looked out of the dusty windows, a little like eavesdroppers, but privileged, too. The bus crawled through the town of Carmel and over a hill to the brown Mission Carmelo with its crooked dome, and there the young driver pulled to the side of the road and put his feet on the dashboard while his passengers were led through the dark old church.

When they returned to their seats some of the barriers traveling people build about themselves were down.

"Did you hear?" said the prosperous man. "The guide said the church is built like a ship with a stone keel and hull deep in the ground under it. That's for the earthquakes—like a ship in a storm, you see. But it wouldn't work."

A young priest with a clean rosy face and a pride in his new serge cassock answered from two seats behind: "But it has worked. There have been earthquakes, and the mission still stands; built of mud and it still stands."

An old man broke in, an old and healthy man with eager eyes. "Funny things happen," he said. "I lost my wife last year. Been married over fifty years." He looked smilingly about for some comment, and forgot the funny things that happen.

A honeymooning couple sat arm in arm. The girl squeezed tightly. "Ask the driver where we're going now."

The bus moved slowly on, up the Carmel Valley—past orchards and past fields of artichokes, and past a red cliff, veined with green creepers. The afternoon was waning now, and the sun sank toward the seaward mouth of the valley. The road left the Carmel River and climbed up a hillside until it ran along the top of a narrow ridge. Here the driver cut his bus sharply to the roadside and backed and pulled ahead four times before he had faced around. Then he shut off the motor and turned to his passengers. "This is as far as we go, folks. I always like to stretch my legs before we start back. Maybe some of you folks would like to get out and walk around."

They climbed stiffly from their seats and stood on the ridge peak and looked down into the Pastures of Heaven. And the air was as golden gauze in the last of the sun. The land below them was plotted in squares of green orchard trees and in squares of yellow grain and in squares of violet earth. From the sturdy farmhouses, set in their gardens, the smoke of the evening fires drifted upward until the hillbreeze swept it cleanly off. Cowbells were softly clashing in the valley; a dog barked so far away that the sound rose up to the travelers in sharp little whispers. Directly below the ridge a band of sheep had gathered under an oak tree against the night.

"It's called Las Pasturas del Cielo," the driver said. "They raise good vegetables there—good berries and fruit earlier here than any place else. The name means Pastures of Heaven."

The passengers gazed into the valley.

The successful man cleared his throat. His voice had a tone of prophecy. "If I have any vision, I tell you this: Some day there'll be big houses in that valley, stone houses and gardens, golf links and big gates and iron work. Rich men will live there—men that are tired of working away in town, men that have made their pile and want a quiet place to settle down to rest and enjoy themselves. If I had the money,

I'd buy the whole thing. I'd hold on to it, and sometime I'd sub-divide it." He paused and made a little gathering gesture with his hand. "Yes, and by God I'd live there myself."

His wife said: "Sh!" He looked guiltily around and saw that no one was listening to him.

The purple hill-shadow was creeping out toward the center of the valley; somewhere below a pig screamed angrily. The young man raised his eyes from the land and smiled a confession to his new wife, and she smiled firmly and reprovingly back at him. His smile had said: "I almost let myself think of it. It would be nice—but I can't, of course."

And hers had answered: "No, of course you can't! There's ambition to think of, and all our friends expect things of us. There's your name to make so I can be proud of you. You can't run away from responsibility and cover your head in a place like this. But it would be nice." And both smiles softened and remained in their eyes.

The young priest strolled away by himself. He whispered a prayer, but practice had taught him to pray and to think about something else. "There might be a little church down there," he thought. "No poverty there, no smells, no trouble. My people might confess small wholesome sins that fly off with the penance of a few Hail Marys. It would be quiet there; nothing dirty nor violent would ever happen there to make me sorry nor doubtful nor ashamed. The people in those houses there would love me. They would call me Father and I'd be just with them when it was kindly to be just." He frowned and punished the thought. "I am not a good priest. I'll scourge myself with the poor, with the smell of them and with their fighting. I can't run from the tragedies of God." And he thought, "Maybe I'll come to a place like this when I am dead."

The old man stared into the valley with his eager eyes,

and in his deafened ears the silence surged like a little wind blowing in a cypress tree. The farther hills were blurred to him, but he could see the golden light and the purple dark. His breathing choked and tears came into his eyes. He beat his hands helplessly against his hips. "I've never had time to think. I've been too busy with troubles ever to think anything out. If I could go down there and live down there for a little—why, I'd think over all the things that ever happened to me, and maybe I could make something out of them, something all in one piece that had a meaning, instead of all these trailing ends, these raw and dragging tails. Nothing would bother me down there and I could think."

The bus driver dropped his cigarette in the road and stepped it into the dirt. "Come on, folks," he called. "We ought to be getting along." He helped them in and shut the doors on them, but they crowded close to the windows and looked down into the Pastures of Heaven where the air lay blue like a lake now, and the farms were submerged in the quiet.

"You know," the driver said, "I always think it would be nice to have a little place down there. A man could keep a cow and a few pigs and a dog or two. A man could raise enough to eat on a little farm." He kicked the starter and the motor roared for a moment before he throttled it down. "I guess it sounds kind of funny to you folks, but I always like to look down there and think how quiet and easy a man could live on a little place." He thrust the gear lever; the car gathered speed and swept down the grade toward the long Carmel Valley and toward the sun where it was setting in the ocean at the valley's mouth.

EXPLANATORY NOTES

3 *Carmelo Mission*: One of the Franciscan missions established in California by the Spanish. Initially known as Mission San Carlos Borromeo and now called Mission Carmel, it dates from 1770 and was moved to its present site, in the Carmel Valley, in 1771.

3 *manzanita*: Also known as the madrona shrub, an evergreen indigenous to California bearing edible red berries called madrona apples.

15 *Melachrino cigarettes*: Brand name of a Turkish-tobacco cigarette produced by M. Melachrino and Company, popular in the early decades of the twentieth century.

18 *Furies*: From Greek and Roman mythology, the Furies were female deities of vengeance who punished the perpetrators of unavenged crimes.

29 *Dresden vase*: Valuable vase of hard porcelain, usually highly decorative, produced in the area of Dresden, Germany.

43 *troglodytic*: Primitive, bestial, or primeval in appearance; the troglodytes were prehistoric people who lived in caves.

47 Ivanhoe *and* The Talisman: Historical novels by Sir Walter Scott (1771–1832). *Ivanhoe* (1820) details the chivalric exploits of the disinherited Wilfred of Ivanhoe and his efforts to win the hand of the Lady Rowena. *The Talisman* (1825) offers an account of the Third Crusade, including a story of forbidden love between the Scottish knight Sir Kenneth and the English Lady Edith Plantagenet.

47 *Zane Grey*: A popular author of western novels. Grey's *Riders of the Purple Sage* was published in 1912.

47 *James Oliver Curwood*: A writer of adventure and nature fiction, Curwood was born in 1878 and died in 1927. Among his novels is *The Valley of the Silent Men* (1920).

47 The Sea Wolf, The Call of the Wild: Adventure novels by

Jack London (1876–1916). *The Sea Wolf* (1904) tells the story of Humphry Van Weyden, an unwilling cabin boy who sails on the seal-hunting voyage of the *Ghost* to the waters off Alaska. *The Call of the Wild* (1903), the most popular of London's works, recounts the adventures of a dog who is sold to gold-rushers and becomes wild, living in the forests of Alaska. Both works were popular among young boys.

48 *changelings*: Children of elves and fairies secretly substituted for human children.

48 *gnomes*: Ageless creatures, resembling dwarves, who dwell in the Earth and guard treasure.

54 *Napa*: City at the southern end of the fertile Napa Valley, approximately thirty-five miles northeast of San Francisco.

55 *Russian Hill*: Upper-class residential area of San Francisco with many large houses and gardens; it is located on the burial grounds of Russian seal hunters.

61 *cinerarias*: Perennial herb-related plants originally from the Canary Islands, cinerarias have heart-shaped leaves and clustered flowers, usually tinted white, red, blue, or purple.

73 Travels with a Donkey: Published in 1879, this book by Robert Louis Stevenson recounts his travels with a donkey and his encounter with a Trappist monk in the Cévennes region of the French highlands. Probably a source for Steinbeck's title *Travels with Charley*.

74 *Velasquez'* Cardinal: The painter Diego Velázquez (1599–1660) completed his *Cardinal Astalli* between 1650 and 1651. This portrait is noted for the animated features of the Cardinal's face.

75 Kidnapped: A novel by Robert Louis Stevenson, published in 1886, which details the adventures of David Balfour, an orphan sold by his uncle to a slave ship. David becomes a cabin boy, joins in taking over the ship, and finds himself in the Scottish Highlands after the ship runs aground.

75 *essays of David Grayson*: David Grayson, the pen name of Ray Stannard Baker (1870–1946), was a journalist, popular essayist, and the authorized biographer of President Woodrow Wilson.

75 Adventures in Contentment: Published in 1907, this book by David Grayson purports to be the journal of a farmer offering didactic stories and essays.

75 *influenza epidemic*: The most severe outbreak of influenza in modern times, the epidemic of 1918 claimed 20 million lives worldwide, including approximately 550,000 in the United States.

76 Treasure Island. Immensely popular Robert Louis Stevenson novel, published in 1883. It presents the adventures of Jim Hawkins in search of treasure aboard the *Hispaniola*. A mutiny led by Long John Silver is eventually overcome by Jim and his friends, the treasure is secured, and Jim returns to England.

77 *Atlantis*: Legendary island mentioned in two of Plato's dialogues. Atlantis was swallowed up by the ocean after its inhabitants became wicked.

77 *Incas*: A Native American people centered in Peru and dominant in South America between 1100 and the Spanish conquest of the continent in the sixteenth century.

78 *Parthenon*: Temple of the Greek goddess Athena, located in Athens on the Acropolis. The temple was constructed in the mid-fifth century B.C.

79 *Junius' Encyclopedia*: Perhaps a reference to the *Etymologicum Anglicanum* (*English Etymology*), composed by Franciscus Junius the Younger. It stimulated interest in Old English. The reference here may refer simply to a set of encyclopedias owned by Junius Maltby.

82 *Carthaginians*: Inhabitants of Carthage, one of the greatest cities of antiquity. Carthage, a trading center, was located on the North African coast, near the present-day city of Tunis.

84 *Gallic wars*: Military campaigns between 58 and 50 B.C. in which the Roman emperor Julius Caesar conquered Gaul, or modern-day France.

84 *Trafalgar*: At the Battle of Trafalgar in 1805, Admiral Nelson's British ships defeated Napoleon's fleet. Trafalgar is on the Atlantic coast of Spain, just north of the Strait of Gibraltar.

88 *Hengest and Horsa*: Brothers who were leaders of the first Anglo-Saxon settlers of Great Britain between A.D. 446 and 454.

88 *Gato Amarillo*: Spanish for "yellow cat."

89 *auto-da-fé*: Punishment administered by the Inquisition (religious trials in Spain between 1478 and 1834), usually burning at the stake for heretics.

90 *Guinevere*: Wife of King Arthur and lover of Sir Lancelot in the Arthurian legends; her affair with Lancelot precipitates the destruction of Camelot.

90 *Bastille*: The storming in 1789 of the Bastille, a medieval fortress in Paris used as a prison, marked the beginning of the French Revolution.

91 *Lacedaemonians*: More commonly "Spartans," a people known for their stoicism and skill at warfare. *Thermopylae* is a narrow mountain pass in Greece where the Spartans held off the greatly superior Persian force for several days before being killed to the last man. Thermopylae has since been associated with heroic valor in the face of great odds.

102 hombre fuerte: Spanish for "strong man."

102 *General Vallejo*: A soldier, born in Monterey in 1808, who protected northern California from Russian expansion and Indian raids. He was also instrumental in establishing a California independent from Mexico in 1836.

123 *Vasquez*: A famous highwayman in Monterey county, Tiburcio Vasquez (1835–1875) was captured in Los Angeles in 1874 and executed for murder in San Jose the following year.

131 *Leviathan*: A reference to the sea monster in the Old Testament (Psalms 74:14). The word has come to designate anything of a large, monstrous size.

150 *Millet's "Angelus"*: A painting by the French artist Jean-Francois Millet (1814–1875) depicting a peasant couple praying in a field in response to the churchbells announcing the prayer of "The Angelus."

150 *Elaine*: In Arthurian legend, her love for Sir Lancelot is platonic and pure, as opposed to Guinevere's sensual and adulterous desires. Elaine dies from her ardor for Lancelot, and

her body is transported to Camelot, where her tale is told to King Arthur.

169 *Aztecs*: A Native-American civilization in Mexico, the Aztecs were conquered by the Spanish conquistador Hernando Cortes in 1519.

173 *the Michelangelo* David: Michelangelo's most famous sculpture, completed in 1504, depicts the biblical hero David with a sling over his left shoulder, presumably preparing to face Goliath.

174 *Herodotus . . . Xenophon . . . Thucydides*: Greek historians. The *History* of Herodotus (ca. 484–420 B.C.), the first account of the ancient world, provides the details of the Greco-Persian wars. The works of Xenophon (ca. 431–352 B.C.) provide insight into the culture of ancient Greece; his *Anabasis* covers the march of Greek soldiers from Sardis to Babylon. Thucydides (died ca. 401 B.C.) is best known for his *History of the Peloponnesian War*, an account of the conflict between the city-states of Athens and Sparta.

185 *Georgics*: Virgil's (37–29 B.C.) poem is remarkable for its practical instruction into agricultural practices and agrarian virtues.

185 *Varro on farming*: Marcus Terentius Varro (116–27 B.C.) was a Roman author whose work was intended to promote the greatness of Rome. His essays cover agriculture, rural life, and animal husbandry.

186 *Rochester lamps*: Kerosene-burning lamps popular in the 1880s and 1890s, with a pear-shaped glass cylinder that protected the flame from drafts.

198 *Seventeen Mile Drive*: Scenic drive along the Monterey peninsula, along which lies Pebble Beach.

ALSO BY JOHN STEINBECK

Fiction:

The Acts of King Arthur and His Noble Knights
Edited by Chase Horton
Foreword by Christopher Paolini
ISBN 978-0-14-310545-9

Cannery Row
Introduction and Notes by
Susan Shillinglaw
ISBN 978-0-14-018737-3

East of Eden
Introduction and Notes by
David Wyatt
ISBN 978-0-14-018639-0

The Grapes of Wrath
Introduction and Notes by
Robert DeMott
ISBN 978-0-14-303943-3

In Dubious Battle
Introduction and Notes by
Warren French
ISBN 978-0-14-303963-1

The Moon Is Down
Introduction and Notes by
by Donald V. Coers
ISBN 978-0-14-018746-5

Of Mice and Men
Introduction by Susan Shillinglaw
ISBN 978-0-14-018642-0

The Pearl
Introduction by Linda Wagner-Martin
Drawings by José Clemente Orozco
ISBN 978-0-14-018738-0

The Red Pony
Introduction by John Seelye
ISBN 978-0-14-018739-7

Sweet Thursday
Introduction and Notes by
Robert DeMott
ISBN 978-0-14-303947-1

To a God Unknown
Introduction and Notes by
Robert DeMott
ISBN 978-0-14-018751-9

Tortilla Flat
Introduction and Notes by
Thomas Fensch
ISBN 978-0-14-018740-3

The Winter of Our Discontent
Introduction and Notes by
Susan Shillinglaw
ISBN 978-0-14-303948-8

Nonfiction:

***The Log from the* Sea of Cortez**
Introduction by Richard Astro
ISBN 978-0-14-018744-1

Travels with Charley in Search of America
Introduction by Jay Parini
ISBN 978-0-14-018741-0

Collections:

The Portable Steinbeck
Edited by Pascal Covici, Jr.
Introduction by Susan Shillinglaw
ISBN 978-0-14-310697-5

The Short Novels of John Steinbeck
ISBN 978-0-14-310577-0